Katie,
Enjoy
Isaiah
He binds up the broken-hearted...
Blessings
Janet W. Ferguson

MW00636500

Going Up South

Southern Hearts Series

Book 2

Janet W. Ferguson

Copyright © 2016 Janet Ferguson

Southern Sun Press LLC

All rights reserved. No part of this publication may be reproduced, distributed or transmitted in any form or by any means, including photocopying, recording, or other electronic or mechanical methods, without the prior written permission of the publisher, except in the case of brief quotations embodied in critical reviews and certain other noncommercial uses permitted by copyright law.

Publisher's Note: This book is a work of fiction. Names, characters, any resemblance to persons, living or dead, or events is purely coincidental. The characters and incidents are the product of the author's imagination and used fictitiously. Locales and public names are sometimes used for atmospheric purposes.

Scripture quotations marked (NIV) are taken from the Holy Bible, New International Version®, NIV®. Copyright © 1973, 1978, 1984, 2011 by Biblica, Inc.™ Used by permission of Zondervan. All rights reserved worldwide. www.zondervan.com The "NIV" and "New International Version" are trademarks registered in the United States Patent and Trademark Office by Biblica, Inc.™

ISBN-10: 0-9974822-6-5
ISBN-13: 978-0-9974822-6-3

Acknowledgments

If anyone mentioned they'd traveled to Honduras or Guatemala, I cornered them and asked about a hundred questions. The place I described in this story is a mixture of all the experiences that were described along with a few memories from the very rustic Sardis Lake Church Camp (I was guilted into being a counselor at Sardis-by ministers Tom Perkins and Jerry Neill, but I ended up loving it) and my own trip to Guatemala with Praying Pelican Missions. My thanks go out to:

God for loving and searching out prodigals like me

Surgical nurse, Lisa Cantrell, who is my friend and cheerleader and has answered emails for a few years now about her medical mission trips with Health Talents International. Bless her heart! I hope to travel with her someday. Also, Rick Harper with Health Talents International Guatemala

My niece, Dr. Courtney Middleton who spent a year serving as a missionary in Honduras and I bug her with all sorts of questions, medical and mission wise. It was her idea to focus on the issue of dengue fever

My great niece, Calie Swartzlander, who shared her Honduras experience and my nephew, Brad Lister, described his Honduras iguana experience

Linda Sue Neill who sent pics and described her interesting truck rides through Honduras and other experiences

My son, Luke, for allowing his mom to chaperone his youth group to Guatemala, and his youth minister Jonathan Woods for planning and organizing the trip

Volunteer proofreaders Angela Young, Kathy McKinsey,

Karla Patterson, Marilyn Poole, and John Lawry

My husband, Bruce, for supporting me

My daughter, Mary Kristen, for reading my manuscripts twice

My sister, Betty Lister, and my niece, Heather Simoneau, English teacher and technical writer who've edited manuscripts and blogs

Neddie Joye Tolleson, Melissa Thompson, and Beth Hansen, who read the first rough draft and encouraged me

My amazing ACFW critique partners, Mentor author Misty Beller, Editor Robin Patchen, Cover artist Paper and Sage

My dog and several cats who sit on or beside me while I write, the reason pets end up in all my stories.

…to bind up the broken-hearted…

Chapter 1

Another sleepless night. Early morning light peeked through the top of the new drapes. The bedroom remodeling had finally ended, but Cassie Brooks still couldn't sleep. New paint and bedding did little to erase the memories of her unfaithful husband. She slipped out of bed and went through her morning routine.

Walk the dog. Study her Bible. Exercise.

She had plenty of extra time.

After she dressed, her high heels clacked against the mahogany flooring through the house and into the garage. She set the alarm and locked the door to the Victorian-style mansion Evan had insisted they buy. Way too large for their family of three, even more so now that there were only two, but Evan had always lived for prestige.

The heavy scent of blooming sweet hedge saturated the humid Mississippi air as she tossed her carry-on bag into her minivan and sat. She settled behind the wheel and backed out. While winding around the short five blocks to pick up her friends, a yawn worked its way from her mouth. This would be a long day. First, a drive to the Memphis airport, then hours on a flight to L.A. At least she could sleep on the plane.

When she turned her minivan into the driveway of Jill and Nick Russo's house, Sarah Beth McCoy already waited on their sidewalk, a suitcase in each hand. Cassie parked and climbed out. As she neared, the big tears rimming Sarah Beth's swollen brown eyes came into view.

This would be a tough trip for her sweet friend. An anxiety disorder made leaving Oxford hard enough on the woman. Plus the fact that they were leaving for a funeral all the way back in Los Angeles.

Reaching for Sarah Beth's bags, Cassie steeled herself. She'd come to support her friends. "Here. Let me throw those in the back. You sit wherever you feel most comfortable in the van."

Fear carved hard across Sarah Beth's forehead as she walked beside Cassie. "That would be nowhere."

"You poor thing." A deadly car accident could mess up a person. After situating the suitcases, Cassie wrapped Sarah Beth in an embrace. "I'm sorry you're still struggling."

"I'll make the trip with God's help. And yours." She sniffled and brushed at the moisture on her cheeks. "Thanks for offering to go with us. You're a good friend."

Cassie led her toward the front passenger seat. "I wanted to help. Besides, Benjamin's at his father's this weekend." Another reality she'd yet to get used to.

The door of the quaint gray cottage opened, and Jill emerged onto the broad front porch with her baby snuggled close.

As they neared, Cassie grinned. "What a bundle of cuteness. Can I take him while you get the car seat?"

"Sure." The tall, thin blonde lay the infant across Cassie's arms. How quickly time had passed since the difficult birth of the little guy. Jill had been ill the entire pregnancy, and they'd worried so much over her.

With the car seat in place, Cassie strapped him in. The baby grinned and cooed. "Such a ham. You should bring him to my garden for a photo shoot. He'll be natural in front of a camera."

Jill's blue eyes flashed a warning at Sarah Beth.

What did that mean? Did Jill have a problem with taking pictures of the sweet baby? Cassie shook her head. "You know, time passes so quickly. I can't believe my little boy's a teenager now. I took a ton of pictures, and I'm so glad I did." She eyed Sarah Beth's midsection. "Just think, in six months, you and Jess will have a little baby, too. I wonder what he or she will look like."

The lines on Sarah Beth's face loosened a tad. "If I had my wish, he would look like my husband. A little Jess McCoy." Tears filled her eyes again and clung to her lashes.

Cassie's heart squeezed at her friend's suffering. "I admire your bravery. You don't have to go to your boss's funeral. And you could've asked Jess to leave his fishing trip with his father, but you're doing this. I'm proud of you."

A half chuckle came from Sarah Beth. "I'm pretty sure you're the brave one, Cassie—flying to L.A. with a new mother, a baby, and a pregnant woman who suffers from agoraphobia."

With a slow blink, Cassie nodded. Sarah Beth had a point.

~~~

Dylan Conner straightened his blue tie in the mirror of the funeral home's side hall, then swiped his fingers through his auburn hair. The visitation area was packed. A lot of people knew Bill Rogers.

Funny how quickly life could change. Only ten days ago, Dylan had visited Bill in his upscale office. Now Bill was gone. One of his few real friends.

Show business held a special kind of loneliness few could understand. No wonder so many celebrities lost their way and ended up abusing alcohol or drugs. Life in the spotlight brutalized a person.

He'd had another friend in Bill's advertising agency's office. Once. A tall, funny brunette with dark eyes and a smile that lit up a room. Too bad she had to go and marry that jock Jess McCoy. Sarah Beth and Bill had worked together for years, and they'd been close, but would she be able to overcome her anxiety and make the long trip from that little Mississippi town to L.A.?

A warm ache settled in the vicinity of his heart. One could hope. He'd love to see her again. Even if she never felt the same way about him. Of the women he'd known over the years, none were as sincere. Real even. Not that he planned to settle down or raise a family. Too many bad memories of his own louse of a father kept him from taking the plunge. Maybe Sarah Beth was better off with McCoy. With the football coach, she could have a family.

With him, all she'd get was life in the fishbowl. She'd made
~~~

the right choice.

As he made his way back toward the main lobby, the ornate entrance door of the funeral home swung open, and *she* walked through. Dylan's breath caught. Sarah Beth had come.

Memories had to be haunting the woman. Visitations where she'd been the one standing and greeting people for hours. Her parents and grandmother. Her boyfriend's funeral—the death that sent her running back home to Mississippi.

Sarah Beth wrapped her arms around herself as she trailed behind Jill and a cute redhead carrying a baby. They neared the receiving line, where mourners in high-priced suits and designer dresses offered condolences to the grieving widow. How many had truly loved Bill? How many were here just to peek at the celebrities who would attend the advertising exec's funeral?

Jill introduced the redhead to someone ahead of them. But Sarah Beth stopped, gripping the corner of the wall that curled around to the hallway on the far side of the lobby. What was wrong? Was she going to pass out?

Her eyelids slid shut.

Dylan rushed to her side and looped his arm behind her back. A familiar pair of brown eyes met his.

"I wasn't sure you'd be up for the trip." Dylan allowed his lips to lift into a small smile.

Sarah Beth fell into his shoulder, tears rolling from her cheeks onto his suit coat. He may've had a crush on the woman, but they'd also been friends. And he knew what she'd been through after Adam's death.

"Come over to a chair. Let's talk, and you can give yourself a minute before you offer condolences to Carol."

"I'm just a little dizzy."

She let him lead her away from the crowd to a wingback chair by the wall. The trip must've taken a lot out of her. Dylan rubbed her hand. "A funeral wasn't the way I would've wanted your first visit back in L.A. to happen."

"I really wanted to be here for Carol. At least I had someone to travel with, since Jess was out of town."

"Still married, though, right?" Couldn't hurt to ask.

"Yes, Dylan, we're still together."

"Always looking out for you, you know."

She gave him a faint smile. "Right."

"Seriously, though." He paused to pull his thoughts together. "I thought highly of Bill. He had a way about him that made me feel comfortable. I dropped by his office when I was in the area." He caught her eye for a moment. "I liked to check up on you, too. Get the scoop."

Jill appeared with the baby in her arms now, the petite redhead at her side. "Sarah Beth, you vanished. I was worried about you."

Dylan stood and looked at Jill and the infant. "Hello to you, too."

Jill's lips clamped shut, and she dropped her gaze.

Guess she hadn't expected to see him here. The one night he'd spent with Jill last year had been a mistake. Thank goodness, the rendezvous hadn't made the tabloids like the whole Sophia fiasco had. There was no reason for Jill to be acting like an angry ex-wife or anything, though. He'd treated her with respect the times he'd seen her at Bill's office.

Maybe he should be extra polite. Dylan stood and hovered over the baby. "Who is this? Yours?"

Jill turned the infant over her shoulder to face the other way.

He moved around her and made eye contact with the little guy. "He's a good-looking boy. What's his name?"

"Michael James Russo." Her voice cracked as she answered.

"James was my grandfather's name. I like it." The baby's lips curled as he made garbled sounds. "Can I hold him? I think he wants to play."

"He spits up a lot."

Dylan flashed his best grin and held out his arms. "I like to live dangerously. Remember?"

A toothless smile covered the baby's face. He chortled as Dylan covered his eyes and played peekaboo.

Jill finally let go of the child, but her face drained of color.

Talk about overprotective mothers. She needed a chill pill.

The redhead moved near and peered over small designer glasses at the baby. The elegant chandelier above her reflected off the thin lenses. "Hi, I'm Cassie. Our little pumpkin seems to think you're hilarious."

"I'm Dylan. Kids love me. They see me as one of them."

Sarah Beth's mouth twisted. "No doubt."

Dylan lifted the baby up and down. "He's so light. How old is he?"

Neither Jill nor Sarah Beth spoke.

Blue-green eyes sparkled up at him as Cassie pressed her index finger to her chin. "About three months?"

Sarah Beth jerked herself up from her seat. "He's probably light because Jill was sick for so long, but the doctor says he's fine." She motioned across the room. "I'm ready to get back in the receiving line, and it's my turn to hold Michael."

Two high-strung women? Definitely lowered the romantic interest level. At least their friend Cassie seemed normal. Dylan laid the baby in Sarah Beth's arms. "Are you sure you're okay now?"

"I am."

Whispering, Jill whisked Sarah Beth toward the long line of well-wishers.

What in the world was going on with those two?

Dylan walked with them and studied Michael as he waited in the line of friends who'd come to pay their respects to Bill's family. He stayed close as they reached Bill's wife, Carol.

There was something about that baby.

And the women's strange attitudes. He didn't know Jill that well, despite his one night with her. But Sarah Beth was usually pretty laid-back.

Three months old. How long had Jill been gone, anyway? Not a year even. And last summer… A little ball of anxiety planted itself in Dylan's stomach.

"You came." Carol embraced Sarah Beth and held her. "I know how hard this trip must've been for you." When Carol released her, they both wiped tears from their cheeks. "I can't believe it. Bill and I finally got things together, and we were going so strong…" She shook her head. "He got on that small plane and…"

Sarah Beth clasped Carol's hand. "I know it doesn't take away your pain, but I'm glad y'all did get to have some time." Her voice broke. "Bill was a father figure to me."

Dylan stepped around the people between himself and Sarah Beth and laid his hand on Carol's shoulder. "Bill was the same for me, and I'm truly sorry for your loss."

Her eyes downcast, Jill added, "Exactly what I was going to say. I had the utmost respect for him."

"Your son's precious." Carol reached for Michael's tiny fingers. "And I'll always treasure our trip to Paris. It was a turning point in our marriage." She smiled up at Sarah Beth. "Oh, Bill told me you're expecting a baby, too. Congratulations. You deserve some happiness."

A lump formed in Dylan's throat, and his eyes dropped to Sarah Beth's midsection. "You're pregnant?"

"Just a little."

"That's not a thing." Dylan raised an eyebrow. Pregnant? Sarah Beth? So quick. She only married in December. "I think you mean not very far along."

Concern wrinkled Carol's brow. "But you're planning to go to Honduras to see the clinic and the chapel this summer?"

Sarah Beth bobbed her head.

"You know, Bill hoped to join your group for the trip." Carol sniffled, then cleared her throat. "I should speak to the other guests. Please, come by the house when this is over so we can talk."

Sarah Beth and Jill took off as soon as they passed Carol, mumbling something about the baby needing a diaper change. But he caught a glimpse of them scooting out the front door in a hurry. Maybe he'd go by Carol's, too. She'd invited them all, hadn't she?

Michael. All the way to Bill's house, the infant's smile replayed in Dylan's mind. Maybe he was imagining it, but Michael looked a lot like his own baby picture hanging at his mother's home in Boone, North Carolina. He'd been with Jill one night. What month—?

His throat closed. It couldn't be.

Once he reached Carol's home, Dylan let himself inside. The redhead sat on the couch in the living room with the baby. He stopped and bent down to eye level with the boy. "Hey, fella. It's me again."

Michael grinned. A cute little guy. A strange feeling wrenched around his chest like a giant rubber band. What was that?

It almost hurt.

Who was he kidding? He finally acknowledged the simple math that had been working itself out in his head since he'd climbed into his car. This baby had his hair, his eyes, even his smile.

This was his son. Michael. And no one had bothered to tell him.

Chapter 2

Cassie squirmed as the actor stared at Michael in her arms. Dylan Conner sure did love babies. He'd been grinning and talking gibberish to the child at the funeral home, and now he knelt in front of her, staring.

What was she supposed to do? She'd never watched his movies, but she knew his face from the covers of those magazines in the grocery store checkout. And they didn't do him justice. The man was stunning. Green eyes, auburn hair, and prominent cheekbones—picture-perfect facial structure. No wonder women swooned over him. Not that she ever wanted to get involved with another man. That ship sailed when Evan humiliated her in front of their friends and their law firm. The entire town. One heartbreak to last a lifetime. A bitter chuckle slipped from her lips. As if the famous actor Dylan Conner would ever be interested anyway.

The temperature in the room seemed to be rising. Heat crept up Cassie's neck. Perhaps she should move to another location. Maybe outside for a few minutes to catch a breeze. "If you'll excuse me, I need to stretch my legs a bit."

Dylan stood and stepped back, his eyes never leaving Michael. "Where would I find Sarah Beth or Jill?"

"Sarah Beth's in the kitchen. The woman loves to eat, even more now that she's pregnant. I think Jill's in the ladies room."

For a fleeting moment, his gaze met hers. A hint of moisture glazed over his eyes. This trip became stranger with every passing moment.

~~~

Bright lights and the scent of chicory flooded Dylan's senses as he entered the kitchen. Sarah Beth stood counting scoops of coffee into a filter. Sarah Beth was Jill's best friend.
~~~

Surely she knew about Michael's paternity. Why hadn't she told him?

Dylan tamped down the grenade exploding in his chest and forced out words. "Drinking coffee while pregnant? Thought that was a no-no?" With cautious steps he joined her and held out his hand. "Here, let me."

"Shh, I'm counting. I'm not going to mess up this time." As she put the last scoop in, she glanced up at him. "I won't drink any, but the smell alone gives me a jolt of energy."

He should probably try to ease into his question, but he couldn't do it. Too many thoughts and feelings and fears churned in his mind. He met her brown eyes. "Are you my friend, Sarah Beth?"

She turned on the coffee maker, cleared her throat, and let out a weak laugh. "Of course."

But would she tell the truth? "And you're a Christian—you're not supposed to lie."

"Is that a question?"

The runaround had to stop. His hands dropped to the marble counter with a slap. "Here's a question. Is Michael my son?"

She bit her lip and stared at the dripping coffee. A solemn hush stretched between them.

"Your silence answers loud and clear." How could she? Dylan spun away and stormed out of the kitchen.

"Wait." Her footsteps clattered on the tile floor behind him.

In the living room, he found Jill and paused beside her, his fists squeezed into balls. "I need to talk to you. Outside."

Jill sucked in a gasp of air, dropped her eyes, and followed him to the front yard of the ranch-style home. Sarah Beth shadowed them past a group of Cypress trees.

Once out of earshot of the other guests, Dylan stopped and stared at Jill. "Why didn't you tell me?" He paced, ramming his fingers through his hair. "Did you think I wasn't good enough to be a father? How dare you? Do you realize who you're dealing with?" He had to get out of there and think. Where was the car?

"Dylan, it was one night." Jill's palms turned up. "We never hung out again."

His legs took a life of their own and jogged down the drive. Both women followed, Jill grabbing his arm. "If I'd told you, wouldn't you have thought I was just after your money? I wasn't trying to fool you. I didn't think you would…"

He jerked his arm away. "What? You didn't think I would care to know I had a son? You didn't think I was human?"

"No, no." Jill mashed her hand to her forehead. "I didn't know what I was going to do. Sarah Beth begged me to stay with her because I was sick. Of course, I knew she wanted me to have the baby. There wasn't a plan. Things just happened."

"Guess what? More things may *just happen*." He slung open the door of his black Audi.

Sarah Beth grabbed the car door. "Dylan, wait. Please."

"Why should I?"

Sarah Beth's eyes pleaded. "Let's go for a ride and talk. Just you and me."

Her words softened the fury in his chest. He rounded the hood of the car to the passenger side and opened the door. "Get in."

Chapter 3

Dylan was Michael's father? Outside, under a large sycamore, Cassie patted the baby's back and nuzzled her face against his velvety cheeks. Had she heard right?

Not likely she could misinterpret the admission. But how should she proceed? Jill still stood where Dylan and Sarah Beth had left her, head-in-hands.

Pretending to be preoccupied with the baby could work. She could act like she hadn't heard anything.

Michael's fine auburn hair brushed against her cheek as he turned his head. Should she say something? Maybe she could offer legal help.

No. What was she thinking? Since Evan's betrayal, she'd relegated that part of her life to almost nil—a few minor legal issues for friends plus her pro-bono work. A custody battle with a celebrity the caliber of Dylan Conner could evolve into a cross-country tug-of-war played out in the media.

But the warmth of the little man in her arms poked at her heart. After her own ex had heaped humiliating gossip on her family, she hated to turn her back on Jill and Michael if she could help.

Her feet moved toward Jill. A soft moan from under Jill's hands picked at Cassie's resolve. The least she could do was offer. "Jill?" She kept her voice soft. "I overheard."

"The rest of my baby's life, he'll be hounded by sleazy papers, and Dylan's probably going to hire some expensive lawyer to sue for custody. I should've known something like this would happen." Her voice garbled with sobs. "I don't deserve to be happy. I've messed up too many times, but Nick—he's good. I hate that I've dragged my husband into this mess. And sweet little Katie, too."

"Does Nick know about…?" If not, Jill may be in for even more trouble.

Jill lifted her face. "He knows everything. Nick's an amazing man and father…" Her voice trailed off.

Cassie cleared her throat and took a deep breath. "I've mediated some difficult cases successfully. But if mediation isn't an option, you'll want the attorney who handled my divorce and custody case. He's the best around. Especially against a hostile, wealthy opponent."

Shaking her head, Jill stared at the ground. "I don't think Nick and I could afford your attorney."

"Maybe mediation can work, then. It's worth a try, and I won't charge you anything."

"Okay, I guess." She released a shaky breath. "I need to call Nick."

Did she really just offer to mediate a child custody case between Jill Russo and Dylan Conner? How was this going to affect her teenage son? The last thing Benjamin needed was more drama.

· · · · ·

After Sarah Beth slid into the passenger seat, Dylan stomped the gas pedal and sped down the drive. His head swirled between fury and panic. And something else he couldn't name. The baby's smiling face pinched at his heart. The innocence.

They rolled along the curvy canyon roads that clung to the mountains leading down to the Pacific. He needed to focus on the hairpin turns that came one after another, especially with the sun sinking on the horizon.

A whimper came from the seat next to him. With the heights and the curves, Sarah Beth must've been freaking out. He slowed the car. "You okay?"

"Yes. No." She groaned. "I'll text Jill and tell her not to wait around. Michael will be getting tired."

His anger subsided at the thought of the sleepy baby. His sleepy baby.

He glanced at Sarah Beth. She was rubbing her palms

together. Was she having a panic attack? His house wasn't much farther. He'd stop there so she could get out.

Sarah Beth took in a deep breath then released it with a whoosh. "Dylan, I'm sorry. I was afraid, at first, that Jill would end the pregnancy. Later, I warned her she couldn't keep this from you forever, but she worried what would happen if the paparazzi found out. What would life be like for the baby? Then, she got really sick. The doctors sent her to the hospital in Jackson, because the baby wasn't growing."

Fear like a razor sliced at his chest. "Is he okay now? He's really small." The thought needled him. "I could've gotten better doctors. I can take him to a specialist, the best specialist."

"I think he's going to be fine."

He scoffed, and his spine stiffened. "But you don't know, do you? I can get him the best of care."

"I didn't know you wanted to be a father. What about your career?"

Dylan opened his mouth, then snapped his jaw shut. They reached the end of the road and turned out onto the coastal highway. As night fell, they approached the gated driveway leading to his hillside mansion.

Sarah Beth stared as he punched in the code. "We're at your house?"

"I need to think." He pulled into the garage and parked.

"What am I supposed to do?"

Dylan shrugged. "Come in."

Her teeth chewed her bottom lip. "I need to make a phone call first."

No doubt to her jock husband. "I'll be inside." Abandoning her, he slammed the car door. He deactivated the alarm and left the mansion's door ajar.

Inside, the weight of the revelation crashed down on him. He was a father. Memories tumbled through his mind as he paced the kitchen. His mother weeping. Kids pointing while teachers whispered in hushed tones. The day he left the school cafeteria and never went back.

A few minutes later, Sarah Beth tapped on the door. Dylan crossed the room, swung it open wider, and then returned to the kitchen. The bright lights only served to make the situation more surreal. "Something to drink?"

"No." She lagged behind him.

He grabbed a beer. After a long swig, he glared at her. "I'm guessing you want to sit outside. You and your rules of propriety and all. Some rules. They must not apply to telling the truth." He pointed to the deck off the living room.

Her mouth twisted, but she followed him through the mansion without answering. His words had to sting. She hadn't actually lied, but she hadn't told him, either.

They reached the wooden balcony which offered an unobstructed view of the ocean. The wind from the Pacific chilled the air as they plopped into the cushioned beach chairs.

Sarah Beth wrapped her arms around her legs and hugged them to her chest. Was she shivering? Crying?

A twinge of guilt soured Dylan's stomach. The woman had gone through so much pain in this town. Her boyfriend's tragic death, and now Bill's funeral.

"Dylan, I still don't know how I could've handled this better." Words squeezed from her throat between sobs. "Jill didn't want me to tell anyone at first. I didn't tell Jess or Nick until she was hospitalized, and it slipped." She sniffed twice. "After that, life happened."

Now his stomach twisted. None of this was Sarah Beth's fault. He stood and hurried inside to grab a blanket from the sofa. He wrapped it around her shoulders. "Here. You're freezing." He caught his breath and sighed. He couldn't stand to see her cry. "I wish you were the mother of my child." His fingers pushed through his hair. "It's not your fault. It's Jill's. She put you in an awkward position."

"No, no, no. This isn't about me. You and Jill need to work out what's best for Michael. The baby's the one who did nothing wrong. He needs the adults in his life to put his welfare above their own."

The moonlight blurred as his eyes filled with moisture. "Are you saying he'll be better off without me?"

She reached out and took his hand. "I don't mean… Why don't you come to Oxford and get together with Jill and Nick? Try to work something out…maybe a plan everyone…well, maybe everyone won't be happy with it. But work out a plan everyone can live with."

He studied her hand on his, then pulled his away. "I'm on location for at least two weeks, but I may travel down South before the Honduras trip."

"What Honduras trip?" Her voice was shrill.

"I'm going to Honduras the same week your Oxford group's going. Dr. Rodriguez moved down there a couple of months ago to live and work at the clinic."

"But why?"

What was she freaking out about? Was her husband that jealous? "Why am I going, or why did Dr. Rodriguez move?"

"Both."

"Dr. Rodriguez wanted to be on the front line of the epidemic. He's still searching for a cure, but he wanted to treat patients. The dengue virus is moving up into the States. Cases have been confirmed in Florida and Texas. He's passionate about this."

"Like Adam." Sarah Beth let out a shaky breath. "I've been out of touch with Dr. Rodriguez since I married in December."

"Anyway, I'm going because I've invested a lot of money. And I know you find this hard to believe, but I care." The darkness outside and the emotional day only served to add to the black void inside his soul. A heavy emptiness he'd carried for years. A fact he blamed on his own father.

"But, Dylan, it's dangerous for you down there. You're famous, and criminals could kidnap you for ransom."

"Criminals could kidnap *you* for ransom. And you're pregnant."

She huffed. "Not that again. Jess and Mark have both been freaking out about me going there since they found out about the baby."

They sat minutes without speaking, ocean waves crashing,

lulling Dylan's anger and hurt.

Sarah Beth rose and placed a hand on Dylan's shoulder. "I care about you, and I love that little baby. I pray this all works out." She pulled her phone close to her face. "It's getting late. I should go to the hotel."

"I'll take you."

Her palm popped up. "I'll call a cab."

"Fine."

Thirty minutes later he returned to the deck. Alone. The way he spent most of his life. Of course that had been his plan. Never to marry. Never to put a kid through what he'd been through. That was what he'd thought he'd wanted once. Now that he'd seen Michael…

But what did he know about raising a child?

Chapter 4

Headlights flew past in a blur as Cassie sped down Highway Six. The Mississippi sun dipped low in the cloudy sky, and her foot grew heavy with thoughts of her own custody case and scandalous divorce. It hadn't been national news, but in her small town, it had provided plenty of fodder for the gossip mill. Her divorce had been so rough, and the fact that she and Evan had worked at the same firm made it even more difficult. She hadn't practiced much law since.

Once parked in front of Sarah Beth's house, Cassie set a fast pace toward the front door with the magazine tucked under her arm. If you could honor the rag with the title of *magazine*. She groaned. The timing couldn't be worse. And she hated being the bearer of more bad news.

She hesitated before knocking. Sarah Beth would be upset, and Jess, of course, but no point in postponing the inevitable. Gossip would be all over Oxford in no time. At least Jill and Michael had dodged the bullet.

Cassie tucked her keys into the pocket of her ivory blazer then squeezed at the knot forming in her shoulders.

A large dog barked, and the door opened. Coach Jess McCoy waved her in. "You're just in time for a late dinner. Chicken Parmesan. I'll get Sarah Beth." The former Florida star quarterback smiled as his wife's name left his lips.

This was going to be harder than she'd thought. She followed him into the entrance hall and waited. The dog stood drooling by her side.

A minute later, Sarah Beth appeared dressed in yoga pants and a long T-shirt. "Hey, come on in and have a seat." She led Cassie to the eclectic living room. A bold mix of modern art and antiques had been scattered over the space in a way that screamed Sarah Beth.

As she neared the sofa, Cassie held up the paper. "I don't normally look at this trash, but was at the grocery store a minute ago, and the picture caught my eye. I don't believe anything these gossip rags print."

Sarah Beth grabbed the tabloid. "I don't understand…" Her mouth dropped open. "Oh my stars." Shrieking, Sarah Beth's fingers curled around the edges. "What kind of jerk takes pictures in a funeral home?"

Jess looked over his wife's shoulder and gawked. "That's at the funeral home?"

"I was woozy when I first got there, and Dylan helped me to a chair. And apparently held my hand for one second."

Redness rushed to Jess's cheeks, and a fire lit in his eyes. He took the paper and ripped it in half. "I'd love to tackle that guy, just knock him on his backside. He's always trying to weasel his way into your life."

Sarah Beth rotated and circled her arms around her husband's neck. "Nothing has ever happened between me and Dylan, and nothing ever will."

"But he'd love for it to. I bet he said as much while you were there, even knowing you're married and pregnant with my child."

Cassie cleared her throat. She'd witnessed much worse in her law practice, but these were her friends. "I'll just let myself out. So sorry."

Sarah Beth backed away from Jess and took her arm. "Stay for dinner. We'll change the subject."

"Stay, Cassie." Arms crossed, Jess gave his wife a cynical look. "But I'm right, aren't I? What did Dylan say? I want to know."

She let go of Cassie's arm and returned to her husband. "He said something offhand like, 'I wish you were having my baby instead.'" Sarah Beth caressed Jess's cheeks. "He has a crush on me. Don't tell me women have stopped throwing themselves at the hot football coach just because you wear a ring." She fingered a strand of his blond hair then traced his jawbone.

"Dylan doesn't know what love is. Not the love like I have for you, or like Nick has for Jill."

Holding in a groan, Cassie toed the polished pine floor. She should make a run for it. Watching this love fest pinched her bruised heart.

Jess sighed. "If I didn't love you so much, I wouldn't want to pommel Dylan." He pulled her in closer. "And I love our child so much already." A smile crept across his lips. "If this is a girl, her dates better show up in full pads."

Two more seconds, and she was out of there. Cassie chuckled, a pathetic attempt at reminding them of her presence. "Having a football coach for a dad may be right up there with having a father called Big Roy." The tension in the room dropped a notch. For them, anyway.

Sarah Beth bobbed her head. "Or an FBI agent for a brother."

"It'll be tougher, trust me." Jess clucked his tongue. "Go wash your hands for dinner, ladies."

Sarah Beth released him, and he disappeared into the kitchen. She grinned at Cassie. "He's the best cook. You have to stay. You can take a plate home for Benjamin, too."

Why not? She'd just lurked through two awkward marital scenes. And Benjamin had eaten out with friends from church.

As they entered the living room, a scream sliced the air.

Jess sprinted back out of the kitchen. "What's wrong, Sarah Beth? Are you hurt? Is it the baby?"

Cassie glanced around, heart racing. *What was wrong?*

Sarah Beth pointed through the glass of the back door. "Look."

Their enormous dog stood on the step with her head down, cowering. In her mouth was a tiny black and white kitten.

"You scared the life out of me, babe." Jess yanked open the door, squatted, and removed the animal drenched in drool.

Sarah Beth's big brown eyes blinked back tears. "Poor kitty."

The kitten squirmed in his hand as he stood. "Whoa. It's not dead. It's purring."

Whining, the dog raised to her hind legs.

Cassie peered over his shoulder. "Aw, it's cute. I don't see any bite marks. Can it walk?"

"I don't know. Hold the dog, and I'll see." Jess set the cat down on the floor.

Sarah Beth clamped her arms around Gingie and brought her back on all fours.

The kitten scampered to the dog, who whined again and nudged the ball of damp fluff with her nose.

"Should I let Gingie go?" Sarah Beth looked to Jess.

"You can try it, I guess."

The dog lay down and rolled over, and the kitten climbed on her.

Jess let out a huff. "Maybe Gingie thinks it's her baby."

"That's like something you see on the Internet." Cassie shook her head.

The kitten swatted at the huge dog's tail, and by the pout on Sarah Beth's mouth, one thing was obvious. "You have a cat now." Cassie had to laugh.

Jess rolled his eyes and let his head drop back. "And I don't even like cats."

Sarah Beth scooped up the little animal. "I want to run it to the vet's house down the street before we eat. It won't take long." She eyed Cassie and winked. "Will you come with me?"

"Of course." What else did she have to do? And they could talk.

Outside, Sarah Beth linked an arm with Cassie's, despite their height difference. "I'm sorry you had to see our little spat, but I'm glad you were the one to show us the paper. Jess can't stand Dylan, but it's mostly because…"

"Dylan has a crush on you."

"But we were only good friends. Dylan knows that, and deep down, Jess does, too."

The knot in Cassie's neck became a tangled mess. How much more complicated would this custody case become?

~~~

The SUV was out back, so Sarah Beth should be at home.
~~~

Dylan hesitated before he knocked. He'd had fun visiting with Sarah Beth on this porch last year, but he'd also made a big mistake in this town. A mistake named Sophia.

Maybe this visit would end better. He hoped so, for his son's sake. His knuckles rapped on the glass. Growling and barking commenced, then a thud. That crazy dog never did like him.

Jess McCoy threw open the door, his hands balled in fists. "What?" His jaw clenched after he spoke.

Why did that jerk have to be the one to answer? "Is Sarah Beth home?" Dylan craned his neck to look around Jess.

"No." Jess stepped over to block the view.

"Where is she?"

He crossed his arms over his chest. "Why?"

"I wanted to stay in the pool house. I need to try to figure out some things."

"After what you said to my wife, you want to stay here?"

Shoulders squared, Dylan lifted his chin. "And what might that be?"

"You wished she was the mother of your child."

Dylan's jaws snapped shut. She couldn't wait to tell that one. Had they had a big laugh over him? Hands fisted, he spun and stormed down the steps to the car and took off.

Once he hit the highway, the speedometer of the rental car topped ninety before he eased off the accelerator. His fingers loosened on the steering wheel. Why'd he been stupid enough to come to this small town asking for a favor? He should've known it would come to nothing.

No one had ever done him any favors. Certainly not in the little town where he'd grown up. He'd worked for everything he'd gotten. Worked his way through the University of North Carolina and then moved out to L.A., taking odd jobs behind the scenes.

Sure, he'd had a lucky break with his first film. But that was the way life worked in Hollywood. Timing.

Dylan bit back the urge to shout obscenities at the windshield. But he wouldn't give Jess McCoy that much control over him. Why should the guy be such an insecure jerk? Didn't Jess get the girl? The man should be happy. If he had somehow won Sarah Beth's heart, he'd be gloating at all the poor wannabes.

Dylan chewed his bottom lip. Once he reached Memphis and checked in at the Peabody, the situation would change. No more putting him off. A phone call to his attorney would be the game-changer. He had a child, and he wasn't messing around. Jill and the rest of them would find out soon enough that he wasn't a man to be trifled with.

~~~

Cassie groaned and picked up her phone. She entered the number Sarah Beth had given her. Dylan Conner's generic voicemail picked up on the first ring.

"This is Cassie Brooks in Oxford, Mississippi. I'm trying to reach you in regards to Michael Russo. Please call me at your earliest convenience." She left her number, hung up, and puffed out a sigh.

For the first time since her divorce, she was in lawyer mode. Sarah Beth had told her not to worry about any of the marketing work until all this mess was settled. Cassie studied cases, precedents, and arbitration agreements that might be applicable. The celebrity custody battles she'd read about were ugly. *I pray that an agreement is possible, Lord. Bend and soften all of the hearts involved somehow.*

Outside the window, office lights went out one by one as she worked well into the evening. She had plenty of time. Benjamin had weekend plans, fishing with his grandfather in Alabama.

She unlocked the screen on her phone and pulled up Benjamin's picture with her father. The bittersweet truth assaulted her, punching holes in her composure. The man she'd chosen to marry would never be the kind of father she'd been blessed to have. At least Dad finally had another man in the family to hang out with. Her two favorite men. Possibly only favorite men. Ever.

The phone in her hand chirped. That was fast. She accepted
~~~

the call. "This is Cassie Brooks."

"You called about my son." Dylan's voice was matter of fact, devoid of emotion.

"I am calling in regards to the papers you served Mrs. Jill Russo today. She's interested in mediation. Would you be willing to explore the option before or instead of going to court? These issues are difficult enough, but your position in the public eye could make them even more so. Through mediation, you could avoid the unwanted publicity for yourself, and most importantly, for your son."

"*Now* Jill admits Michael is my son?"

"She's willing to admit he's your son. I would suggest, however, you proceed with a paternity test. As a mediator, I'll do my utmost to be fair and nonpartisan. My goal will be to look out for the welfare of the child and find a solution that would be workable for both parties. The mediation itself is not legally binding. But we could work it into a form, which, once agreed upon and proposed to the court, would be binding."

The line stayed silent for a pregnant moment. "I don't know."

"Mr. Conner, I have a son. If you're like me, you want what's best for your child. If the mediation works, everyone gains, especially Michael. If it doesn't, you can let the custody lawyers duke it out. I hope you'll choose to try mediation for the good of your child."

Dylan let out a deep breath. "It's not legally binding if we can't agree?"

"Correct. Check with your attorney if you like."

"Don't worry, I will. *If* I agree, when would we start?"

"When can you come to Oxford?"

Another moment of silence followed. "I'm close by."

"I have one trip out of the country in May, but other than that, my schedule's open."

"Let me guess. You're going to Honduras with Sarah Beth?"

"I'm going with the same group."

Dylan hissed. "She put you up to this."

"No one put me up to anything. In fact, I would prefer not to be involved for unrelated personal reasons. But, if you agree to the mediation for the benefit of your child, I'll be impartial. Like I mentioned, you can always let other attorneys take over later. If you come—and I hope you will—bring a family member or friend. It helps to have another person on your side. Maybe a sibling or parent."

"I could bring my mother, I guess and try it. She doesn't travel much, but she might if she gets to see her grandchild." His voice softened. "Can we be with him?"

Something in his tone touched her heart. "Seems like a fair request. Get me the date of arrival when you make arrangements."

"Okay."

"And Mr. Conner…"

"Yes?"

"You're doing the right thing."

After they ended the call, she pictured the way Dylan had smiled and made faces at the baby in L.A. The man couldn't be all bad, could he? But even if he wasn't, with all the convoluted relationships, would they ever be able to work out an agreeable solution?

Chapter 5

I ask for wisdom, Father. Help me be quick to listen, slow to speak, and slow to anger.

The doorbell interrupted Cassie's prayer, and painted toenails click-clacked as her dog raced to greet the guests. Cassie pushed away from the kitchen table and took quick steps to catch up. Near the door, the white poodle stood waist-high, wagging her pompom tail. "Mimi, not everyone likes dogs."

Mimi cocked her woolly head.

Cassie turned the knob and swung open the wood-and-glass front door. With somber faces, Jill and Nick stood on the porch. Jill's eyes were red as she snuggled Michael close.

"I hope you don't mind the dog."

Nick waved her off. "We pet-sit for Sarah Beth's big mutt."

"This is Mimi."

Mimi sat and offered a paw.

Jill managed a weak smile. "Cute. She's so big. Is she a standard poodle?"

"Yes. My mother bought her for me when I was going through my divorce."

Nick bent down and scratched behind Mimi's ears. "She's obviously smart. My little girl, Katie, would love to see her. Her hairstyle and pink bows crack me up."

Cassie motioned for them to follow her. "The groomer goes all out, no matter what I tell him. Come have a seat in the parlor."

As Jill sank into the antique Chippendale sofa, the wrinkles that furrowed her brow and forehead relaxed for a second. But a sharp rap at the door brought them right back. She swung her gaze that way, then looked at her husband. "I'm not sure how I'm going to get through this."

Cassie squeezed her shoulder. "I've prayed for each of you this morning. Did you get to read through the book of James like I suggested?"

Nick nodded and took Jill's hand. "We read it together. I'm definitely going to need to tame my tongue."

"Finding a mutually satisfying agreement will be difficult, so when you feel like you want to blow up, pray. *Hard.*" Cassie turned back toward the entrance hall. "Nick, grab Mimi's collar while I answer. I better not keep them waiting."

A small gasp came from Jill. "Them?"

"Dylan's mother came."

Jill turned to Nick. "I never pictured him having a mother."

One side of Nick's mouth cocked up as he took hold of the dog. "Me either. Just spawned or something."

"Way to tame that tongue, Nick." Cassie left them to answer the door. Would Nick be able to keep his cool? If not, he could blow any chance of negotiation.

On the front step, Dylan and a pretty, gray-haired woman waited. His mother's face held a warm smile. Maybe she would be an asset. Unless Dylan inherited his acting talent from her.

A ripple of tension ran through Cassie's jawbone. Why had she offered to do this? She pressed her lips into a smile. "I'm Cassie Brooks. Welcome to my home."

"I'm Sheila." Dylan's mother extended her hand, but her gaze traveled around the room. "Oh, I love old Victorian houses. Dylan built me a Victorian replica on a mountain in Boone, North Carolina."

Cassie eyed Dylan. "That was a really nice thing for a son to do."

He said nothing.

Okay.

"Follow me." She led them into the parlor.

Once they'd entered, Sheila's eyes lit up at the sight of Michael. "My word, that baby is the spitting image of my Dylan." Her kind smile appeared genuine. "You must be Jill. I'm Sheila, Dylan's mother." She crossed the room and reached toward Michael's tiny fingers, caressing them. "I never thought I'd be a grandmother." She glanced back at Jill. "I admit the circumstances aren't what anyone would have chosen, but God will work things out."

Nick studied Sheila, his expression unreadable, while Jill's eyes watered as Michael took the woman's finger.

Shoulders rigid and still silent, Dylan stared at Michael.

What was he thinking? Cassie motioned toward the loveseat and side chairs. "Let's sit down and talk."

When everyone got situated, Cassie opened a notepad. "What I prefer is to offer each person an opportunity to speak uninterrupted on various issues I'll bring up. We'll simply go around the room, and I'll take notes. Then, I'll give you another chance to respond if you feel the need. Would anyone else like to take notes?" She motioned toward a stack of paper and container of pens.

"I would." Nick helped himself to what he needed.

Dylan pulled out his phone. "I'll use this." His voice was flat.

Mimi left the spot where she'd rested by Nick and stood in front of Dylan with paw extended.

Dylan's brow lifted. "Part of the mediation?"

Cassie looked up from her notes. "Oh, sorry. That's Mimi."

With a side-glance to his mother, Dylan shook Mimi's paw.

Mimi inched over to Sheila, who chortled and shook the poodle's paw. "Well, I never in my life. Pleasure to meet you, Mimi."

If only relations between the humans could be so easy.

~~~

Dylan studied this Cassie Brooks. He'd seen the little redhead in California. She was good. Even brought in her dog to lessen the tension. Her sparkling eyes appeared kind and genuine behind her glasses. Were her eyes green or blue?

Wait. That didn't matter. No way was he trusting her. These Oxford people had already been dishonest once.

Cassie cleared her throat. "Dylan, let's start by discussing how you feel about being a father. What kind of father do you
~~~

want to be?"

His mouth went dry. What kind of father did he want to be? All eyes looked to him for an answer. Man, this woman was tricky. "I wasn't expecting that question." He glanced at his mother and gave a bitter smirk. "Nothing like mine."

Sheila shook her head. "Dylan's father…" Her gaze traveled to Jill and Nick. "We would want to keep this confidential, for everyone's sake." After Jill nodded, Sheila continued. "His father made some big mistakes. Illegal mistakes. I gathered Dylan and everything we owned and moved us to Boone. We changed our names, hoping to rid ourselves of that man and the scandal."

Cassie nodded and dropped her gaze.

He didn't want any of their pity. That wasn't the plan. The thought had him itching to get out of there. He moved to the edge of the loveseat, but his mother touched his hand. The woman was like a freaky mind reader. Would she always know his thoughts?

After jotting notes on her legal pad, Cassie looked back at him. "I'm gathering that you don't want to be a nonentity. You want to be a part of Michael's life."

"I want…" He swallowed. He had no idea how to answer this question. He closed his eyes and thought of all the things he'd wanted from his own father. "I want to teach him to throw a ball, watch him when he's performing or playing sports, take him to the doctor if he's sick, teach him to swim and fish…"

"Stuff his father never did." His mother's voice broke as she tried to finish the thought for Dylan.

"But you did, Mom." He took her hand and gave it a gentle squeeze.

"Things a good father would want to do." Cassie sniffled again and wiped at her face. "I apologize. I must be catching a cold."

Her eyes reddened and held tears. She'd suddenly caught a cold? Maybe she wasn't faking. Maybe she was one of those women who cried at the drop of a hat. If so, he couldn't imagine her being a very good attorney. If she was faking, she could outperform a lot of the actresses he'd run across.

A coo caught all of their attention. His mom grinned as Michael chortled.

Releasing a loud breath, Jill lifted Michael toward her. "Do you want to hold him?"

"Oh, yes. Thank you." His mother took Michael, who rewarded her with a smile.

The sight flooded Dylan with warmth. His mother would make a wonderful grandmother if they could work this mess out. He'd see that they did. No matter what.

Cassie motioned toward Jill and Nick. "Let's hear from Jill now. How do you feel about Dylan being a father to Michael?"

Jill clasped her hands together in her lap. "Scared."

Dylan did a double take. Scared of what? Like he'd hurt his own son. His gut simmered. The woman better not claim he'd attacked her or something crazy. She'd be sorry.

Cassie tilted her head and tapped the pen to her lips. "What scares you?"

"I'm scared he'll take Michael, and I won't get to be with him." Her gaze darted to Dylan, then back to the attorney. "Dylan has money, and money is power." Her voice shook. She cleared her throat and continued. "I'm scared of life in the eye of the media. I don't want weirdos with cameras following Michael's every move. I'm scared Dylan may not know how to take care of a baby, and Michael could accidentally get injured. I'm scared Michael would rather be with Dylan than me. I'm scared of almost everything that has to do with Michael." Jill's voice broke, and she bent over. Her husband grabbed her hand and squeezed. "I know I don't deserve to be a mother. I'm not good enough. If it weren't for Nick, I wouldn't have been able to get through all the sleepless nights and crying when we first brought Michael home from the hospital. Being a parent is so hard."

His mother stood, turned, and situated Michael in his arms. Warmth spread through him from the tiny squirming boy.

Standing in front of Jill, his mother placed a hand on her

shoulder. "Oh, sweetie, all new mothers feel like that. It's the hardest job in the world, I always say. The most important, too."

A knife of worry thrust into Dylan's chest. This little baby in his arms was defenseless against crazed fans and reporters. "You're right to worry about the cameras and the weirdos. Maybe it's better if no one knows he's my son for now."

Jill's head snapped up, and she wiped her cheeks. "You're not going to take him?"

Cassie tapped her fingers on the coffee table. "I think we're getting ahead of ourselves. We'll talk about visitation, but first, a major issue is the paternity testing and the birth certificate—"

"I don't need a paternity test. The one night we were together… I just know he's my son."

An awkward silence followed. Cassie inhaled audibly then blew out a long breath. "I would still recommend the testing. Changing the birth certificate will be more difficult, since Jill listed Nick as the father. If you decide to proceed with the change, I'll have paperwork for everyone to sign later." She made a note on the pad. "Let's move to visitation. What are you expecting, Dylan?"

"To be with him… I don't know."

"In Oxford?" Small lines formed above Cassie's brows. "It's not easy for a baby to fly out to Los Angeles for a weekend or holiday."

"I could come when I have time off, maybe buy a place here."

Cassie turned to Jill. "How does that sound?"

"I'd rather he visited with him here, but I'm nervous for him to take Michael without knowing how to take care of a baby right now, even in Oxford."

"That seems like a reasonable concern. Maybe his mother could come, or another friend who's experienced with children. He could also learn from you and Nick what to do."

Jill massaged her forehead. "I guess."

"We can schedule times through me for a while. I'll

communicate each of your wishes, concerns, and schedules. Since Dylan and his mother are here for the weekend, Jill can type up instructions like she would for a babysitter, and they can spend time with Michael before they leave. I think you told me you're not nursing?"

"No, but—" Jill hedged. "They're not keeping him today, are they?"

Fire soared to Dylan's face. "And why not?"

"Wait." Cassie held her hands up. "Let's calm down. Things have been going smoothly." Her eyes grew large, and she looked at Jill. "How about after you take Michael home for a nap? That will give you time to type up the instructions and get bottles together. Then you could bring Michael back here. I'll be home after the CSU mission trip meeting, and Dylan and his mother can spend time with Michael then."

Jill looked at Nick, who nodded. "After his nap."

A bit of the blaze receded, and his mother's eyes caught his. He knew that look. He could almost hear her voice in his head. *Behave yourself, Dylan.*

Chapter 6

From near the stage, Cassie scanned the noisy crowd in the old converted warehouse. Excitement buzzed as students discussed the upcoming mission trip. Benjamin stood beside her on the left, Sarah Beth and Jess to her right. The energy in the room made Cassie's heart pound. What a dream come true to get to go on a mission trip with her son. *Thank you, Lord, that Benjamin is a believer.*

Jess pointed toward a group of football players who'd signed up to go. "More football players volunteered than expected. Once Cole Sanders threw his name in, others followed his lead. I never imagined the quarterback would be interested in mission work. Especially in a developing country."

The lanky thirty-year-old student minister, Chris Hardy, stepped onto the old wooden platform and called the meeting to order. "Glad to see most of the group is present. We'll meet one more time before the trip to organize the donated supplies and make sure everyone has their checklist completed. All of you should have your passports and immunizations at this point. I can't emphasize enough the importance of bringing protective clothing and mosquito netting. There've been some cases of dengue fever reported in villages near the clinic. As we've discussed, the disease is epidemic." He motioned toward Jess. "Coach McCoy's going to explain the work assignments and have you sign up for your top two choices."

On a long table near the front of the stage, Jess placed four papers. "You can choose between four teams.

"One area of service is vector control, which simply means mosquito control. There may be stagnant water nearby, and we'll chemically treat those swampy areas. Also handing out netting to the families. Nothing glamorous, but really important in stopping the spread of dengue fever.

"Another team will work on building projects and repairs in the nearby homes and villages. We'll overhaul water wells, depending on weather and supplies. Experience with tools or a strong back would be helpful. I'll be leading some of my players on this team." He motioned to Sarah Beth. "Your turn."

A grin lit up her face. "If you like kids, the minister, Juan, will head a group who'll lead crafts, organize outdoor games, and provide snacks for the children. Honduras is the size of Tennessee, but it's more densely populated and considered one of the poorest nations in the Western Hemisphere. A lot of the children go to bed hungry, so the snack time is popular.

"The last group will work as compassionate caregivers with Dr. Rodriguez. He's a lead researcher for the cure of dengue fever. These should be volunteers who won't mind interacting with the sick. The work requires a strong constitution and a big heart. You may be changing beds, walking patients, giving out deworming pills, or simply sorting vitamins."

From a large canvas bag on her shoulder, she pulled out a box of pens and placed them beside the papers. "Sign up for two of the teams, numbering them in your order of preference. We'll do our best to accommodate your choices, but no guarantees."

Benjamin leaned close to Cassie's ear. "Mom, we probably rock a tool belt better than most of these guys. Let's sign up for the construction."

Once again, her son's eagerness warmed her heart. "Go for it." She thumped his forearm. "I'm proud of you, you know?"

His lips mashed into a lopsided smile as his eyes met hers for a moment, then pulled away. Like when he was a little boy.

Cassie resisted the urge to fold him into her arms. With so many older students around, she didn't want to push her luck.

At the table, the first student to pick up a pen was the quarterback, Cole Sanders. "Coach, where do you want me?"

Jess placed a hand on his shoulder. "Help with the kids.

Keep the arm safe."

"I don't know much about any of it." Cole hesitated, his tall form hovering over the paper. "Maybe I shouldn't have volunteered for this trip."

"You're being a leader, and a quarterback has to lead."

The words lifted the worry from Cole's face. He wrote his name on top of the list to work with the children.

Another student, Audrey Vaughn, stood behind Cole. The corners of her lips curved upward as she gazed at the quarterback when he turned around. "How'd you do on your final?"

"I made a C, thanks to your tutoring."

"That's great. I knew you could do it. What'd you sign up for?"

Before Cole could answer, an enormous body wedged its way between the quarterback and Audrey. Cassie pulled Benjamin back as Jess moved closer. This looked like trouble.

Grant Vaughn, the university's biggest offensive lineman, grabbed a pen and pushed it toward his sister. "Audrey, sign up with my group. Mom said to keep you safe."

Ah. One protective older brother.

"You'll have to sign up with me." Audrey signed the paper below Cole's name, turned, and walked toward the exit.

Grant puffed out his chest and scowled at Cole. "Stay away from my sister. Remember I've got your back on the field. Or not."

Jess squared off with Grant. "Enough."

Through gritted teeth, Cole spat out words. "Coach set up the tutoring with your sister, not me."

Grant jabbed a finger toward Cole. "I've heard how you talk about girls, and I've seen the trash you look at on your computer."

Cassie's heart rate accelerated as the huge boys stared each other down. It appeared Jess would have a mediation of his own on this trip.

Jess gripped Grant's shoulder and motioned with his other hand for Cole to leave. "Let's go outside and talk, Grant."

With her elbow, Cassie nudged Benjamin. "Hurry and sign up. We need to get home. And steer clear of that train wreck when we're in Honduras."

~~~

An hour later, a head donning a baseball cap and dark sunglasses popped over the fence of Cassie's back yard. "Ms. Brooks. We're back."

Dylan Conner. Cassie's heart sank. They were early. Really early.

Why hadn't she sent her son out to a friend's after the meeting at CSU? Before the movie star and his mother returned? Benjamin had been through enough drama for one lifetime. She held back the sigh that threatened. "The gate's unlocked. Come on in."

Dylan and Sheila came through the gate and ambled along the garden's stone trail to where Cassie held a board for Benjamin to cut with the table saw. "Keep it straight. One more cut."

The saw ripped through the board, the shrill sound tearing the air.

Dylan stroked his unshaven chin. "A woman who knows how to use power tools?"

The puffy circles under Dylan's eyes hadn't been as obvious earlier inside the house. Or maybe she'd been too focused to notice. Even with the shade from his hat, the man looked weary. She nodded toward her sixteen-year-old, who already stood over six feet tall. "This is Benjamin, my son. He started this business to make spending money. We turn scrap metal, windows, doorknobs, you name it, into wall hangings or frames, or an occasional bookshelf. A little store on the Square sells his work."

Sheila pointed toward the woodwork hanging on copper hooks in the open garden shed. "I'd love to buy that gray picture frame. I could take a photo of Dylan with Michael."

Benjamin studied Dylan's face. "You're Dylan Conner, the actor?"

Dylan nodded.
~~~

"I liked that action movie you were in."

"*Current*?"

Benjamin nodded, and one corner of Dylan's mouth lifted. "I had to battle to escape the chick flicks and get into something more manly."

Benjamin crossed over and lifted the gray frame from the hook. "You and your mom take this. Or anything else you want, on the house."

"We don't mind paying." Dylan pulled his wallet from his back pocket.

Cassie shook her head. "He doesn't offer freebies often, so take him up on it."

With a few quick steps, Dylan moved to Benjamin's side and gave his shoulder a squeeze. "I appreciate it."

Cassie pulled off her leather work gloves and unplugged the saw. "We can finish this tomorrow."

"I was ready for a break." He gave his mother a playful nudge. "You slave driver."

Dylan pulled a baseball glove off another hook and ran his fingers across the leather. "You play ball?"

Benjamin's eyes lit up. "Yeah, you?"

That was one thing Cassie missed about having a husband. One of the few. She threw the ball with her son, but she knew it wasn't the same. Would the great Dylan Conner actually—?

"I used to." Dylan pushed his hand in the glove. "You want to throw a few?"

"Bag of baseballs right here." Grinning, Benjamin dug one out and tossed it to Dylan.

Sweat trickled down Cassie's brow, and she swiped at it with the sleeve of her shirt. Maybe Dylan wasn't the jerk Jess and Nick had made him out to be. Too soon for a verdict.

Sheila fanned herself with her hand. "Some heat in this part of the country."

"Good gravy. I'm sorry. Let's you and I chat in the sunroom. I'll pour us some sweet tea, then we can watch the guys through the window and listen for the doorbell, too."

Cassie led Sheila to one of the white wicker rocking chairs

inside her sunroom and left her watching their sons through the glass. After slicing lemon wedges, Cassie filled glasses with ice and poured the tea. This was not how she'd planned her day. Now she'd have to figure out how to explain to Benjamin why a famous actor and his mother were visiting a baby at their house. What would Dylan and Jill allow her to tell him? Why hadn't she thought this through? Obviously, she wasn't ready to get back into the legal profession. With the tea and lemons arranged on a tray, she slipped back out to the sunroom. "Here you go, Mrs. Conner."

"Call me Sheila." She took the glass and held it to her cheek. "Nice and cool. You're good at what you do. I can tell you take your time and get things right."

Cassie stared into the icy brown tea. "I used to think I did." She sighed. "Until my own marriage failed." Why'd she admit that?

"I guess we have a lot in common—a bad marriage, but a son we love dearly."

She prayed their sons turned out better than their fathers.

~~~

A slamming car door caught Dylan's attention. They were here. His son was here. He still couldn't get used to the idea. His chest squeezed every time he thought about the tiny baby that shared his blood.

The hour had passed quickly throwing the ball with Benjamin. This woman, Cassie Brooks, had done well raising her boy. He was polite, athletic, and earned his own spending money.

Dylan pulled off the baseball glove. Would he do as well parenting Michael? "I think I hear my…" He kicked at the grassy lawn. "Um. I need to go inside to talk with some people."

"Thanks for throwing with me." A smile covered Benjamin's face as he took the glove.

"I enjoyed it." Dylan found the back door and let himself into the sunroom where he'd seen his mother and Cassie chatting earlier. What in the world had his mother said about
~~~

him? Once that woman started talking…

The chairs were empty so he continued into the house. He glanced around the posh kitchen with its marble countertops and top-of-the-line appliances. In the living room, an elaborately carved mantel and fireplace anchored one wall. Obviously Cassie had money. But even though the spacious mansion held antique furniture and art, the place still maintained a homey and welcoming air.

A little girl walked through the front hall dressed in a purple princess costume. "I like your house, Ms. Cassie. It looks like a castle."

Cassie's red hair was pulled into a tight bun, and the sides of her eyes crinkled behind her glasses when she smiled at the girl. "And I like your outfit."

"Mommy bought it for me. I get to be the princess while you're babysitting Michael. I'm going to have chicken nuggets *and* see a movie." She put her hand to her forehead. "It seems like forever since I had a night out."

Why hadn't he been told there was another child involved? The girl wasn't Jill's, so she had to be Nick's daughter. How would she be with Michael? Was she good with his son? He moved to stand by his mother in the hall.

The little girl eyed them both. "Hello, I'm Katherine Marie Russo. You must be Uncle Dylan and Aunt Sheila. Daddy told me you're visiting from California. You can call me Katie. My brother is Michael. He can't eat real food or put small things in his mouth. He might choke. And he has to be changed a bunch of times a day, so he won't get diaper rash. You don't want that." She held up one finger. "I forgot to tell you not to lay him on anything and walk away. He might roll."

His mother gave him a sideways glance. "Mississippi seems to have polite children and pets."

Dylan squatted down to Katie's level. "You seem like a good big sister. Do you like having a brother?"

Katie sighed. "Yeah, but it's hard work, let me tell you."

~~~

Cassie covered her mouth to hold in a laugh. She shot
~~~

Benjamin a look as he slipped up beside her. Now he pretended to cough to conceal a snicker. At least he didn't laugh out loud. Nick's daughter was so adorable.

Nick shuffled by with a load of equipment.

Sheila let him pass, then stepped toward Jill and the baby, arms raised. "Y'all have a great time with the princess. We'll be careful with Michael."

Jill flinched, but handed her child over. "His bottles should be refrigerated until you need them. But I fed him right before we came. He has diapers and wipes, plus a cream for when you change him because he has a little rash." She bit down on her bottom lip. "Cassie has our numbers. Call us for any reason at all. Don't hesitate."

Nick returned and placed a hand on the back of Jill's arm. "Ready to go?"

Snuggling the baby closer, Sheila gave Jill a tender smile. "Between the four of us, he'll be fine, but I'll call if anything out of the ordinary comes up. I promise."

Once they left, Sheila passed the baby to Dylan. "Here you go, son."

An expression of sheer joy filled his face, misted his eyes. Gently, Dylan nuzzled Michael's cheek with his own. "You are perfect."

The intimacy pinched Cassie's heart, and she took a step back. "I should give y'all some privacy. Make yourselves at home in the living room or wherever."

"You don't have to." Dylan's eyes met hers. "Just go about your normal life."

As if that were possible.

Before long, the late afternoon passed into evening. Cassie and Benjamin cleaned up the outdoor equipment, changed, and ordered deli delivery for all of them. The vast array of baby contraptions Nick had brought still sat beside the couch as Michael nestled in someone's arms the entire time. Even Benjamin held him.

A muscle in Dylan's cheek twitched. Was he nervous about a teenager holding the baby? Cassie snickered. "You think you're nervous now, just wait till Michael's sixteen and driving."

"Don't." Dylan's fingers raked through his short, auburn hair. "It's overwhelming enough as it is."

His mother smiled from her perch in the wingback chair across the room. "You'll do fine. Your knees may be worn out from praying like mine, though."

"I guess I put you through the ringer a time or two."

Her arms crossed her chest. "A time or two?"

"Maybe three?"

"Right, son." She pressed her lips together, but her eyes held a smile.

Headlights flashed through the front door, and Cassie pushed to her feet. "They're back. I'll go let them in."

Once the door cracked, Jill brushed past Cassie and Dylan. "Thanks. It's late, we better take him." She scooped Michael from Benjamin's arms.

The stress of the situation had obviously taken a toll on the frail blonde. Blotches spotted Jill's skin, and her stiff movements looked almost painful.

Cassie trailed her to the car, and Dylan followed.

He leaned on the car as Jill strapped Michael in his car seat. "I have to take Mom home tomorrow and fly back to Los Angeles the next day, but we're free in the morning. Can we visit for a couple more hours?" His eyes pleaded. "I'm not sure when I'll be back."

No answer came, only an audible inhale from pursed lips. Nick placed a hand on her back. "Maybe Dylan and Cassie could watch Michael while we go to church."

Cassie held her breath. Jill's cooperation could make or break this mediation.

Chapter 7

A tiny spot on the glass in the sunroom drew Cassie's attention, but she refused to get distracted. She'd cleaned the glass once this week already. That's all she would allow herself. She took a sip of her coffee and glanced outside at the blooming day-lilies.

So far, so good, Lord. Turning her attention back to the well-worn pages of her Bible, she jotted notes in her new journal. The verses settled the worries churning around her head.

Benjamin appeared, wearing a polo with khaki shorts, and popped the tab of his soda. "I like Dylan. He doesn't act like he's famous or anything. I wish I could tell my friends I threw a baseball with Dylan Conner."

"But you know you can't, right? We talked about it."

"I know. We don't want those trashy papers to know he's here. And it was hard enough for you and me, having people whisper behind our backs in Oxford. I'd hate to have the whole world staring at me like he has to deal with."

"I'm glad you understand, but I'm also sorry for what you went through." She searched his face for a reaction.

Eyes downcast, he fiddled with the pop-top on his can. "Me, too."

The fact that her son had intimate experience with this sort of gossip ripped at her gut. The fact that his father had caused the gossip infuriated her. How could Evan have been so selfish? She slung the journal onto the glass top of the wicker table.

A car door slammed outside. "Good gravy. Someone's here already. They're early. Again. And I haven't even pulled up my hair or put on my glasses."

"Just go let them in."

She didn't have much choice. What was with this guy and being super early?

When she pulled open the front door, Dylan's jaw dropped. "With your hair always in that bun, I never knew it was that red. It's like fire."

Cassie clawed at her neck. The thermostat must've broken, the room was hot. "You're early."

Undeterred, Dylan took a step closer. His hand grazed a long strand on her shoulder.

Sheila smacked his arm. "Dylan Conner. Don't touch her hair."

Sidling next to Cassie, Benjamin laughed. "People always want to touch it if she leaves it down. Half the time, she wears a baseball cap when she goes out."

"I'll put on a fresh pot of coffee." Cringing, Cassie wheeled toward the kitchen. "I made apple turnovers earlier this morning. Make yourselves at home." *Lord, help me keep calm.* When this all started, she'd never imagined Dylan Conner would be in her home, making friends with her son, and touching her hair.

The smell of warm apples and cinnamon by the oven soothed her nerves. A bit. With any luck, she could settle the mess and be finished soon. She needed to figure out how they could give Dylan some time with Michael without Jill falling apart.

Benjamin slipped up beside her. "Mom, can I stay home from church with y'all?" He gave her his little boy look. "I'll go to the youth service tonight."

Sighing, Cassie relented. "I guess." The situation grew more complicated by the minute.

The two hours after Jill delivered Michael were pleasant, even enjoyable. It had been a long time since Benjamin was that little. She studied her son sitting with Dylan. They both smiled and made faces at baby Michael.

Maybe she should've tried to give Benjamin a brother or sister. But even before everything came to light about her husband, instinct warned her Evan had been up to something, way back then. Late nights at the office, volunteering for trips to take depositions… He always seemed to find a reason to stay away from home. At least he'd made an effort to attend Benjamin's ballgames.

Watching Dylan brought back a few happy memories. Much like Evan had been with Benjamin, Dylan was nervous about holding Michael at first. As Dylan's anxiety fell away, his son enthralled him. He'd posed at least a hundred questions to her and his mother about parenting.

As soon as church let out, Jill and Nick must've hightailed it over. They were in and out in minutes, taking Michael with them.

Dylan's hands sank into his pockets as he watched them drive away.

Cassie put a cautious hand on his back. "You did well. How do you feel about the way your first visit went?"

His eyes closed, and he swallowed hard. Then he fixed his gaze on her. "I feel like you're a miracle worker. I never imagined I'd get to spend so much time with him this weekend. Thank you."

"I pray great things continue for Michael. And you." The quicker the better, so her and Benjamin's life could get back to normal.

~~~

Dylan kissed his mother's cheek as he left her home in the mountains. It was time to make the hundred-mile drive from Boone to the Charlotte airport. The tree-lined mountain roads normally relaxed him. But not today. He longed to be back in the baking humidity. Back in that other small town. Back in Cassie's living room, holding his son.

Michael had stolen his heart. Completely. There was nothing he wouldn't do for his little boy. Even move, if he had to. How could he make the huge decisions ahead? Not just now, but a lifetime of decisions. Where would he find direction? The thought of it overwhelmed him.

At least he had his mother. She'd been a good parent, sheltering him as much as she could, moving to Boone and
~~~

changing their names. Always the encourager, from baseball to acting, she'd given him the confidence to dream.

Still, a part of him missed having a man to talk to, to throw a ball with.

He'd give that to Michael.

He didn't know this man, Nick, who Jill had named as Michael's father. The man must've known the baby wasn't his, but he didn't seem upset that his wife gave birth to another man's child. What did that make the guy?

Either really nice or an idiot. Maybe both.

Whatever the case, Michael was the top priority. As soon as the filming of the next scenes on his current project ended, he'd catch a flight back down South to Oxford.

Chapter 8

"Thanks for inviting Benjamin to go boating with you." Cassie followed her son through Sarah Beth's front door.

"You're welcome." Sarah Beth scuttled around, pushing things into a canvas bag. "You sure you won't join us?"

"I didn't inherit my father's sea legs. Even Jacuzzis nauseate me."

In the living room, Nick stood drinking coffee with Sam Conrad. Cassie waved. "Y'all watch over my boy."

A groan came from Benjamin as he rolled his eyes. "Really, Mom?"

Sarah Beth locked arms with Cassie. "I'll watch out for him. I'm not skiing because of the baby. This is a surprise for Jess."

"What's the occasion?" Worrying about Benjamin skiing with four capable adults did seem a little silly. So many teens gave their parents real reasons for anxiety, but Benjamin wasn't one of them. She'd been blessed with an easy child.

A truck rumbled out back. "He's here. Hide." Sarah Beth pushed them toward the laundry room, where they all squeezed in and peeked through a crack in the door.

Like Jess wouldn't notice their vehicles parked out front.

The back door rattled, then opened. "I got the watermelons you wanted. Do we have company?"

"Close your eyes, Jess. I have a surprise for you."

"Can I set the watermelons down first?"

"Okay, then don't move." Sarah Beth waited a second for him to unload his arms, then picked up a ski vest from behind the door and held it up, waving for them to come out. "You can open your eyes now. I know I'm a couple of weeks late, but in honor of our first date anniversary, we're going waterskiing today!"

"Sounds perfect." Jess greeted all the guests, then nestled her in his arms and kissed her. "Thanks for planning this."

Groaning, Sam let out a series of forced coughs. "Now that I feel like losing my breakfast, let's go."

"Don't be a hater." Jess's forehead crinkled as he surveyed his wife. "But, can pregnant women ski?"

"I'm just going along for the ride. I want to be careful." Her hand went to her midsection. "There's so much to think about—having a kid."

Sam nudged Nick. "Where's your hot wife? Home with the rug rats?"

"Classy, Sam. Yeah, my hot wife is at home with my children. It's a wonder you keep your job with your mouth."

"Don't worry about my job." Sam motioned to Cassie. "She's one of my best customers. I'm good, right?"

"Sam's a fantastic money manager. Couldn't be happier."

A satisfied smirk lifted Sam's lips. "Enough chit chat. Let's roll." He nodded toward the door, then eyed Cassie.

"Y'all go on. Don't worry about me."

Jess held up a hand. "I need to change." His keys and cell phone clattered as he threw them on the counter.

Once he left the room, Sarah Beth sighed. "This is going to be great."

Disappointment stabbed at Cassie's insides. Wouldn't she love to have that kind of relationship? Those hopes had been crushed and swept out the door along with her heart and her pride over a year ago.

The phone on the counter vibrated with a text. Sarah Beth grabbed it and stared. An almost guttural growl came from her throat. "Sean Jessup McCoy."

Maybe things weren't as rosy as she thought. She'd already witnessed the Dylan-tabloid scene. "Benjamin, let's step outside while they get the equipment."

At that moment, Jess reappeared wearing his swim trunks. "What's wrong? The grocer assured me the watermelon was ripe."

"Not the watermelon. This." Through gritted teeth, Sarah

Beth forced out words and held up the phone. "Explain why that Sophia woman is sending a picture of herself to your phone." Sarah Beth's hand shook as she squeezed the phone with white knuckles. "I could crush this."

Jess shook his head. "I can't control what the crazy woman does. I delete stuff like that."

One fist went to Sarah Beth's hip. "How often does she send *stuff like that*, and do other women send *stuff like that*?"

Nick motioned toward Jess. "In his defense, women have been texting all kind of messages to Jess since he quarterbacked at Florida. He didn't know them, didn't know how they got his number. I wouldn't put it past Sophia to text him just to cause problems."

"Um." Benjamin spoke from beside her. "It's a thing some girls do now. Not cool, though."

So her son knew about lewd texts? Did girls send him pictures…? *Stop.* Cassie closed her eyes. Not going there. Her son was growing up, and they lived in a fallen world.

Sarah Beth sat and punched into the phone's settings. "Humph, I blocked her number."

Rubbing the blond stubble on his chin, Jess let out a loud exhale. "I should've told you she still tries to contact me, but you can check our phone records. I haven't texted, called, or emailed her back. I ignore and delete."

"I'll be needing the password to your computer and email."

Her husband gave her a tender look. "All my passwords are Sarah Beth-1."

His words contorted her mouth and set her lips to quivering. "I'm sorry. These pregnancy hormones make me crazy… I…" Her voice broke.

"I like that you're a little crazy." Jess's arms wrapped around her waist. "We're still learning how to navigate these issues as newlyweds. I freaked out the other day, too." His chin brushed her forehead.

She wiped her nose and patted his chest. "You're right. Let's go."

Sam groaned again. "Thank goodness. You're killing me

with all that mush."

A sinking feeling overwhelmed Cassie. If only her own marital problems could've been solved that easily.

~~~

At seven o'clock that evening, Cassie sat on the edge of Sarah Beth's couch. On the loveseat across from her, Sarah Beth and Jill made faces at Michael. A growl rumbled through Cassie's stomach. She'd forgotten to eat lunch. Again. Oh well, the pork chops Jess and the guys were grilling by the pool would be ready soon.

Just outside the screen door, Katie dangled a string up and down, giggling as the kitten jumped higher and higher.

Covering the side of her mouth, Sarah Beth whispered, "Jess hasn't had any contact, at least on his end. I may not know how to cook, but I'm not technologically challenged. I checked everywhere."

Jill furrowed her brows. "But you know he loves you, and your relationship has to be built on trust."

"I know, and he said he was glad I'm a little jealous, but that I don't have anything to worry about."

Cassie's mouth went dry, and her gaze fell to the ground. "There's a fine line to walk between trust and being caught off guard...like I was. There's so much temptation out there." Had she really said that out loud?

Sarah Beth moved across to sit beside her. "Your husband cheated on you?"

Why had she brought this up? Without raising her eyes, Cassie nodded. The bitterness she'd fought so hard against stooped her shoulders and choked away words.

"I didn't mean to dredge up a sore subject."

Cassie pressed on a smile. "It's okay. You were still living in L.A. then so you missed the drama, but I never want you to walk on eggshells around me. Why don't we go check and see how long till the meat is ready? I know you're starving after a day on the water."

"You know me all too well."

"You two go ahead." Jill caressed Michael's head. "It's too
~~~

muggy for baby boy."

"We won't be long." A change of space might lighten the moment. Cassie followed Sarah Beth out the back door.

They approached the men. Gesturing with broad movements, Nick questioned Sam. "Why were you wasting money in a casino? Can't you find something else to do with your time and money?"

Lifting one shoulder, Sam shook his head. "Oxford may be great for college students, young couples, and retired people, but for a single man in his late twenties…not so much. I get bored."

The guys quieted when the ladies joined them, and Jess held up a spatula. "I'm cooking as fast as I can."

Sarah Beth laughed. "He knows me so well. I'm starving lately and craving pork. At least this week."

"*Lately* you're starving?" Nick's face screwed into a frown. "You've been a pig since I met you."

"Not all women are bone thin, like your wife. Some of us like to eat."

Cassie took a step closer to Sam. "I overheard you saying you're bored. Why don't you join our crew going to Honduras? Serving those less fortunate than ourselves can be a great cure for boredom."

Sarah Beth's upper lip curled. "I don't think Sam would be interested."

Pointing the spatula at her, Jess scoffed. "You don't know until you ask. That's a great idea, Cassie." He turned to Sam. "What do you think?"

"I hate to say this, but…Sarah Beth is right. I can't see myself on some dirt floor with no AC, eating beans and rice with a bunch of dirty little kids."

"It's not that bad. We stay in a facility that's like a dorm. The floors are concrete, and there are fans. It's plenty cool at night because of the mountains. You'd be pleasantly surprised. The scenery is gorgeous, and I can guarantee you will not be bored."

Everyone waited for Sam's response.

He waved them off. “Stop staring at me. I’ll look into it and get back to you. Don’t get your hopes up, though.”

A nervous sigh came from Sarah Beth. “If Dylan Conner can do it—”

“Don’t bring that guy into this.” Jess shot her a look.

Tension zipped around the circle of friends. Cassie cleared her throat. “Anyone can change. Especially on a mission trip.” She hoped.

Chapter 9

Two weeks had passed in a blur. Dylan shut the door to his rental car, stepped into the Mississippi humidity, and edged toward Cassie's white Victorian home. As soon as his shoot had finished, he'd changed his flight that had been scheduled back to Los Angeles, and headed down South. Why should he wait? If this visit went as well as the last time—

Heated voices carried from the front door left ajar, and he halted his pace in the shadow of the immense turret that jutted from the roof.

"Baby, come on." A man with a twangy Southern drawl whined. "I made a mistake. Can't you forgive me?"

"Stop it, Evan." Cassie's voice. Not yelling, but authoritative. "You wanted a different kind of life. You don't get to have your old one back."

"I'm nothing without you."

"You have a *new wife*. And baby. I'm civil to you because of my faith and because of our son. I'll communicate with you only in matters concerning him. Don't let yourself into *my* house again."

"Come on." The man lowered his voice. "I was your first and only. You can't desert me."

His muscles rigid, Dylan took a cautious step closer. This guy gave him the creeps. How did a nice girl like Cassie ever get mixed up with such a slime-ball?

Cassie let out a long huff. "Let me enlighten you on a little secret. After our divorce, people came to me with information about you—some of it marital, some of it professional. I took the evidence and created electronic files that I've stored in more than one place. I sent a copy to my father."

The man sucked in a breath. "You sent it to Big Roy? He's

gonna kill me."

"If you mess with me or Benjamin, I'll have you disbarred. I think you can guess why."

"I thought you were better than that, Ms. Perfect, all high and mighty."

"You humiliated me and your son." Her pitch rose a fraction. "You cost a young man his life. And you dare criticize me? I should've known in law school not to get involved with you. Trusting you was the biggest mistake of my life. I believed you when you said you loved me—that you were my *best friend for life.*"

"You *are* my best friend." His tone softened. "And I miss you. We could leave now and go anywhere in the country and practice law. Benjamin's old enough. He doesn't need you to mother him all the time."

With quiet steps, Dylan moved onto the porch. The weasel made a big mistake with that Benjamin comment. What a loser.

"This is the last time I'm telling you. Our pre-nup was clear. Our divorce was clear. Unless it's about our son, don't contact me. And don't show up here again unless it's for a scheduled visit with Benjamin."

The opening in the door pulled wider to reveal Cassie glaring at her ex-husband. She held a white-knuckle grip on the wood frame.

Evan grabbed her arm. "Give me a chance."

Cassie threw Evan's hand off. "Get out." The dog stood close by and growled.

"Or what?" His voice was cool. "You'll call Daddy? Sic that ridiculous dog on me?"

Heat flowed through Dylan's chest and arms. Neither had noticed him standing on the edge of the porch, but he wasn't letting this guy stay another second. Dylan marched over and inserted himself between the two. "The lady said get out, and that's what you should do."

"What? Who are you?" The man's forehead scrunched together.

Cassie stepped back inside, and Dylan glanced long enough

to see her snatch her phone from a long table near the doorway. Cassie spoke slow and with emphasis. "I *will* call my daddy. *Your* daddy. The police. And your new wife. Whatever it takes to get you to leave." Her eyes seared Evan. "In a heartbeat."

He spun on the heels of his ostrich cowboy boots and stomped to a Mercedes parked down the street.

Once the jerk drove off, Dylan ran his fingers across Cassie's arm. "Did he hurt you?"

"He wouldn't, but I need to cool down." She covered her eyes with one hand and took deep breaths. "Thank the Lord, Benjamin's not here."

"His father sounds like a real loser. No offense."

Dropping her hand, Cassie cocked her head and aimed her gaze at him. "How much did you hear?"

"Enough."

Her blue-green eyes filled with tears. Pain was obvious in the tense line of her lips. "I guess you think less of my mediation skills. I can't even manage my own marriage."

One would think he'd doubt her now. Instead, his heart tugged him toward her. "Could you use a hug?"

A small attempt at a laugh escaped her pink lips. "What?"

Without hesitation, Dylan pulled her into his arms. "I haven't known you long, but I've seen enough to know you deserve better."

Cassie rested her head on Dylan's shoulder for a moment, then stiffened and pulled away. Her hands ran down her starched navy skirt as if to straighten it. "I'm sorry. I was thrown off balance. He appeared with no warning." She wiped a tear with her fingertip. "Speaking of… What are you doing here?"

~~~

The muscles formed a knot at the base of Cassie's skull and twisted down her shoulders. Not only had she lost her composure in the first meeting, now she'd let this man comfort her—in his arms. How much more unprofessional could she get?
~~~

Mimi scurried to Dylan and sat in front of him, paw extended. The pink bow from the groomer sprouted from the white fluffy fur on top of her head.

A smile spread across Dylan's face and revealed dimples in each cheek. "Bonjour, Mimi. Good to see you again." His eyes returned to Cassie. "I finished a shoot in New York and was standing in the line at airport security and thought, I can't wait to see my son." He shrugged, his innocent expression reminding her of a child's. "I changed my ticket, flew to Memphis, rented a car, and here I am."

"But what are you doing *here*?" She pointed at her porch.

He gave her a sheepish look. "This town doesn't have enough hotels. Apparently, there's a baseball tournament this weekend, and the closest available room is some place called Pontotoc, Mississippi." He paused and ran his fingers through his hair. "I don't really have any friends here. I thought you might know someone who has a house or condo for rent."

She waved him in. "Does Jill know you're in Oxford?"

One side of his mouth lifted. "No." He glanced around. "Are you sure I can come inside? I know Sarah Beth has rules about men being in her home when she's alone."

Cassie raised an eyebrow as she closed the front door behind him. "Sounds like a good rule. Should I be worried?"

"I'm safe enough." His eyes locked with hers.

The knob rattled in the kitchen, and Benjamin burst through the garage entrance. His backpack hit the old church pew by the door with a thud. "You're back."

Dylan crossed the room to shake Benjamin's hand. "This small town must be growing on me. I'm trying to figure out a place to hole up for a while."

"Stay here. This is a huge house, and it's just me and Mom."

A boulder lodged in Cassie's throat. Really, Benjamin?

"I couldn't put your mom out like that."

"It'd be fun. I have a baseball game tonight. You could come watch." He looked past Dylan. "Right, Mom?"

A wave of heat ran up Cassie's back. She kneaded her neck with her knuckles and chewed the inside of her cheek. What should she say? They certainly had room, but talk about unprofessional. Of course, she was friends with Jill and Nick, too. That was what put her in this predicament in the first place. And she wanted to make things easier.

This would be convenient. For a day or two.

She needed to answer. If she was going to do this, she should offer her room, since she didn't really know the man well enough to have him sleep in a room upstairs near her son. "The hotels will probably empty after the weekend. You can stay until then. You can have my room, and I'll sleep upstairs in one of the rooms by Benji."

Her son groaned. "Mom, I asked you not to call me that anymore."

Dylan laughed and clapped Benjamin's shoulder. "My mom used to call me Dill. I kind of miss it now. At your age, not so much." He studied Cassie. "Are you sure you don't mind?"

"It's fine." She pretended to scowl. "You know most of us down South are armed, right?"

"No need for firearms." Dylan inched closer and whispered, "I was scared enough when I heard something about a father named Big Roy."

A small laugh escaped her lips. Judging by the look on his face, Dylan was serious. Let the actor be scared of Daddy, too. "You should be."

"I'll run out and grab my suitcase."

After he darted through the door, she sighed. Her head throbbed. A massage might help. Not normally something she treated herself with, but to get rid of all this tension…

Dylan traipsed back in, carrying a small suitcase and backpack.

"Follow me, and I'll show you where to put your things."

She led him down the hall to her room. Her brain wasn't cooperating after the day's unexpected course of events. No words came to mind. So much for casual conversation. At least she'd cleaned the house. She'd need to move some clothes upstairs for the weekend. They stepped inside. "This is it. I'll change the sheets, and grab the things I'll need. You can use that closet." She pointed at the closed door. "It's empty. It belonged to…"

"The jerk who just left?"

"Yep, the jerk."

He plopped down on the plaid reading chair in the corner and kicked his loafers up on the ottoman. "This room looks just like an ad for Ralph Lauren."

Her jaw dropped. Good gravy, how could he know? "I did copy an ad I saw for Ralph Lauren. The decorator finished not long ago. I'd wanted a change since… Funny you noticed, though."

Dylan leaned back and closed his eyes. The man had long lashes. "I'm usually thumbing through magazines to see what junk they're writing about me, so I probably saw the ad a dozen times. Plus, I fly a lot. More magazines."

She pulled a set of sheets from the antique chifferobe and dragged the old ones off the bed. "Does it bother you? The stuff they write?"

Dylan's shoulders lifted. "I hated they got pictures of Sarah Beth. She's been through enough without having to deal with more drama."

"I heard when you visited her here last year you wore some pretty outlandish costumes. Now you're only hiding behind the sunglasses and baseball cap?"

His green eyes opened and found hers, his expression serious. "I was trying to protect her when I came to visit. And I thought it might make her laugh if I looked ridiculous. She needed to laugh again after Adam died."

A ripple of sympathy pulled at her gut. He'd wanted to cheer up Sarah Beth? She smoothed out the covers. "Sounds like you really cared about her."

Dylan stood and crossed the room to his suitcase he'd left by the closet. He unzipped it, rummaged through his clothes, and held out a T-shirt. "I told myself after my dad left, I'd never marry or have kids. It wasn't fair to put them through a divorce. Sarah Beth is probably the only woman who made me reconsider the marriage thing."

"We're not so different then. After my divorce, I promised myself to never go through that kind of pain again." Or put her son through the grief again. "I hope Benjamin doesn't feel the way you do about marriage and family, though. I hadn't considered that he might shut himself off."

"Benjamin won't turn out like me. Hey, I hadn't planned to have a kid either. Maybe I'll take the plunge someday." He grinned at her. "You may change your mind, too. You know, never say never."

Chapter 10

Dylan struggled to open his eyelids. One side of his face was sheltered under a flowered sheet. The other groggy eye scanned the room. Where was he? And what was that noise? Pale blue silk drapes. Not a hotel suite.

"Cassandra Jane?" A deep, Southern voice boomed from nearby. "We're here for a visit. Wake up, you sleepyhead."

Sleepyhead? Cassandra Jane? *Cassie.* His attractive host.

Dylan peeked out from the covers. An enormous, bearded man stood in the doorway, aviator sunglasses resting on a head of red hair peppered with gray. Two women stood with him, both blonde, one a good bit older.

The younger of the two gawked. "That's a man in the bed, Daddy, and the bedroom looks different."

Oh, crud. How could he escape? Dylan tried to focus his fuzzy brain while his heart battered his ribs.

"Are we in the right house?" The monstrous man turned to the girl—who looked to be in her early twenties. "Emma Catherine, go check the house number and see if we're in Cassandra Jane's house."

"We're in the right house, Daddy." Emma Catherine frowned. "And you know I hate when you call me that double name." Her frown turned to a giggle. "Maybe Cassie picked him up. She is single, now."

No. No. From bad to worse. This had to be Big Roy. Would the guy notice if he crawled under the bed? Maybe he shouldn't make any sudden movements.

The older woman stepped nearer. "Cassandra wouldn't do that. *She's* a good girl."

His throat tightened. The situation could prove hazardous to his health. His eyes scanned left and right once more. No escape. He may as well surrender. Sitting up, he gathered the sheets to his chin. "Um, the hotels were full, and Cassie was kind enough to put me up for the weekend. She and Benjamin are sleeping upstairs. I'm Dylan Conner."

A squeal erupted from deep within Emma's throat. The earsplitting sound was worse than Sarah Beth's dog. She pounced on the bed, crouching above his pillow. "Dylan Conner? Like Dylan Conner, the actor?" Her lashes fluttered inches away from his.

"Get back here, Emma Catherine." The big man pawed at his belt. "Dang, I left the pistol in the car. I'm gonna check into this mess. Houseguest, huh…"

Not good. A crazed fan and a redneck looking for a gun. No wonder Cassie's ex was scared. Big Roy should've been called Ginormous Roy, and apparently, he was usually packing. Dylan scooted toward the opposite side of the mattress. It had been a while since he'd wanted to run out of a woman's bedroom. Except for maybe the catastrophe named Sophia.

The older lady rubbed the large man's arm. "Settle down, Roy. There's a reason Cassandra has a man here."

Big Roy eyed his wife, his mouth twisting as if deciding whether to attack.

Emma scrambled closer, pulled her cell from her pocket, and clicked. "You don't mind if we take a few selfies together, do you?"

A thousand times yes, he minded. Could the Cassie he knew really be related to this girl? Or Big Roy?

A flame of blazing red hair arrived at the bedroom door, like a flare being answered at a shipwreck. Help, at last.

"Good gravy. Mom? Dad? What are y'all doing here?"

Roy encased Cassie in his arms, lifting her off the ground. "We came to visit my girl. Why's there a man in your bed?"

"Please tell me you didn't barge into my bedroom."

"Your sister's got her phone out taking pictures of the intruder right now. Do I need to fetch my pistol?"

"Oh, Daddy, no." Cassie spun and dashed to her sister, grabbing the phone. "And you. No pictures. I'll take this."

"I could make some money with those." Emma turned to Dylan, eyes half open. "Or just stare at them every night before I go to sleep."

Chin dropping to her chest, Cassie gave Dylan an apologetic look. "I'm so sorry." Her eyes squeezed shut. "Quit acting like a stalker, Em."

"Fine. Give me my phone back."

"After I delete the pictures."

Escape time. Dylan hopped up, slipped a T-shirt over his head, and ran his fingers through his hair. Thank goodness he'd worn pajama pants.

Cassie let out a loud exhale and motioned limply. "These are my parents, Ruby and Roy Bosarge."

The way Cassie's ponytail bounced with her frustration made Dylan smile. The situation was rather humorous. Or it would be, assuming he lived through it.

Roy crossed the room in three strides and shook Dylan's hand. Hard. "Sure enough, I recognize you now. I liked that shoot-em-up movie you were in. Sorry about getting all riled up. Who would've thought?"

Smiling, Ruby joined them. "Any friend of Cassandra's is a friend of ours."

Cassie shoved a thumb toward Emma. "And the slightly obnoxious one is my sister."

Flashing her white teeth, Emma smiled. "A fan."

Though the danger seemed to have passed, he'd better pour on the charm, just in case. Dylan made eye contact with each family member and offered his best smile. "It's totally understandable that you were thrown." He grinned at Ruby. "Let me guess. Jane Austen fan, right?"

"You're good." Ruby gave him a knowing look. "I love Jane Austen's writings. I named my daughters after Jane, her sister, Cassandra, and her characters Emma, Catherine, Elinor, and Elizabeth."

"How many daughters do you have?"

"Just three. Cassandra Jane, Emma Catherine, and Elinor Elizabeth. Cassandra is the oldest. You can probably tell, definitely the mature child. No doubt you can guess Emma is our late-in-life baby. And a blessing." She glanced toward the young woman.

Roy motioned down the hall. "Is Benjamin upstairs? I wanted to fly up and carry him to a Braves game. The ladies thought they could spend the day here."

"I don't know what Benjamin has planned. He played a game last night, but they lost, and they're out of this tournament."

"I'll go ask him right quick." Roy turned back and stroked his beard. "The actor can tag along, too. I have room in my plane."

Ride in the plane with him? "Let me check my schedule." If Jill wouldn't let him have Michael this afternoon, being on the big guy's good side seemed like a wise choice.

~~~

A horrible idea. Cassie rolled her shoulders to fight the tension forming a tight cord from her neck down her arms. Yet here she was at Sarah Beth's front door with her headstrong baby sister. Mother had tried to reign Emma in, but that worked about as well as flying a kite in a tornado. Sarah Beth had insisted they come for supper, so here they were.

The door flew open, and Sarah Beth stood with her large dog beside her. "Welcome. Glad y'all came. We have plenty of food."

The least of Cassie's worries. "This is my mother, Ruby Bosarge, and my sister, Emma."

"Nice to meet you both. Come meet Kim, our student minister's wife."

Kim, a smiling strawberry blonde, shook Mother's hand. The back door swung open, and the scent of charcoal and herbs drifted in, along with the muggy warm air. Jess entered carrying a tray of what looked like pork chops and zucchini. Sarah Beth must still be craving pork.

"Where's Benjamin tonight?" Jess slowed as he passed.

"My father decided to fly up today and take Benjamin to a Braves game." She introduced her family to Jess.
~~~

"Good to meet you. Can I take that for you?" Her mother was ever the gracious Southern belle.

"Whoa. Hel-lo, Jess." Then there was Emma. The gleam in her eyes and the gawking. How boy crazy could one girl be?

Cassie elbowed her.

Emma opened her mouth. Again. "You should've seen my daddy's face this morning when he saw that actor Dylan Conner in my sister's bed. It was hilarious."

The room fell silent. Stares circled among the friends.

Cassie's temples pulsed with a full-blown tension headache. Maybe a migraine, too. "It's nothing like that sounded. Dylan flew in from New York to… All the hotels were filled, so he stopped by to see if I knew someone who might rent a condo or something. Benjamin all but insisted that he stay with us until Monday when the hotels clear out."

"That man tries to weasel his way in wherever he can." Jess set the tray on the counter with a thud. "Don't trust him, Cassie."

Lines wrinkled her mother's forehead. "What's he done? He wouldn't hurt Benjamin, would he?"

Sarah Beth shook her head and waved them off. "Oh, no. He's just a bit of a flirt."

"A bit?" Jess shot her a hard look.

"Sounds like somebody's jealous." Emma teased in a sing-song voice.

"Emma Catherine." Her mother tugged Emma's elbow. "You're a guest here." She turned to Sarah Beth. "I'm sorry. I had to invest in hair dye when this one was born. The gray started as soon as I brought her home from the hospital."

Emma crossed her arms in front of her ample chest. "Callin' 'em as I see 'em."

Sarah Beth smothered a laugh with her hand.

The spatula in Jess's hand aimed at Sarah Beth. "Be nice, or Gingie and that cat are getting your pork chop."

"Gingie will eat it in one gulp."

The corners of Jess's mouth turned up.

"And you wouldn't?"

After Jess returned to his cooking, Sarah Beth lowered her voice and leaned toward the ladies. "Dylan wanted me to go out with him, so it's kind of a sore subject."

Emma pointed her finger toward her mom. "Told you."

"And he's not someone Cassie would want to go out with, anyway." Sarah Beth motioned toward the sofas, and the ladies followed her lead and sat. "Dylan's not ready to settle down, and I don't think he's got his spiritual life together, if you know what I mean."

"Not really, but Cassie's first man wasn't all that great either." Emma's blue eyes rolled.

"Emma!" Her mother let out a long sigh. "We're here five minutes, and you've embarrassed our host and now your sister?"

Could this get any worse? Her mother was her best friend, and she wanted her to visit. But Emma? Another story. It was hard to believe they were related. Cassie trudged over to the window to keep from saying something she shouldn't. *Tame the tongue.*

Her mother followed and slipped her arm across her shoulders. Her gentle touch always soothed away stress.

Behind them, Kim cleared her throat. "After we eat, we have worship over at the Christian Student Union. Other young people Emma's age will be there. Come with us. There's music and a coffee bar."

"I'm in," Emma squealed.

Oh no. Kim would be sorry she asked. Cassie squinted as she looked through the glass pane. "What's with the holes in your backyard?"

Sarah Beth moved alongside Cassie and her mother. "My cat who thinks she's a dog digs holes with my dog who thinks she's the cat's mother. Crazy, right?"

Cassie had to laugh. "Why aren't Jill and Nick here tonight?"

Sarah Beth studied her hands before she spoke. "Jill's been dealing with the baby blues."

Jill had been exhausted and hadn't felt well, but no one had disclosed this diagnosis. "How long has she been suffering from postpartum depression?"

"Since Michael was born. Why?"

"That can be bad. Sometimes dangerous."

"I'm sure it's awful, but Jill's not dangerous. She loves that baby. She was feeling a little better, but then with Bill's death and the stress of dealing with… Please, keep this confidential, if you know what I mean."

Another reason she shouldn't have offered to mediate this case. The list kept getting longer.

Chapter 11

"Kim and Chris must have the patience of saints to take Emma with them." The cord of tension that had wrapped Cassie's scalp loosened. She eased her minivan out of her driveway. "Thanks for having us over for dinner and riding with me to drop Mother off." She glanced at Sarah Beth. "How are you feeling?"

"Hungrier, if that's possible. But I'm power walking for exercise. Jess runs one loop through the neighborhood, then I join him, and he power walks with me. I know some people run when they're pregnant, but I'm being super careful." She giggled. "He looks hilarious power walking—and totally handsome, of course. Every day I'm amazed at how much I love him." She cleared her throat and stretched her long arms in front of her. "As you know, we've both had to come to terms with jealousy and trust issues. But overall, I feel blessed beyond measure."

A weak smile was all Cassie could summon up. A familiar ache in her chest resurfaced. Her own first year of marriage had been much the same. A handsome husband. A quick pregnancy. But even then, she'd had her doubts about Evan's faithfulness. Without evidence, she'd pushed them aside as petty jealousy. He was an ambitious, young attorney trying to move up in his career, in society.

But in the end, he'd been guilty beyond reasonable doubt. Would there ever be complete closure to the wounds? She'd salvaged what was left of her heart and sealed it off from everyone but Benjamin.

"Did I say something wrong?" Sarah Beth asked. "I do that a lot."

"Of course not. I'm glad you're happy. It's just, I never

thought this would be my life. A divorced, single parent. I tried to do things right. I said no to alcohol, drugs, guys. I focused on my studies, went to church. Still, my marriage blew up in my face. All the things I entrusted to Evan, he discarded like yesterday's garbage."

"How are you doing spiritually with all this?"

Cassie swallowed at the lump in her throat. "I cling to the Lord. Sometimes it feels like He's all I have that's real in the world besides my son. I know I'm blessed, but I get lonely, and it still hurts." She huffed. "I mean, what's wrong with me? Am I too boring, too unattractive? Why would Evan have needed to turn to other women?" Glancing at Sarah Beth, she shook her head. "I shouldn't unload on you like this."

"I had the same questions about myself when Adam didn't want to marry me." Cassie had heard a bit of the story about Adam. He and Sarah Beth had been together for years. When she returned to her Christian faith, she moved out of their shared apartment. Eventually Adam became a Christian, reached out to her, and seemed to want her back. Almost immediately afterward, they were together in the car accident that took Adam's life. Sarah Beth had never been the same.

She continued. "I felt like there must've been something about me that wasn't pretty enough or interesting enough. I thought maybe I wasn't lovable. I sure don't have all the answers about men, but I'm a good listener when you want to talk, and I can pray for you."

Sarah Beth slapped a palm against her thigh. "If there's one thing I know for sure, there's nothing wrong with you. Evan was an idiot. I always wanted to be petite like you. And your red hair is stunning, not that you let anyone see much of it. All the work you helped me with for the university was perfect. Of course, it took me a while to find out you were an attorney hiding out in my campus office. No wonder."

The kind words lifted a bit of the heaviness that had settled around Cassie's heart. "The work I helped you with was fun and challenging. I enjoyed it. And I couldn't bring myself to work at the law firm where everything happened."

"Was he with someone from the office?"

Pain nudged its way back in. "Another attorney's wife." She eased the van into the Christian Student Union parking lot. "I better go see what my baby sister's getting into at the CSU."

Sarah Beth smirked. "She seems like a handful."

"You don't know the half of it."

~~~

From across the dimly lit converted warehouse, Kim gave Cassie a stiff look and signaled with a finger wave. Emma was near the stage where the local favorite musician, Bryan Freeman, sang and played guitar. Cassie made her way over as he finished a song.

A loud whoop and an ear-piercing whistle spewed from Emma.

Bryan's blue eyes widened at his new fan's appreciation, but he recovered with a grin in her direction.

Emma hovered over him as he gathered his guitar into the case. "You, mister, have got *the* voice. I mean I was melting right there in my sandals from the first note."

He closed the last clasp and stood. "I give all the glory to the Lord."

"You should go to Nashville. I mean, I'd pay to hear you." She grinned and batted her eyelashes. "Though, I hope you wouldn't charge me too much."

Poor guy. Cassie stepped in to try to save him. "Very nice, Bryan. This is my little sister, Emma. She's visiting from Mobile."

"Are you going to school here?" Extending a hand, Bryan shook Emma's hand, then Cassie's.

Emma ran her finger along the painted railing near the stage. "I was at Alabama, but I took a break this year. I couldn't decide what I wanted to do."

Took a break? Is that what they called it when the university booted you out?

"Happens to a lot of people." Bryan motioned toward the groups of students mingling around the room. "You want me to introduce you to a few students?"
~~~

Cassie slipped her hand behind Emma's back. "Maybe we should go?"

"Not yet." With a twist away from Cassie, Emma locked arms with Bryan. "Let's hit it." She pointed. "Start over there with those guys talking to Coach McCoy."

"The football players?"

She patted his arm. "Perfect."

Trailing behind them, Cassie sighed. Exactly as she'd feared. Damage control was the best she could do now.

Dropping Bryan's arm, Emma interjected herself into the midst of the football players. "Hey, Coach McCoy, I'd love to meet your friends."

"Sure, Emma." Jess introduced his players and Audrey Vaughn, who was standing with her brother, Grant.

Emma poked Grant's bicep. "You've got some guns there. Is this your girlfriend?"

Grant smiled and, if it was possible, the huge lineman puffed up a little more. "Sister."

Leaning close to Audrey, Emma attempted a whisper. "Who is that magnificent guy behind Coach McCoy?"

"Cole Sanders, the university's starting quarterback."

"I bet he knows some plays. Does he have a girlfriend?"

This conversation needed to cease and desist. "Emma, I'm exhausted." Cassie nudged her sister. "And we should go hang out with Mom."

Emma's eyes flashed. "I've been with Mom every day for the past year." She turned to Audrey. "You like him, don't you?"

Audrey's spine stiffened. "I'm just his tutor."

Gripping Emma's elbow, Cassie tugged.

"I wish I could stay longer." Emma pointed a thumb at Cassie. "But my sister's on my case."

Audrey squinted. "Are you going to Honduras with us, too?"

No. No. No. Cassie had hoped to omit this information until after the fact.

Emma's mouth fell open. "Cassie's going to Honduras with

y'all?" She turned her attention back to Cassie. "I want to go."

Not a chance. "It's too late to sign up. It's a mission trip, not a vacation. Besides, I'm looking forward to spending time with Benjamin."

"Blah, blah, all right." She stared back at Cole and chewed her lip. "I wonder if Mom and Dad would let me stay up here with you for a while."

Cassie shook her head and led Emma to the door. "Now's not a good time. I'm still sorting through my own stuff. I just can't."

Emma's lip pooched out as her shoulders slumped. Such a pitiful expression, too.

A smidgen of sympathy sliced through Cassie's annoyance. "Maybe when they let you try college again. You could check out school here." *Since Alabama probably wouldn't let her back on the campus.*

Emma perked up. "I can convince them to let me come in the fall. Especially since you're here. They might let me. Maybe even for summer school."

Cassie glanced heavenward. *Lord, help us all.*

~~~

The afternoon at the ballgame eased some of the sting of having to wait another day to see Michael. Dylan held in a tired sigh. His surprise visit hadn't set well with Jill. She'd claimed to have plans.

Small bumps and jolts along with the twilight view across the plane's windshield lulled him into a deep state of relaxation. He fought to hold his eyes open. Not that he didn't trust Big Roy's piloting, but the guy had to be exhausted. Flying after a full day watching baseball would leave anyone fatigued.

Benjamin snoozed in the back seat, worry free.

That was trust. What would it be like to have a father like Big Roy?

He'd never know. Cassie was blessed to have good parents. No doubt, Roy was a little on the eccentric side, but the man was easy to like—his deep, rich laugh and the way he showed affection to Benjamin. The guy had talked to everyone at the
~~~

Braves' ballpark, from the vendors to the players they'd met after the game. He spoke with equal respect and interest to all.

Dylan glanced back. He liked Benjamin, too. They'd laughed and cheered, even though the home team lost. In fact, he couldn't remember having such a good time at a baseball game. That was the kind of fun he wanted his son to have someday.

~~~

The hum of the garage door opening sent Cassie to her feet. *Thank you, Lord.* She trusted her father with her little boy, but the thought of them flying in that small plane sent her maternal instincts into overdrive. Of course, she really shouldn't think of Benjamin as her little boy any more. He'd passed her height years before.

A second later, the door opened. Benjamin held out a mesh bag of autographed baseballs. "Dylan got us in to meet the players. They signed the balls after Dylan took pictures with them. You should've been there."

A nice surprise. Cassie studied Dylan's chiseled face. "That does sound fun. Thank you."

Dylan clapped her father's shoulder. "I had a blast with Benjamin and my new friend Roy." He pointed at Cassie. "You should come with us next time, though."

Her father let out a hearty chuckle. "I found me a new travel buddy. Dylan knows baseball and can get us in anywhere. And he's not afraid to fly with me. That's a hard combination to find."

Dylan cupped one side of his mouth as he leaned toward Cassie. "I rediscovered prayer."

"I said a few myself." She snickered. "Funny, I thought I'd be doing yard work this weekend. Who knew I'd have a house full of company. But I'm pleasantly surprised."

"Mom, you gotta get out more." Benjamin rested a hand on her shoulder. "Why don't you and Dylan go up to Memphis for dinner or something?"

Cassie's neck burned. Now her son was sending her on a date. She scratched at her collarbone while she tried to recover.
~~~

"Benjamin Evan Brooks, I have a life, thank you."

"Sure enough, Benjamin has a point." Nodding, her father crossed his arms at his chest. "No need to sit around this big house like a bump on a log. Get out and live a little."

Could things get more embarrassing? "Daddy, please."

Dylan eyed Cassie. "We could go to Memphis. I've heard about the great barbeque."

Was he teasing her? Cassie cocked her head and scrunched her nose. She turned and called up the stairs. "Emma, Dylan Conner's back."

A shriek echoed down the halls, then footsteps thumped across the wood floors above.

A crooked smile traveled up the sharp angles of Dylan's face. "Devious. Your father told me you were a smart one."

Emma bounded down toward Dylan. "I hate that I have to leave tomorrow. I haven't been able to spend much time getting to know you."

He threw a glance at Cassie. "Your sister can give you the scoop." He cleared his throat. "I'm taking her to Memphis for a dinner date soon."

"Get out." Eyes wide, Emma stomped her foot. "You and Ms. Perfect are going on a date?" She turned to her father. "Daddy, are you okay with this?"

"Sure enough." He stood a little taller. "I suggested it."

Cassie put her hand to her ear. "I think Mother needs me in the other room." How had she lost control of this conversation?

~~~

Cassie stuffed the sheets from the guest rooms into the washer and pushed the button. Her parents left early, Emma dragging behind, half asleep. It would've been nice to have them another day, but the quiet was pleasant, too. Besides, Dylan had finally worked out a time to get Michael. They didn't need Emma around asking questions.

The last of the dishes from breakfast were put away, and the roast for the evening meal was thawing in the sink. A steaming cup of chai tea and a book waited in the sunroom.
~~~

She slipped into the white wicker chair facing the bird feeder in the back yard, and Mimi rested at her feet.

The tea warmed her throat as the spicy brew slid down.

"Reading anything good?"

She hadn't heard Dylan approach. "A book about medical missionaries in developing countries." She lowered the book to her lap and glanced at him. "I'm trying to learn as much as I can before we go."

Dylan sucked in a deep breath and stretched his arms over his head, eyes closed. Hair stuck up at the back of his head, and sleep lines ran across his perfect face. A look more natural than the ones on the cover of all those magazines. And cute.

Opening his eyes, the corners of his mouth lifted. "What are you smiling at? Thinking of our future date in Memphis?"

Why had Benjamin and Daddy ever brought that up? "Your hair's sticking up." And she wasn't smiling, was she? She darted her eyes back toward the book. "Would you like some chai tea?"

"Direct me, and I'll get it myself."

"I don't mind." She set her book on the light blue vintage table and stood.

"I'll shadow you, so next time I won't interrupt your reading."

His hand brushed against hers as he reached to push open the door. She wouldn't acknowledge the touch. Or the sensation that lingered on her skin.

One cabinet after the other, she opened and described the contents. "Make yourself at home, but don't feel like you can't ask where something is."

"I'm good at memorizing things once I get a look. It helps with my work."

Cassie turned to stare at him. "Are you saying you have a photographic memory?"

"When I need to. For example, I vividly remember your fiery red hair that day you left it down." His gaze traveled from her hair to her eyes. "And I noticed your green eyes have flecks of blue when you aren't wearing those fake glasses."

His observation unnerved her. "What fake glasses?"

Dylan held out his hand. "I wear costumes for a living, you know. Let me peek through your lenses."

"That's not necessary." Cassie dropped the tea bag into the water, then offered the mug. He was tall, but not as tall as Daddy. And slimmer, with deep green eyes. Eyes that noticed things. Memorized things. She needed to be more careful. "Do you want milk or sugar?"

"Your costume makes sense for your occupation. I'm not knocking it. You want to keep the focus on business. Not your pretty hair and eyes."

His words hung in the air.

She rotated back toward the sunroom. "Let me know if your memory fails and you can't find the milk and sugar."

Chapter 12

Cassie prayed during her quiet time for her words and actions to be pleasing to the Lord. His guidance through the next few weeks of mediation would be all that saved her. No matter how much she planned, the fragile situation could change like the direction of the wind. Which way would it blow this week?

As long as Benjamin was around, she wasn't as concerned, but once he left for school today, she'd be alone with Dylan. That could be uncomfortable. After her Bible study and morning workout, she cooked the ten slices of bread she'd soaked in a bowl of eggs mixed with milk, vanilla, and cinnamon. Now all she needed to do was sauté the sliced bananas for a minute. She slid the slices into a hot skillet.

As she finished, Benjamin appeared. "French toast. My favorite." He rounded up his backpack, then stood alongside her, waiting for a stack. "Trying to impress Dylan?"

She gave his head a playful flick. "See if I make *your* favorite again anytime soon."

"Touchy subject."

"After the awkward matchmaking over the weekend?" She shot him a lopsided smile.

"Something smells delicious. I had to find the source." Clean-shaven and a smile lighting his deep green eyes, Dylan entered the kitchen.

"Mom's cinnamon French toast with sautéed bananas." Benjamin rubbed his stomach and then took his plate to the table.

Dylan sucked in a deep whiff and joined Cassie at the coffee pot. "Sign me up." When she pushed a plate of French toast drizzled with real maple syrup in front of him, a sigh escaped his throat. "Diet's ruined."

Benjamin hooted and pointed at them. "Did you plan matching outfits last night?"

"What?" Cassie swept a glance over Dylan. Khaki shorts, a blue polo, and a white baseball cap. The same as her. She swiped her Ray-Bans from the counter. "What kind of sunglasses do you wear?"

Dimples appeared on his smooth cheeks as he pulled the exact pair out of his pocket. "Looks like we're twinsies. I can change."

How awkward. "We're just going to get Michael."

"Unless some of those photographers find you." Benjamin took his plate to the sink and rinsed it. "It would be hilarious. Dylan Conner and his date in matching outfits."

Not that again. Why was her son so obsessed with fixing her up with this actor? "Babysitting isn't a date, and I'm too old for Dylan."

Dylan tapped her nose with his forefinger. "Only four years. That's not too old."

"How do you know?"

His eyes met hers. "I asked your father."

More awkward and weird, too. She shut off the stove, put away the ingredients, and grabbed her keys. "Bye, Benji. Be amazing today. I love you." She motioned to Dylan. "Let's go get Michael. I've missed holding him." Plus she needed something to distract herself from this man and this insane situation.

With his fork shoveling at his plate with one hand, Dylan held up the other hand. "I've missed him, too. But can I finish my breakfast? This is good."

Something in his green eyes reminded her of a little boy. But then they twinkled and glanced down at her lips. No. Not a little boy at all.

~~~

A wreath with a blue bow still hung on the white wooden door, announcing Michael's birth. Dylan bit the inside of his jaw. Too bad he hadn't gotten to be there. As he imagined the scene at the hospital, something tore inside, like the ripping of
~~~

an old wound. He corralled his thoughts back to the present. There was nothing he could do about missing his son's birth now.

The house looked nice enough. Well-kept. Small, but quaint like most of the houses on the street. He glanced at Cassie beside him as he tapped on the door. Her sleek red hair barely showed with the bun and baseball cap. Too bad about that, too. He'd love to see those blazing locks. And touch them. A stupid thought. The mediation was too important to screw up with flirtations. His son was all that mattered.

No one answered, and no sounds came from inside. Cassie moved around an oak rocking chair and peered into the long window across the porch. "She knew we were coming, right?"

"I texted her last night. I'll call." He punched Jill's contact on his phone. This had better not be some kind of trick. If it was, there'd be a price to pay. He wasn't putting up with manipulation. "No answer."

Cassie's lips twisted. "Let me see if it's locked." She knocked again, then pushed the door open. "Jill? Is everything okay?" She walked into the dark house and down the hall calling her name.

Dylan shadowed her, taking in the home's modest decor and listening for any sign of life.

A baby's coo came from the second bedroom, and they followed the sound into a nursery painted pale yellow. On the floor, Jill lay beside Michael, who played with a plastic baby toy that hung above him.

Cassie fell to her knees above Jill. "What's wrong? Are you okay?"

No response. Dylan bent down and gave Jill a gentle shake. "Jill." He patted her cheek. "Wake up."

Jill's eyes fluttered open. "Oh, no. Is Michael okay?"

"He's fine. Are you sick?" Cassie lay the back of her hand on Jill's forehead.

"I felt weak. I couldn't… My joints ache."

"Have you been exposed to the flu?" Fearful, Dylan touched Michael's forehead. Soft and cool. Thank goodness.

"Nick and Katie had a little spring cold last week, but nothing like flu."

"I'll pack some things for you and Michael." Cassie stood. "We have to get you to the hospital. Something's not right."

With a wobble, Jill pushed herself onto her elbows, then lay back on the floor. "I can't."

Dylan slipped an arm under her. "Let me help you." She was skin and bones. No wonder she was weak. Maybe she just needed to eat more. But she'd said there was pain in her joints. What if she'd lain there all day, his son crying for a bottle in a dirty diaper? His jaw clamped shut, but he kept his touch gentle as he helped her to Cassie's van.

Meanwhile, Cassie turned the air on, went around to the back, and strapped Michael in the infant seat. Then she placed the baby bag and another duffle between the captain's chairs. The woman was efficient.

Looking once more at Jill's frail state before shutting the door, a wave of nausea swept through Dylan's body. If this was the flu or worse, would his son catch it? What if something terrible happened? The baby was so tiny. How would he take care of a sick infant? He glanced back at Michael. The baby's color was good. Maybe he would be all right.

The short drive proved the hospital was closer than he realized. One plus for small towns. But would the place have the technology to treat Michael if he did get sick?

Cassie put the van in park. "Dylan, call and ask Sarah Beth to be prepared to pick up Katie after school while I call Nick to tell him to meet us at the hospital."

Her competence eased the sick feeling in his stomach. Why did he put so much trust in a woman he barely knew?

At the ER, Cassie checked in at the window for Jill. She spoke to the nurse in a professional tone and explained the situation. "Which doctor is in today?"

When the nurse gave a name, Cassie patted the counter. "Please let him know Cassie Brooks is here with the patient."

Moments later, a man in blue scrubs pushed through the double doors. "Cassie Brooks. Great to see you." He extended his hand. "Do you like the improvements to the ER?"

Cassie returned the handshake. "Very pleased. I'm glad we were able to raise the funds." With her head, she motioned toward Jill. "This is my dear friend. I found her passed out at home. She has a baby. I'd appreciate it if you could take good care of her. Her husband's on his way."

"Of course. Let's bring her on back. Y'all can come with her, if it's okay with the patient."

"Yes." Jill managed a little nod.

With Michael in his arms, Dylan trailed behind the wheelchair. An orderly rolled Jill into a small, curtained area. Cassie had worked her magic again. They'd still be waiting if she hadn't intervened.

Fifteen minutes later, Nick entered and strode to his wife's side. He placed one hand on Jill's cheek. "You should've told me you were this sick. I would've stayed home. Do they know what's wrong?"

"It's probably nothing." Eyes barely open, Jill rested her hand on top of his. "I feel bad for putting you through all this, plus the expense."

What? Why was she worried about finances when she was clearly ill? Dylan's gaze left Michael to study Jill's expression. "If money's an issue, I'd be glad to help."

A razor might've cut less than Nick's searing stare. "I can pay for my wife's medical bills, and if I couldn't, I'd sell everything I own to make her well."

"You'd do anything except take money from the terrible Dylan Conner." Scoffing, Dylan rolled his eyes. "I owe you child support anyway."

Cassie put her hand on Dylan's forearm, giving him a gentle squeeze. His teeth bit down on his tongue. He'd keep the peace. Now wasn't the time to poke the hornet's nest.

They sat in silence until a doctor entered. His badge read Dr. Renner. "Jill, I'm sorry to hear you're still feeling poorly. I'd hoped you'd perk up after our last visit."

Nick let go of Jill and stood. "I'm no doctor, but this isn't postpartum depression. She's not well, and I'm ready to get to the bottom of it. Do I need to take her to Memphis or Jackson to a specialist?"

"Let me see what test results we have so far." Dr. Renner scanned her chart and then removed his glasses. His hand went to Jill's cheek. "How long have you had that rash?"

"Rash? I thought it was just the sun. Um… A couple of weeks ago, I guess, Nick built two rocking chairs for the front porch so we could spend time outside. I get a bit of sun sitting out there, and my face has stayed red."

He lifted Jill's hand, pressing along her wrists and knuckles. The pressure caused her to wince. "How long have your joints been this tender?" He continued, examining and pressing each joint.

"I've been achy for a while, but it got a lot worse last week."

He felt along the glands under her jawline and ears. "Has anyone been sick?"

"Nick and Katie had a little cold last week."

The doctor took a deep breath and exhaled slowly. "I'm sorry I didn't think of this when you were pregnant. There's no definitive test, but a series of criteria and markers. I'll need to call in a rheumatologist. You have the markers in the blood tests and the physical symptoms of Lupus. The butterfly rash across your face is a classic Lupus rash presentation."

Visibly shaken, Nick stood between the doctor and his wife, as if he could shield her from the diagnosis with his body. "How serious is this?"

Dylan's stomach tensed. Sure, he was ticked off at Jill, but he didn't wish some dreaded disease on her. If only they'd see he wanted to help.

The doctor replaced his glasses and moved to address his answer to Jill. "Lupus is an autoimmune disease. There's no cure, but it's manageable. Treatments have vastly improved over the past decades.

"Patients tend to have flare-ups when the immune system is active, so exposure to the cold may have caused the disease to become more active, plus the sun can exacerbate the symptoms. A short course of steroids will give you a boost.

You'll need to think about starting an antimalarial drug. It helps, but you'll take it indefinitely, and there's a slight chance of vision loss. Very rare, though."

Dylan's eyebrows furrowed. "Antimalarial drug? Does she have malaria?"

"No. The antimalarial drugs help send lupus into remission. It may take a couple of months to feel the change, but I want the specialist to manage her disease. I'll call and see if he can come by today and get her feeling better."

Tears trickled down Jill's face, and Nick sat on the side of the bed, caressing her head.

A somber quiet fell over the room. They should go and let them process the diagnosis. Dylan nudged Cassie's elbow.

She nodded and moved to the edge of the hospital bed. "We'll keep Michael as long as you need us to. Sarah Beth's picking up Katie. Don't worry about anything but getting well."

Nick's mouth formed a tight line. "I'll call soon."

The pacifier wiggled up and down in Michael's mouth, his little eyes staring up with an intense gaze as he snuggled against Dylan's chest. As they left the room, the warmth of his son in his arms sent a wave of marvel through him once again.

Part of him understood why Jill had kept the truth from him. But that wasn't her choice to make. The other part of him—still furious. Now Jill was sick. Really sick. Would she be able to care for their son?

The sunlight startled Michael as they exited through the automatic doors of the ER. His tiny eyes scrunched closed. Dylan shielded the baby's face with his hand. He'd shield him from as much hurt as he could. From now on.

Chapter 13

It had been a long time since Cassie had shopped in the diaper aisle. Which brand stopped those baby-boy leaks? So much she'd forgotten about infants in the past sixteen years. She threw two of the top brands into the cart.

Around the next aisle, Cassie eyed the organic dark chocolate bars, some with almonds. A must-have for stress relief. She picked one. Then threw a second in as well.

"Mmm, that looks good." Sarah Beth's voice spun Cassie around. Her arms were filled with packages of sour gummy worms. "Stocking up on chocolate? The solution for many of life's problems."

"How right you are." Cassie chuckled. "I'll probably inhale both on the way home. And how are you?"

"You really want to know?"

"Dylan has my cell if he needs help with Michael."

After tossing her candy in her basket, Sarah Beth wrapped her arms around herself. "Seeing Michael makes me so eager to have our baby. A little boy with Jess's blond hair and brown eyes." She sighed. "But can I take that little baby to a daycare and leave? Should I hire a nanny at the house? That would mean the nanny got to spend time with my child while I slave away on these campaigns to make other people money. Is it worth it?"

Cassie's heart squeezed for her friend. She'd faced the same dilemma with her legal career. "Let's pay and go have coffee in the deli."

Once they'd gone through the line and settled at a table, Sarah Beth devoured a lunch of baked chicken with turnip greens and black-eyed peas while Cassie nibbled at the first chocolate bar. A chiming cell interrupted their talk.

"Oh goodness. I better answer." Sarah Beth's elbow knocked over her tea as she struggled to pull the phone from her bag. "That ringtone's for the office in L.A." After throwing napkins at the spill, Sarah Beth lay the phone on the other side of her plate and pressed the speaker button. "Hello, this is Sarah Beth." She wiped the table, then piled the soggy mess in her cup.

"This is Max Davis. I'm taking Bill's position."

The man's tone was blunt.

"I look forward to working with you."

"That's the problem. You're not really working with me, because apparently Bill gave you some cozy arrangement—for what reason I can't fathom. You're going to need to be here in our office from now on."

Cassie eyed her friend's face. Lines formed between Sarah Beth's brows, and a vein in her forehead popped out. The new boss wasn't starting off on a good note.

"Is there a problem with my work?"

He cursed. "You're two thousand miles away, picking and choosing which accounts you want."

Uh-oh. If the way Sarah Beth's lips curled was any indication, the whole conversation had her friend's blood boiling. "It's gone fine up until now."

"You need to decide if you're in or out. Let me know by the end of the week."

"Hang on for a second, Mr. Davis."

A long sigh ensued on the other end of the line.

Sarah Beth muted the phone. "I think I just got my answer."

"What will you do? Resign?"

A slow smile spread across Sarah Beth's face. "In a way." She picked up the phone and texted a message faster than anyone above the age of eighteen should be able to do. "Can you check this for typos?"

What was her friend up to? After reading the email, Cassie laughed, head shaking. "Looks perfect." The woman did have business savvy.

Unmuting the phone, Sarah Beth spoke in a sweet, and a bit

overly perky, tone. "I'm back. You should have my resignation in your inbox. I copied the partners. I'll send all my accounts over to them along with an offer to hire out as a consultant. From Oxford. Two thousand miles away." She cleared her throat and smiled. "I did warn them that my consulting fees will be considerably higher than what I'm making now. Have a good day, Mr. Davis." With that, she hung up.

"Are you okay?"

Nodding slow and even, Sarah Beth shrugged. "A little numb, but good. Jess and I had talked about me taking a leave of absence anyway." Her lips pulled down at the sides. "What would Bill think if he were still—?"

"He'd want you to spend time with your family." But her resignation meant Jill would be out of a job, too. Had Sarah Beth considered that?

"Oh, no. It's time to pick up Katie at preschool." Sarah Beth glanced around. "Want to go with me?"

"Sure."

Thirty minutes later, they were back at the grocery store. Katie pointed from her vantage point in the huge, blue rolling shopping buggy contraption. "Get that one, Miss Sarah Beth."

Sarah Beth grabbed the roast and threw it in the buggy.

Behind them, Cassie followed, picking up after them. The rolling monstrosity toppled a stand of pretzel bites they'd just passed. The quicker they bought the items necessary for Katie's dinner recipe, the better. The adorable child wanted to give cooking lessons to Sarah Beth.

"Is this all we need?" Sarah Beth scratched her head.

With more confidence than any executive Cassie had ever met, Katie nodded. "That's all. Daddy and I make supper in the Crock-Pot all the time. If you have it set on low, you can't burn it. Just put in all the ingredients in the morning, cover with the lid, and turn it on. Since it's later, we'll have to turn it to high, but I'll be here to remind you to check the food."

After they completed Katie's list, Cassie dropped off the diapers and checked on Michael. And Dylan.

His grin confident, Dylan insisted he was fine, which

worked since Sarah Beth begged Cassie to secretly supervise the roast experiment. The woman was not a cook. Cassie shuddered at the times she'd tasted Sarah Beth's attempt at using the coffee pot.

Chatter filled the kitchen when Cassie let herself in Sarah Beth's house. Katie's cute Southern drawl prattled on about the ins and outs of the children and teachers at her school, the art they'd made, and why. Cassie pictured Katie as a teacher. Or more likely a principal someday. Maybe even superintendent, the way she was orchestrating dinner.

The ingredients lined the counter. "Can I help?"

Sarah Beth sat on the floor rummaging through a cabinet. "I'm looking for the Crock-Pot." Then she stood and crossed the room. "I know. It's with our wedding gifts in the laundry room closet." Thuds and clatters followed. "Found it. Still in the box."

When Sarah Beth set it on the counter, Katie ran her small fingers down the side of the box. "First get some scissors and cut the tape."

Cassie laughed. "I think she's got the opening-the-box part. It's the cooking that's a problem."

With the box open and the crockpot plugged in, Sarah Beth gave Cassie a wide grin as they seasoned the roast and vegetables. "This is so exciting. I might be able to do this."

"You might." Katie held up a tiny finger. "But you have to be careful not to mix up things like sugar and salt. Oh, and don't pour the salt through the blue container with a spout. Too much comes out."

Obviously, she'd seen Nick make that mistake or done it herself. "Now all y'all have to do is put the lid on, right?"

"That's all. I think Uncle Jess will be proud of this supper we're making." Her little mouth twisted. "When will my mommy feel better?"

Sarah Beth's eyes widened as she washed her hands.

Poor thing. Cassie squatted down to eye level beside Katie. "As soon as the medicine starts working. Kind of like when you get a bad cold. It takes a few days."

Minutes later, Jess rambled through the back door, Gingie on his heels. He sniffed. "Is someone cooking?"

Katie tore out from her spot to hug his legs. "Uncle Jess."

He laid his phone and keys on the counter then scooped her up into a tight hug. "Hey, squirt. I heard you were here." He shot them a worried glance.

Before either could say anything, Katie continued. "I taught Miss Sarah Beth how to make a roast in the Crock-Pot for your supper. It'll be ready in a few hours."

His forehead mashed against hers. "You taught my wife to cook?"

Giggling, she nodded. "Yes, sir, Uncle Jess."

"Good job, Katie. I came home for a minute to check on you ladies." He set her back down and nodded toward the back hall. "Can I talk to Sarah Beth and Cassie in the other room?"

His phone beeped, and Sarah Beth snatched it up. Her fist clamped around the phone, and her jaw clenched. "Yes, Katie, can you wait in here with Gingie and the kitty for a couple of minutes?"

"I'm five-years-old. You can walk to the back of the house, and I'll be fine."

"Oh, of course." Sarah Beth managed a weak smile before she turned and tromped away.

Cassie followed. Not this again. Jess better look out. The look on Sarah Beth's face could only mean he'd gotten another text from that Sophia woman.

In the hall, Jess spoke in whispered tones. "I got a text from Nick. How's Jill?"

No words came from Sarah Beth as her arms crossed over her chest.

Cassie swallowed back the discomfort. "Jill has lupus. I've already done some research. She should get better, but it may take a few months. We'll all need to step up to help out."

"Of course. We'll do whatever we can to help."

Lips quivering, Sarah Beth shoved the phone at Jess. "Here. You got another text just now. Not from Nick." Her chin lifted as she held his gaze.

Puzzled, Jess's dark eyes scanned the phone. "I blocked her. She must've gotten another phone number."

The hall seemed to be shrinking. Cassie shifted on her feet. "I'll be in the other room with Katie."

"Wait, Cassie." He reached toward Sarah Beth. "Have Cassie hire a private detective. Check the phone bill. I'm not cheating on you."

She'd really rather not be in the middle of more of her friends' personal business. The Jill and Dylan thing was plenty. Cassie cleared her throat. "A restraining order might help. I could give you a contact of someone who would handle the process."

With a sniffle, Sarah Beth shook her head. "The woman's nuts. That might make her more obsessed." She tipped Jess's chin and managed a smile. A nervous giggle followed. "Oh, and I needed to tell you I quit my job today."

"Wow." Jess stared for a moment, then nestled her close. "You'll have more time with me and the baby."

"I'm going to say goodbye to Katie then take my leave." Emotion strangled Cassie. Why hadn't Evan taken it that well when she'd wanted to stay home with Benjamin? In the end, she'd compromised and only worked part-time, but the man seemed to be resentful of the fact he had to work fulltime and she didn't. Even though they'd had plenty of money in the bank.

Chapter 14

Hospitals. Dreadful places. Especially twice in one day. But Jill begged to see Michael before bedtime, so Dylan slid into the back of the van with his son as he'd done earlier that morning. Cassie drove. Only a couple of roundabouts and one streetlight slowed their travel back to the small medical facility after the perfect day with Michael and a pleasant evening with Cassie, though she'd been more quiet than normal.

No way would he do a goodnight visit every time he had visitation with his son, but Jill was sick. And he'd been able to spend much more time with Michael than expected. Although the thought of keeping a baby all night unnerved him a little. Or a lot. If it weren't for Cassie, he might've chickened out.

He glanced around the minivan. Leather interior and that new car smell. Nice for a soccer mom. Which he wasn't. But his vehicle choice might have to change now that he was a father. "This looks brand new. Why'd you buy this when Benjamin's old enough to drive? It's not like a teen boy's gonna let you haul him and his buddies around."

Cassie's mouth twisted into a pucker before she spoke. "Evan hated minivans. He vowed we'd never own one, so the day after the divorce was final, I sold the Mercedes he'd given me and bought this."

"That's actually pretty funny." Dylan chuckled. "In a sneaky sort of way. You seem even-tempered—patient, like someone who keeps her head during conflict, but you have a dry humor that someone would only catch if they were paying close attention." Their eyes met in the rearview mirror—the glints of blue in the sea of green vying for his attention. *Say something else, idiot.* "Thanks for agreeing to have us stay with you instead of moving to a hotel."

"I'm not letting you sit with that sweet baby in a hotel when we have more than enough room. And honestly, Benjamin's smiled more in the few days you've been here than he has since…"

A knot formed in his throat.

He knew exactly how Benjamin felt. "It's hard on a boy being disappointed by his father like that."

Wrinkles crossed Cassie's forehead as she pulled the van into a parking spot. "What do you mean *like that*?"

An unfortunate slip. "Uh, I mean like when a father is unfaithful and embarrasses the family."

The van slowed to a stop in the lot, and Cassie craned her neck to face him, eyes blazing. "Did he talk to you about it?"

Dylan lifted one shoulder. "A little. He and I have some issues in common. We both went through more than the average kid does during a divorce." Would the attorney start a cross-examination now? He'd already said more than he should on this short drive, but he couldn't seem to stop himself.

He struggled to unhook the car seat. "Why are these contraptions so complicated?"

The automatic door on Michael's side opened with a quiet hum. She was already out and reaching for the buckle. "Let me give it a shot." She glanced up, and her expression softened. "Thanks for being a friend to him."

Dylan reached across the seat and caught her petite hand in his. "I admire your strength. You could've run back to your parents in Mobile, but you stuck it out here."

Lips trembling, her usual composure fell away. A sudden gust of wind freed a strand of hair from where she'd tucked it up in a bun under her cap. It blew across her cheek and glimmered in the sunlight, contrasting with her ivory skin. "I figured I had to face people some time—might as well get it over with. The Deep South is a small world, and gossip would've followed me. I'm fine. It hurt more to see Benjamin endure the drama." She tucked the hair back under her hat. "Okay, *fine* may be an overstatement, but I'm healing."

She was so strong. The ugly gossip hadn't destroyed her.

Swallowing, he stretched his legs out of the van and scooped up Michael. "Since the day my mother and I left my dad, I've worried about a time when everyone would know the truth about the man. Even more so once I came into the public eye. Waiting on the bomb to drop is almost worse than… Maybe not, I don't know."

He fell in step beside her through the parking lot. When they reached the sidewalk, Cassie halted and pressed her hand on his forearm. "Your mother did something heroic in moving you both to Boone to protect you."

Splinters of reality punctured his confidence. Should he put his own child through the difficulties of being a celebrity's son? "The truth about my father will come out someday. I've seen it happen to other celebrities. I wonder if we're not better off just telling everything up front." He kissed Michael's head. "It's confusing, the overwhelming need to protect these little people."

Cassie gave him a penetrating look and smiled. "Spoken like a true parent."

Her comment sent warmth through him. *A true parent.* That's what he was now.

After they entered the double doors of the hospital, silence fell between them. Cassie picked up her pace. Probably hoping no one would recognize him.

The door to Jill's hospital room was ajar. Cassie lifted her hand to knock but hesitated.

Bits of conversation drifted out the door. "I feel like God's punishing me for my sins."

Sarah Beth's voice came in hushed tones. "Jill, you haven't done anything worse than I have, and God's not punishing you. We live in a fallen world, but God's grace is strong enough to cover all of our sins. Following Christ doesn't give us a get-out-of-jail-free card. We'll still have troubles. The thing is, we have hope, despite all our pain—a hope for joy and a future in this life and the next."

A man spoke. Maybe Jess. "I'm the worst of sinners. If anyone deserves punishment, it's me. I don't know why he's blessed me, but I know I don't deserve it."

Dylan held in a groan. He didn't know why Jess had been blessed either. From his standpoint, the guy didn't deserve Sarah Beth.

Michael sneezed. Loud. *Good one, buddy.*

"Is that Michael?" Jill's voice and a sniffle came through the door.

Cassie stepped forward. "We didn't want to interrupt."

"Come in."

Keeping his eyes down, Dylan took Michael and laid him on Jill's lap.

Jill craned her neck to make eye contact. "I appreciate everything you've done to help."

Nice. And surprising. "You're welcome."

Michael kicked and cooed for his mother. Such a cute little guy.

"Did you have what you needed? I should've given you a key to the house."

Cassie held up the camouflage backpack. "We went shopping this afternoon." She chuckled. "My third time today. I picked out a manly baby bag for Dylan, and he bought one of every item in the store we could possibly need, including a travel bed."

"We?" Jess's voice was low.

A ball of fury swept through Dylan, and he clenched his fists. "I—"

"Dylan's staying at my house." Cassie's tone stayed light as her gaze drifted to him. Her eyes seemed to be begging him to calm down. "I insisted. I can't stand the thought of that sweet baby in a motel, and Benjamin and I have plenty of room."

Nick carried Katie through the door.

"I found some delicious ice cream." Katie held up a cone of soft serve vanilla.

Sarah Beth put her hands on her hips. "And you didn't bring any to the pregnant woman?"

"I'll go get you some." Dylan inched toward the door. "I could use a walk."

Jess gave him a hard look, but Sarah Beth gripped his arm. "Thanks, Dylan."

He turned to Cassie before he left. "Can I get you some, too?"

"No, thanks. I had a few doses of stress chocolate already."

A couple of stress cocktails would be nice. Of course, that's what landed him in this situation in the first place.

~~~

Cassie's gaze tracked Dylan. He'd handled that situation well enough. In fact, he'd handled the whole day rather well. She was proud of him for keeping his cool.

As soon as he was out of earshot, Nick threw his hands up. "Cassie, what are you doing? You can't trust him. We appreciate that you're trying to help us, but I think you've become too personally involved."

Jess pointed a finger at her. "You don't know what you're getting into."

A loud huff came from Sarah Beth. "We were just talking about how we're all sinners, and God forgave us. I don't think it's our place to judge anyone—including Dylan. Cassie's an intelligent woman, and she can figure out what she thinks of Dylan by herself."

Cassie stood motionless. Too involved for helping watch the baby when Jill was in the hospital? She opened her mouth to speak, then closed it. Her neck burned, and someplace in her gut did, too.

The book of James. Remember, tame the tongue. Slow to speak. Quick to listen.

Glaring at Nick, Jill held Michael out toward Cassie. "I'm getting tired. Would you and Dylan mind taking him home for the night? It's his bedtime anyway. I, for one, don't know what I would have done without you, and I'm glad you're personally involved."

The heat in her neck receded, but she probably still shouldn't speak. She nodded and cradled the baby in her arms.

It was hard to stay mad around adorable children.

~~~

Dylan lowered Michael into the blue plastic bathtub after testing the water with his elbow, as Cassie directed. Something about her gave him confidence.

"You're doing fine." Her voice was calm. "Babies do become rather slippery when you try to get them out."

His expression must've revealed the fact that his stomach sunk to his toes when he pictured Michael crashing to the floor.

"I'll have the towel ready. Don't worry." She pointed to the counter. "Now add a dab of baby wash on the washcloth to get under the chin and arms. Then wash his head."

"His hair can't be dirty. Why am I washing it?"

"It can get dry, flaky skin."

Michael kicked his little feet like he was swimming in the Olympics. Dylan alternated between fear and amusement at the antics as he did as Cassie directed. "He seems to like the warm water."

"I've heard some babies are scared at first, but Benji loved his baths. He still loves the water."

Dylan gently let warm water cascade down the baby's head, removing the soap. When a little trickle dripped into his face, Dylan held his breath, but Michael just smiled.

Cassie held out one of the new hooded towels they'd purchased. "Whenever you're finished, I'm ready to catch him."

Holding his breath, Dylan lifted the wet baby out toward her. She swaddled him in the yellow towel that had eyes and a duck bill on top, and she headed down the hall toward the master bedroom. Dylan wiped his brow, exhaled, and followed. "That was scary, but fun. I worked up a sweat just giving him a bath, how will I ever teach him to drive?"

Cassie flashed a grin over her shoulder. "It gets easier with practice. Before you know it, you'll have that down." She sighed. "But then they grow, and you'll get to figure out the next stage."

"So the challenge never ends?"

Once she laid Michael on a changing pad, she shot Dylan a

mischievous glance. "I'm only sixteen years into it."

"Not comforting." He chuckled and pulled open the plastic diaper package. "I'll dress him." He laid the diaper on the pad and slipped it under the baby. Fumbling around with the plastic contraption, he shifted Michael from side to side while the baby squirmed and kicked. Where was the tape? "Why won't this go on?"

Her hand brushed his as she flipped the diaper around. "Backwards." She smiled again. "And you better hurry. Baby boys can…um, catch you off guard."

He laughed as her ivory neck blotched, but her composed expression never faltered.

The diaper tape stuck to the front on both sides. No gaps. "Finally. There you go, buddy." He glanced at Cassie and her splotched neck. "So, you had Benjamin while you were in law school?"

"Two days after graduation. We married the summer after our second year. Our fathers weren't happy with our decision, and both insisted on a pre-nup. I guess they hoped we'd wait if they asked us to sign, but we didn't. Now, I'm kind of glad. Financial divisions were much easier when—"

"Mom? Dylan?" Benjamin's deep voice carried down the hall.

"We're in Dylan's room, dressing Michael for bed." Cassie called back.

Dylan's room?

Mimi and Benjamin jogged in, the smell of the outdoors trailing them. "I went for a ride with Mimi. She loves hanging her head out of my Jeep."

Cassie raised an eyebrow. "As long as you're watching the road, not the dog."

Benjamin scratched behind Mimi's ears. "I'm careful. Aren't I, Mimi?"

"Speaking of careful…" Cassie motioned toward the dog. "I know we trust Mimi, but she's still an animal. We should be sure to stay between her and the baby until she's used to him. Sometimes animals get jealous."

Dylan had the sudden urge to take Michael and bolt.

"I'm just being extra cautious." Cassie patted his back. "There are so many things I'd never think of."

Benjamin threw his head back and laughed. "That's what moms are for. To think up all the horrific things that could possibly happen and worry about them. Then nag their kids."

Rolling her eyes, Cassie shook her head and smiled. "Because it's so much fun for us."

Benjamin smiled at Michael and crooned, his voice now an octave higher. "Hey, Mikie. Hey, guy. Whatcha' doin?" He held his hand out, and Michael took his finger. "I always wondered what it would be like to have a brother."

Cassie's smile drained away. "You have a half-brother in Memphis." She cleared out of the room in seconds. "I'm going to clean up the bath stuff, and then I'll make his bottle."

Sweet Cassie. Why would a man do her that way?

~~~

Cassie ran through the day in her mind as she grabbed a last sip of water before going up for the night. Dylan looked nothing like the confident movie star she'd met in L.A. Instead, he seemed like a typical new father trying to get the hang of things. Watching him give Michael a bath—that fearful look on his face, his hands so gentle with the little guy… Had Evan ever been involved when Benjamin was that small? It seemed so long ago now, but she couldn't remember her ex ever helping out.

Dylan insisted on taking the night shift with Michael. They'd fed him and laid him in the travel bed scooted up right next to the king-size bed in the master bedroom.

Dylan's room she'd called it. An embarrassing slip. She'd noted the strange look on his face. What was he thinking?

The new high-tech baby monitor with both video and sound lay on the counter. It wouldn't hurt to take it upstairs with her. Just in case. Her mothering instincts couldn't help but worry about whether Dylan would wake up when Michael cried.

At three a.m., he did. Dylan's deep voice filtered through
~~~

the speaker, singing until he'd soothed the baby back to sleep. A nice voice, too, from what she remembered in her drowsy state.

The next morning, she gathered her hair up in a bun and slipped on her sandals when the monitor scratched and crackled, Michael obviously fidgeting in his crib.

After hustling down the steps, she crept into the room, lifting Michael before Dylan woke. The baby smiled.

In the hall, she kept her voice at a whisper. "You're happy in the morning, like my Benji. Not so much like his father, though." Ugh. She wished she hadn't thought of Evan again. Must be all the baby memories dredging up the past. "Let's think of something pleasant, like getting some breakfast, little man."

She had Michael changed and fed by the time Benjamin came down ready for school. The baby kicked and wiggled in a blue and green bouncy seat a couple of feet away from her on the floor. "I have pancake batter ready to put on the griddle, and the bacon is ready in the microwave."

"I have one of those state tests today that they torture us with." He sat down and rummaged through his book bag. "Do you have more of the number two mechanical pencils I like?"

She pointed across the room before pouring the rich batter onto the sizzling griddle. "In the drawer. Watch him while I cook the pancakes. Oh, and do you have lunch money or do you want to take lunch?"

"I'll take one, I guess." He zipped the backpack and sat on the floor by Michael. "Mom, do you like Dylan?"

The spatula slipped from Cassie's hand to the counter with a clatter. Why would he ask that? Had she given off some signals, or was she flirting with Dylan? Benjamin surely meant as a friend. She cleared her throat. "Yes. Do you?"

"Like…do you want to go out with him?"

Not what he meant at all. Recovering, at least sort of, she grabbed the bacon from the microwave, then retrieved the spatula to flip the pancakes. "Why?"

"I like him, and I know you and Dad won't get back

together, with him being remarried and all."

Cassie brought his plate over to the table and pulled out a chair. "Benjamin, I don't have any plans to date anyone."

"Ever? Because, I know some guys at school whose step-fathers are losers, and I was hoping you'd find someone better. You deserve it, and Dylan would be cool to have around."

At least that made a little sense. "I appreciate your concern. If I date, you let me know if you think I'm dating a loser, and I'll take your opinion into consideration."

After Benjamin left for school, Cassie called to check in with Jill to assure her the night had gone well. Instead of her yard work or reading, she turned on some music and dug out her camera and lenses. "Let's take some pictures." She posed Michael in different settings around the house and yard and afterwards, fed him another bottle.

His little eyes slipped shut, reopened twice, his gaze never leaving her face. That warm toasty nestling and those drowsy eyes awakened a love in her that came as naturally as it had with her own son. She caressed his soft head behind his ears.

Time for a nap, little one. Now to get him back in Dylan's room without waking either of them.

No such luck. Dylan stirred when she entered. "Did he just wake up?"

She whispered, "Nap time."

Rolling onto his side, Dylan squinted at his phone. His bare chest slipped out from the sheets, and he gave a sleepy grin. "Oh, wow. Thanks for letting me rest."

She should turn away. Quickly. Or in just a second.

Chapter 15

Cassie inhaled the scent of oranges and cinnamon. Dylan's scent. As if on cue, he rounded the corner into the kitchen. Why did he smell so good? And why was his presence comfortable, yet stirring at the same time? *Say something.* "Can I make you pancakes and bacon topped with real maple syrup?"

"You really know how to spoil a guy. I'd love it, but first things first." He grabbed a mug.

"Here." She poured him a steaming cup of coffee. "Long night, huh? I heard him wake up a few times." She could kick herself for blurting that out.

His lopsided grin only added to her regret. He sipped the hot brew. "You were watching me on the monitor?"

Of course he'd caught her slip.

"I was listening to the monitor, in case you needed me. Not watching."

"Right. What did you hear?"

She turned back on the griddle and uncovered the bowl of batter she'd saved. "I heard Michael cry. I heard you feed him, burp him…sing to him." She poured circles of the creamy mixture onto the griddle. Probably too soon for the metal to have heated to the proper temperature. Why did he complicate her thoughts? Was he staring at her? Her neck burned, so she focused on the expanding cakes.

Dylan moved beside her and craned his neck to see her face. "Are you going to spy on me again tonight, or am I trustworthy enough?" He chuckled. "Or maybe you just enjoy the view?"

Now he was messing with her.

Time for the offensive argument. She kept a straight face as she stared into his sparkling green eyes. "I haven't decided yet. By the way, remember when you asked if I had Benjamin in law school?"

"Yeah."

Inches away, she squared off with him. "Why did you ask?"

He fidgeted. "I put two and two together."

Keep him on the defensive. She lifted one finger toward him. "But how?"

The corner of Dylan's lip lifted. "I heard you talking or maybe asked your dad." His mouth fell open. "You're calling me out for being nosey, aren't you?" He set his cup on the counter and rubbed his palms together. "I have the sudden urge to mess up your hair."

Before she could raise a hand, he slipped out the clip that held her bun in place and tossed it aside. Her hair fell, his fingers sunk through.

She should scoot away. But he did have her hair. Which seemed to be sending electric currents to immobilize her. *Do something.* From behind her back, she gripped a can of whipped cream, then raised it close to his face, her finger on the spout. "Okay, stop. Or I'm going to draw a big happy face on you."

Dylan let out a cackle. "Whipped cream?"

She scoffed. "I *was* going to offer to put chocolate chips and whipped cream on your pancakes, but now I don't think so."

He was so close his breath brushed her forehead—definitely the cinnamon. "You asked for it."

Starting at his mouth she squirted a large whipped smile, then two foamy eyes above his eyebrows. She was about to add a circle starting at the forehead when he grasped her arm.

Through the white trickling down his face, a mischievous smile appeared. "There are a few things you don't know about me." He licked his upper lip. "One, I'm the kind of person that loves to share." With that, he leaned in and rubbed his lips and forehead on her cheeks, spreading the whipped cream across her face.

"Stop." A giggle took over Cassie, even as she tried to stifle it. "I give. You win."

Dylan still held her arm but pulled his face back an inch. "And?"

She frowned. "I don't need you to share."

"And?" He hadn't let go.

"And…I'm a weirdo that may listen to you again on the monitor if I worry about the baby."

Dylan released her arms and smeared some cream near her eye with his hand. "Fair enough." He licked his finger. "I believe I would like chocolate chips and whipped cream on my pancakes. No smiley face, though."

After grabbing a paper towel, she wiped her face, then handed him one. Her somersaulting heart was becoming problematic. She needed to back away and avoid looking at his face. *That perfect face.*

Breathing would be good, too. A whiff of something burning drew her attention. The pancakes. She grabbed the spatula to flip them onto the plate and unplugged the griddle. "Too late for chocolate chips. Maybe next time." She slung the plate on the counter.

Dylan smeared the last of the topping from his temple. A laugh filled his voice. "Cassandra Jane, you are intriguing."

And what did that mean? Her neck itched. Was it blotching again? "I'm going upstairs to straighten up. I'll be down…later."

~~~

The paper towel had partially obscured Dylan's vision, but red dots had definitely covered Cassie's neck. She'd wasted no time taking off upstairs. Had he hurt her? He hadn't touched her neck. Maybe she had a whipped cream allergy.

He wiped his cheek one more time. Or maybe…she'd felt something. A connection.

Hadn't he felt a current run through him? A different kind of feeling than the one he typically experienced with women. A feeling so innocent, yet promising. Was this what friendship with a woman was like? He'd been teasing her about going with him to Memphis because it got a rise out of her. And he'd enjoyed teasing her. Maybe too much.

He dropped the paper towel into the compactor. Being in Oxford wasn't about starting something with Cassie. Being
~~~

here was about his son. But he needed to keep on good terms with this woman for the sake of Michael. She was right about one thing. The press would have a field day if a custody battle went into the courts.

He'd better figure out how to make the situation work.

Without screwing things up.

Chapter 16

A knock sent Cassie scrambling across the linoleum floor past Dylan. She pulled open the thick hospital room door.

"Oh." Sarah Beth stood in the glowing hallway lights, Jess waiting a couple of feet behind. "We can come by later."

The sour look on Jess's face indicated he wasn't pleased about seeing so much of Dylan.

Cassie's gut said to let them come back later, but her mouth didn't obey. "Good timing. We just got here with Michael, and he's dressed up today."

"Come in, y'all, and see Michael in his new outfit." Jill waved them in and then returned her attention to the baby. "I've missed you so much, sweet boy." She rubbed his nose with hers. "Was everything all right last night?"

Across the room, Dylan shrugged but kept his gaze out the window. "Fine. He woke up a couple of times during the night, but Cassie took him this morning and let me sleep in."

Tension smothered the small room. Dylan didn't want to hang out with Jess again, either.

A chair scraped the floor as Sarah Beth pulled close to the bedside and sat. "How are you feeling today?"

"I should be able to go home in the morning. The steroids helped, but I hate thinking about the side effects." One hand pressed over her chest. "The doctor said I had inflammation around my heart and pleurisy in my lungs but doesn't think I have organ damage." She let out a long sigh. "I thought I pulled a muscle sneezing."

"You poor thing." Lines crinkled Sarah Beth's brow. "No wonder you felt so bad. And they blamed it on postpartum depression."

"To be fair, I did have the baby blues, and I don't think I

described my symptoms well enough."

Cassie's phone chimed, and all eyes turned to her. The number didn't register. It might be something about Benjamin. "Hello. This is Cassie."

"Hi, this is Wyatt Meadows, a friend of Sarah Beth's. She gave me your name. I work with the university's law school and wondered if you'd like to get together for lunch tomorrow. We have an opening at the law library if you're interested. If not, we can still have a meal and talk shop."

Cassie glanced at Dylan. "I don't know if I can make it tomorrow. Can I get back with you in a few hours?"

"Of course."

As she hung up, Sarah Beth grinned. "Was that Wyatt? I told him about you."

"Yes." She struggled to keep her face neutral. Why had Sarah Beth given out her number without telling her?

After crossing the room, Sarah Beth took Cassie's hand and squeezed. "You should go hear what he has to say about the position. Besides, he's really a nice guy, and it's just lunch."

Dylan fidgeted with the blind wand for a second and then left his perch at the window to join the circle of conversation. "If you're not going because you're worried about me and Michael, I can handle it."

Sarah Beth held one hand up as if she were a schoolgirl with the right answer. "And I can come over and help Dylan while you're gone."

The sound of Jess clearing his throat twice echoed across the room. He gave Sarah Beth a firm look. "He said he can handle it."

Dylan rolled his eyes.

Sarah Beth should've known Jess wouldn't go for that. And Jess should know by now his wife wasn't interested in Dylan. But hadn't Sarah Beth been jealous of Sophia? Straightening her posture, Cassie pressed words from her dry throat. "I'll call him at a more suitable time to clarify the, uh, lunch ramifications."

An awkward silence followed, tension rising higher, almost

palpable, and tightening the muscles in Cassie's neck.

"Oh, speaking of employment…" Jill spoke at last. "Sarah Beth, I'm going to resign my position as marketing assistant. Nick and I talked, and we think we can swing it."

"Whew." Sarah Beth's shoulders fell forward. "That's good, because I resigned already. I didn't want to upset you while you were sick. The new guy and I didn't see eye to eye."

Dylan took two steps toward the bed. "I want to help with Michael financially."

"I appreciate how supportive you're being." Jill gave Dylan a warm smile.

Inching closer, he raked his fingers through the front of his hair. "I decided to stay in town until we go to Honduras. There's no reason to go back to L.A.—other than I need to buy more clothes."

"Good gravy." Cassie smashed her hand to her forehead. "I haven't even offered to wash your clothes. I can do that tonight."

He looked her way, and his sparkling green eyes brought to mind sea glass she'd found on the beach once. "You've taken excellent care of both of us. Show me where the laundry room is when we get home. I know how to wash clothes."

Home? As his gaze lingered, needles of heat pricked Cassie's neck.

Sarah Beth and Jill exchanged sideways glances. Jill tilted her head. "Cassie, would you and Dylan mind running up to the bakery near the Square to get me one of those huge éclairs?"

Why were they looking at her like that? "Of course." Cassie nodded. "I could eat one myself. What flavor?" And she'd be glad to get out of here.

"Surprise me."

Beside her, Dylan walked toward the lobby without speaking, expression thoughtful.

"It's kind of you to keep offering support for Michael. We should crunch the numbers and draw up the papers."

"I'd like that."

Cassie felt in her pocket for her van keys but came up empty. Not in her purse either. "Oh, I think I left my keys. I'll have to go back."

One side of his mouth lifted. "Mind if I just wait in the lobby?"

"I get it. No problem."

The door was open when Cassie slipped back in.

"Did you see Cassie and Dylan?" Standing by the bed, Sarah Beth motioned wildly. Jess stood behind her, both of their backs to the door.

Cassie froze.

"Girl, how could I miss it?" Jill's voice rose.

"I know, right? Crazy. They're like polar opposites."

"You know what they say about opposites."

The front of Cassie's face tingled. Could they forget the keys and walk home? It was only a few miles.

"I think they're both falling hard. You can see it when they look at each other."

Jess locked his arms around Sarah Beth. "At least maybe he won't be drooling over my wife."

"You finally found a bright side to a situation with Dylan Conner."

Deep breath. Get it over with. "Knock, knock." Cassie hustled in. "I forgot my keys. Be back in a jiffy." *Don't look at anyone. Act like you didn't hear anything.*

Her friendships would never be the same after this case.

~~~

Inside the small bakery, Cassie sipped her decaf and stared at a vintage quilt hanging on the wall. The taste of the decadent pastry blended with the hot brew. She'd only eaten a third of her peach éclair, but her stomach churned, and she pushed the treat away.

She turned her attention to Dylan's serious expression. He'd been quiet as he picked at his food. This situation was hard on him, too.

A thousand questions about him ran through her mind. "Is it difficult for you to be around Sarah Beth?"
~~~

"Not so much anymore." Stirring his coffee, he lifted one shoulder. "I realized when I visited last summer that she and Jess had feelings for each other. We walked into a restaurant, and he was there. The look they shared… You could see it all over their faces. They hadn't even realized yet, but I decided to make my exit. Unfortunately, I made the mistake of leaving with a beautiful sociopath—biggest mistake of my life."

A look? Dylan knew from a single look between Jess and Sarah Beth. What had Jill and Sarah Beth seen today?

Enough. Dylan was opening up about his life. "Was it that Sophia woman?"

"How'd you know?" His intense stare burned into her core.

"I helped Sarah Beth with a few things in the office, ran across your name, and then I saw your picture on the cover of one of those magazines." Guilt hitched in her gut. "If I hadn't, I guess I wouldn't have known who you were. I didn't read the article."

He cocked his head. "You've never seen any of my movies?"

Another faux pas. In fact, it'd been a long time since she'd seen any movie. "Apparently it's true that I don't get out much, but Benjamin and his father saw your latest action film."

Dylan let out a bitter laugh. "It's just as well. You probably wouldn't approve of most of the films. I don't want Michael watching them until he's over twenty-one. If ever."

"I liked going to family movies when Benji was little. You could make some of those now that you have a son."

Dylan smirked. "You and Sarah Beth will have me squeaky clean if I stay here much longer."

"So stay." Her eyes darted to her remaining éclair. Had she really said that out loud?

Chapter 17

Why was this so hard? And suddenly embarrassing? Cassie pulled on her suit coat and grabbed her cream-colored clutch. She was just going to lunch, but thoughts of her conversation with Dylan at the bakery the day before kept replaying through her mind. "I don't need to go, you know. I'm not looking for a job or…anything else."

Dylan leaned against the doorframe of the kitchen with Michael snuggled in his arms. "Go attend your business lunch." His eyes met hers straight on.

A thick silence hung between them, like a balloon dangling midair. She stole one last glance, then gave a little wave. "I'll be back as soon as I can."

At least she'd insisted on taking her own vehicle to the restaurant. She could leave when she wanted, and being picked up at the house like some sixteen-year-old on a blind date didn't sit well. Not like she'd dated anyone at sixteen, or anyone at all besides Evan. And this wasn't a date. She only returned the call to be polite and to discuss the position at the university. *I wish I hadn't let Sarah Beth talk me into this.*

Sarah Beth texted a picture of Wyatt—tall, sandy blond hair, brown eyes. A snappy dresser. Pausing at the entrance of the Italian restaurant on the Square, Cassie scanned the faces of people waiting to get inside the popular establishment. A man in a three-piece suit stood alone under the shade of the green awning, checking his watch. That had to be him.

The guy smiled as she neared. "Are you Cassie?"

She extended her hand. "Nice to meet you."

His firm grip wrapped around her fingers. "I'm glad you changed your mind and joined me. I hope Italian is okay. I got us reservations."

She hadn't wanted to come. Why had she changed her mind? Cassie forced a smile. "Of course."

After they'd been seated, Cassie studied the menu, although she knew everything they offered and what she'd order. At least they served her favorite, chicken Parmesan.

"I love the fettuccine." Wyatt's tanned cheeks spread into a wide smile, revealing straight white teeth." Do you know what you want?"

"I do."

After ordering, Wyatt spoke of growing up in New Mexico and how he ended up teaching at a law school in Mississippi. The apprehension that had roped around Cassie's insides loosened with talk of professors they both knew and developments in case law. The food arrived, and for an hour, they engaged in lively banter over current issues. Debating legal theory always energized her.

She smiled and sipped her sweet tea. "Your students must enjoy your classes."

Wyatt let out a small laugh. "If they're prepared for class, they enjoy it. I'd have to give you an A plus on advocacy and negotiations from our discussions today. You can hold your own. Why aren't you practicing?"

"I've worked part-time and pro bono, but I wanted to raise my son. It was enough that his father was rarely home."

"Do you want to talk to the director about the law library position after we finish lunch? The hours aren't bad, and I think you'd be a great asset."

What did she want? Cassie shrugged. "I'll talk to him, but I'm not sure I'm ready to commit to a full-time position."

Twin lines formed between Wyatt's brows. "Didn't you say your son's sixteen?"

Sounded like something Evan would say. "It makes even more sense to be available when they're teens. More trouble they can get into."

The waitress returned with a check. Wyatt paid, then stood and pulled out her chair. "If you're not interested after the meeting at the library, I hope you at least enjoyed the lunch and the company." His eyes searched hers for some sign.

Her mind went blank, and she scrambled for something to say. "I do like this restaurant."

~~~

The look and feel of the law school building brought Cassie back to college days. "Libraries." She took a deep whiff. "I love that smell. Books, computers, and all that knowledge in one place thrills me."

Wyatt gave her a hopeful smile. "Finally, something that excites you." He motioned her toward an office door. "I'll introduce you to the director. He's expecting us."

At the far end of the room, books lined the walls. Construction had taken place since she'd graduated, and they'd expanded the electronic resources. Though the scene had been altered, overall this still resembled where she'd spent many hours studying.

The director's door loomed in front of her. Did she really want to do this? She smoothed her blazer with her hands. As she did, the cell in her pocket vibrated. She fought the urge to look. But what if it was Benjamin? His father was at least an hour away.

Cassie stopped and checked the number in front of the closed door. "Wyatt, wait. My son's calling. I need to answer and make sure nothing's wrong. He should be at baseball right now."

Wyatt nodded.

She touched to answer. "Benjamin, what is it? I'm in a meeting."

"The coach told me to call you."

Something was wrong—the tone in his voice. "Are you hurt?"

"Not bad. A baseball to the face kind of thing."

"I'll be right there."

~~~

Cassie followed Benjamin into the house. Dark purple bruising circled his swollen cheek and eye, but the doctor assured her there were no fractures. An inch higher, and he might have lost an eye. A shiver coursed through her. Tonight she'd need to keep watch for signs of concussion and make sure he kept the icepack on his cheek.

Benjamin stopped midstride in the living room. "Ssh." He put his finger over his lips then pointed toward the Oriental rug.

Dylan lay across the floor, shirtless, with Michael on his chest. Both were sound asleep. Her breath caught in her throat. They were beautiful.

After Benjamin headed upstairs, the image of Dylan and Michael clung to her and unhitched something locked within. What was this feeling?

Overthinking. That was her problem. A father and son. A lovely father and son lying in her living room. No big deal. She should take a picture for Dylan and his mother. They'd like that. Once Benjamin cleaned up and settled in with the icepack, she pulled out her camera bag.

In the kitchen, she attached the lens and adjusted for a close-up. She tiptoed to the living room and clicked about twenty pictures. Now to load them onto the laptop.

Between checking on Benjamin every few minutes, she cropped her favorites. She couldn't help but notice again how beautiful Dylan and Michael looked lying there. They both shared those long auburn eyelashes and light olive skin. Mimi stood beside her as if studying the pictures, too. Cassie absently scratched the woolly fur on Mimi's back.

"You working for a tabloid now?"

Her fingers flinched as Dylan's voice took her by surprise. "I thought you might want to send a picture to your mom. When I saw you two sleeping like that…" She stood and scooted the chair back. "Here. Sit. Look for yourself. It seemed like the perfect shot. So natural."

As Dylan eased in the chair and scrolled through the photos, his face softened, and he swallowed hard. "Mom would like that. You did an excellent job. Not that I would expect any different."

She re-wiped the clean counters of the kitchen. Were those

tears welling in his eyes?

Brushing a hand across his face, Dylan rose. "You were gone a long time. Does that mean you took the job, or did you just have a really great lunch date?"

"Benjamin called while I was at the law library. He got hit in the face with a baseball. I had to pick him up and rush over to the doctor's office."

"How is he?" His brows knit together, and he closed the distance between them. "Does he have a concussion or did he lose a tooth?"

"They think he's okay."

"I know the best plastic surgeons in L.A., and dentists, too. We can take him if he needs to go, and he'll look better than new." He nudged her arm. "Turn around."

For some reason she complied to the strange request.

His fingers squeezed her shoulders.

Cassie closed her eyes and tilted her neck as Dylan kneaded the taut muscles. She'd become so tense after getting the call from Benjamin.

"I think someone needs a massage. Sit down, and let me work my magic. I've heard I'm pretty good at this."

A massage did sound nice. But awkward. Nevertheless, she inched to the kitchen table and sat while he stood behind her. His hands moved in a circular motion working at the stiffness in her shoulders and neck, the stress melting away. The relief soon switched to something more unsettling, despite no change in his actions. She enjoyed his touch…too much. Her eyes popped open, and she leapt from the chair, knocking it over with a thud.

"I'm better now."

"You sure?" Dylan grinned and turned the chair back upright. "I just got started. You haven't even experienced the piano technique."

"Maybe next time." Her neck was probably the shade of molten lava by now.

His stare weighed heavy on her. "Next time."

"Where's Michael?" Benjamin descended the stairs, holding

the icepack to his cheek. "You guys were passed out when we came in."

"Napping in his bed. I heard you took a hit today. Let me see." Dylan put a hand on Benjamin's shoulder and lifted the icepack with the other. He whistled. "Good one. I know the best doctors in the world if you need anything, but I think you're going to be fine."

Benjamin's eyes gleamed. "It's cool you'd do that for me."

"I care about you." His gaze traveled to Cassie. "And your mom."

Chapter 18

Dylan sat cross-legged in front of the baby quilt, the handmade Persian rug beneath him smooth to his touch. He gazed down at his son. Little arms flailing, Michael kicked and cooed. "Are you entertaining me, buddy?"

Funny how such a simple activity could be so fulfilling. The way Michael mimicked mouth movements as if trying to talk, the constant eye contact, and those toothless smiles filled Dylan's heart to bursting. To think he'd almost missed it all. A surge of bile hit the back of his throat. Maybe he was being too lenient with this custody issue. Feeling sorry for Jill because she was sick was one thing, but what was best for his son? What if she stayed ill for months? Even worse, what if something happened to Jill before they got this mess resolved?

Outside the window, Cassie puttered around the yard like it was perfectly normal having a celebrity and an infant living in her home. Was she the reason he was being such a pushover? He'd known more than a few diabolical lawyers, but surely her plan hadn't been to get her son to invite him to stay there. They'd just seemed to connect. All four of them.

Benjamin strolled in from the kitchen, eating a Popsicle with one hand and holding an icepack on his cheek with the other. He dropped down on the floor and grinned at Michael. "It's like watching the baby channel, waiting to see what he'll do next."

"And no commercials." Dylan scanned Benjamin's profile. He looked nothing like his mother, but he had her good heart. Already, this teenager meant a lot to him. Seeing that dark bruise on Benjamin's face pushed his protective urges into overdrive.

A drip ran down the wooden stick onto Benjamin's arm.

"Are you gonna get in trouble with that melting in here?"

Laughing, Benjamin licked his arm. "Not if you don't tell." He pulled the rest of the treat off in one bite and swallowed. "But Mom says houses are made to be lived in."

A refreshing point of view. One he hoped he could live by with Michael.

~~~

Like most late spring evenings in Mississippi, the sun blazed through Cassie's front entrance hall. The light tap on the door had to be Katie. Cassie reached for the door and smiled at Nick and his daughter. "We've got him ready to go. I'm sure he's missed his big sister."

The smell of cut grass drifted through as Cassie ushered Nick and Katie into her living room.

Nick lifted Michael to his chest. "I don't know how I can ever repay you."

"Dylan did the work, and I got to enjoy holding that darling baby." Cassie ran her hand under Michael's toes and tickled his tiny feet. "We could watch him during the day while you're at work, and at night if you need help." She looked to Nick, waiting for an affirmation.

Dylan stood and punched his hands into his pockets. "We can pick him up and keep him all day. I'm staying until the trip to Honduras in two weeks."

The tick in Nick's jaw said no, but he let out a small sigh. "Landscaping is hectic this time of year. Plus, Jill's still so tired. I don't know when she'll feel like hammering out a solid agreement with you."

Katie gave an exaggerated wave of the hand. "We need the help. You can pick him up in the morning. I'll call you when we're ready."

There was no smothering the laughter. Cassie snickered into her shoulder, but Benjamin belly laughed.

Dylan bent down to Katie's level. "You're such a good big sister. Do you know how to call me?"

"I'll get Mommy to tell me how to spell your name. I can find your number on her phone after that. No problem." She
~~~

lifted one shoulder and blinked.

Nick tousled the little girl's hair. "What would I do without my Katie?"

Once Michael had gone, Cassie led the way into the sunroom with Benjamin and Dylan behind her. They sank into the wicker chairs.

After tossing the icepack aside, Benjamin rubbed his stomach. "I'm starving. Can we go out to eat and maybe catch a movie?"

Dinner out would be easier, despite the fact she'd thawed meat in the refrigerator. "I can't speak for Dylan, but I'm game."

"I'd love to, if you guys aren't afraid of being seen with me."

Benjamin gave a little scoff. "It might be a scandal to be seen with us."

One side of Dylan's mouth turned up. "Just being me is a scandal. Let's go. I'm buying."

Cassie looked down at her crumpled T-shirt. "I'm changing into something clean."

Before she could get up, Dylan tugged her hair loose. "Leave your granny bun and fake glasses at home."

"It's a ballerina bun."

"Well, okay. You can dance a ballet solo for us if you wear it, tiny dancer."

Containing her smile became more and more difficult. Who knew Dylan was so much fun?

Upstairs, she scanned her summer clothes. Nothing seemed right. She rummaged through the closet twice. Why was she having such a hard time finding an outfit to wear around Oxford?

She pushed one outfit after another along the clothes rack. Not shorts. Maybe the sleeveless floral dress and cream-colored sandals? That could work.

Once she'd dressed, Cassie brushed out her hair and let it fall down around her shoulders. Pinning it up helped avoid the inevitable attention the deep red color invited. But something about Dylan's comment... She swept the part to one side, gave it a touch of hair spray, and headed down the stairs.

The look in Dylan's eyes as she hit the bottom step hurled heat from her neck down her arms and back.

His mouth gaped. "You are stunning."

She should say thank you, but the mechanism that sent words from her brain to her tongue seemed to be out of order.

Keys jangled near the door. Benjamin held them up. "Can I drive? I'll be your chauffeur."

That offer switched her brain back into gear. "Our guest may not be ready for a teen driver."

Dylan waved her off. "I'm brave." He elbowed Benjamin. "You can't drive much worse than most of the population of Los Angeles."

"I'm an excellent driver. Much better than Mom."

"Right." Cassie shot him a look.

"Let's go then." Dylan slipped on a pair of dark, large-framed glasses. "I hope this is enough of a disguise." He shrugged. "Worked for Clark Kent."

The man looked adorable no matter what he wore. But she wouldn't dwell on that.

They enjoyed a quiet dinner of shrimp and grits downtown. A smile tugged at the corners of Dylan's lips when the waitress cleared their plates. "Benjamin seemed to manage pretty well despite the facial injury."

"I'm still growing, you know." He patted his stomach. "Anyone else thinking cheesecake?"

Laughing, Dylan slapped his hand on the table. "I don't need to grow. But you go ahead."

"Dylan didn't realize what he was getting into offering to buy you dinner." Cassie pulled out her cell. "I'll check what's playing and the ratings while you scarf down dessert."

"Mom, you don't have to check the ratings. Next year, I'll be seventeen and can watch whatever I want."

She cut her eyes at him. "We'll *see* about that."

"Some kids buy tickets to PG movies and then just walk in the R ones." His head tilted as he scrutinized her response.

"Do you do that?" Her voice rose a fraction. Would he tell

her if he did?

"No, ma'am." His expression seemed genuine.

"Integrity is important." She could only hope he held onto what she'd taught him.

"I know, Mom. Grandpa talks to me about that a lot."

Maybe her father's integrity would make up for Evan's lack of it. She prayed it would.

~~~

Benjamin waved goodnight as he climbed the stairs. "Love you, Mom. Goodnight, Dylan."

"Goodnight." Dylan answered in unison with Cassie.

A strange surge of warmth set Dylan on guard. He'd felt the same way when they sat in the dark theater, Cassie's shoulder touching his. Somehow he'd missed the whole plot. And movies were his business, for goodness' sake.

Cassie glanced at Dylan. "I never showed you where the laundry room was. Can I wash some of your clothes before I go to bed?"

"I'll do it in the morning. But I was wondering if you belong to a gym." He rubbed his hand over his waist. "I'm getting soft with all your good food and no exercise. My trainer's gonna kill me."

"I really am a terrible hostess. We have a gym above the garage."

"You've been kind of busy caring for an infant and his inexperienced father who moved into your home without warning."

"I should've shown you around and made you feel more at home the first day." She pointed toward the kitchen. "You want to have a cup of green tea and sit out in the sunroom for a while?"

The question hovered in his brain. The thought of spending more time with her delighted his senses, but were they growing too close already? His mouth answered without permission. "I'll meet you there in a minute."

~~~

Maybe Dylan changed his mind and went to bed. Cassie set

the teacups on the end table between the two wicker chairs. What possessed her to ask him anyway?

"Hey, sorry. I took a quick shower." His voice jarred her and warmed her at once.

A whiff of citrus drifted to her as he sat down and took a sip of the cup she'd prepared for him. She forced her eyes forward as she savored a lungful. "What *is* it that makes you smell like citrus and cinnamon?"

"Is that a bad thing?" His voice held a hint of insecurity.

"No. I've never smelled men's cologne like that."

"My trainer sells these herbal products. I started buying them when I heard an actress complain about having to do a scene with—I better not mention any names, but she was talking about how bad he stunk. Some other actresses jumped in about what actors had bad breath and so on." He clicked his tongue. "I didn't want to be one of *those guys*. Supposedly, ninety percent of women like this citrus-scented body wash and the cinnamon mouth rinse." His voice lowered. "I hope you're among the ninety percent."

Her tea caught in her throat as though she'd swallowed the lemon wedge. Or a whole lemon. She forced it down with a gulp. "It's nice."

"Do you use your gym, or did you have it built for Benjamin to train for baseball?"

Unable to avert her gaze any longer, she swung her gaze toward him. "I built it, and I use it every day except Saturday and Sunday."

"Really?" Dylan cocked his head to one side, and a damp piece of hair clung to his forehead. "You've been working out since I've been here?"

"Same as always."

He made a dramatic wave. "When?"

"I get up around four forty-five and walk Mimi. When I get back, I do a thirty-minute Bible study. After that, twenty minutes of weights: arms on Monday, Wednesday, and Friday, legs on Tuesday and Thursday. I shower and make breakfast, then wake Benjamin."

"So, you're not very structured."

Again, Cassie choked on her tea, but this time she laughed. "A little." She reached for a napkin to dab her chin. "But I discipline myself to be flexible when it's called for."

"I've never heard someone say they discipline themselves to be flexible. Isn't that an oxymoron?"

"Maybe I'm an oxymoron. Or just a moron. Would you like to join me tomorrow?" Again with the invitations. Babbling, too. Her ribs grabbed at her lungs.

"I believe I would." He stood. "But I'd better go to bed if I'm going to fit into the regimen. You may be tougher than my trainer."

And a desperate moron who needed to keep her mind on doing what was best for baby Michael.

Chapter 19

As he waited by the door for Cassie to unhook Mimi's leash, Dylan wiped his brow for at least the hundredth time. Who knew how humid Mississippi mornings could be? Still, the walk had been the perfect way to wake up and clear his head.

Once inside, Cassie pulled a Bible from a drawer in the kitchen. "Time for coffee and Bible study. Will you be participating in that part of the *structure*?"

"Coffee's a definite yes, but what's involved in this Bible study?"

The preset coffee timer had already worked its magic, and a hazelnut aroma filled the air. She grabbed two mugs. "I do a variety of studies, but once a month, I read the entire book of James. I've done that since I gave my life to the Lord in eighth grade." She glanced up at him. "We could do that today."

"The whole book at one time?" Not exactly his idea of relaxing reading. Especially this early.

"It's only five chapters."

She held out a steaming cup of brew. The slight smile on her pink lips that accompanied the gesture loosened his objections. "Why do you read the same book so often?"

Her intelligent eyes sparkled against her shimmering skin. "I started when our youth pastor led a summer study about taming the tongue. James warns us about being careful with our words. At the time, I felt I needed to work on that. And I never stopped feeling like I could use some help with choosing my words. So I read it once a month. At least." Her voice became more passionate. "There's other meaty scripture in the book. James describes pure religion as helping orphans and widows. He emphasizes honoring the poor."

"I'm sold. Read it to me."

Her chin dropped, and her eyes popped open wide. "You want me to read it to you?"

Wasn't expecting that, was she? He shrugged. "Why not? I guess we could take turns if your voice gets tired."

She stared at him a second, then shrugged. "Let's go to the sunroom." She tucked the Bible under her arm and gathered her cup.

He followed her to the chairs that faced the windows overlooking the manicured back yard. Notes filled the margins on either side of the pages of the well-worn book as she flipped toward the back.

Clearing her throat, she began, her voice quiet at first. As she went on, she spoke with more confidence.

Dylan stirred his coffee, enjoying the sound and glancing out the window. The reading came to an abrupt halt, and he rotated to look at her. "Why'd you stop?"

"That's the end of the book."

"He ends there? Really? What was that last line again?"

"'Whoever turns a sinner from the error of their way will save them from death and cover over a multitude of sins.'"

Interesting way to pull down the curtain. "He writes so much to the rich about how they need to help the poor. I felt like he was preaching to me. Who is this James anyway?"

"He was the half-brother of Jesus. He didn't believe in Jesus, from what we can tell, until after the resurrection. Then Jesus appeared to him."

Dylan chuckled. "That could change someone's mind. I didn't even know Jesus had a brother."

Fidgeting with the arm of the chair, her eyes lowered. "Are you a believer?"

The weight of the question hung between them. Memories of his upbringing in a small church marched through his mind. "I made a commitment as a child, but as I grew older, it seemed the members at my tiny church spent most of their time arguing. I couldn't stand it. It didn't seem like what church should be. When I left for college, I never went back." He propped his chin on his hands and focused on the wooden floor in front of him. "As you can tell, I haven't been living it. You probably think I'm pretty revolting."

She reached across the distance between the chairs. Her hand pressed against his. "We're all sinners. It's Christ's sacrifice that cleans us. I'm no better than you."

"Believe me, you are." A bitter laugh escaped his lips. "Even if I changed, I don't know if I could go to a church. There are so many hypocritical people there."

"Anywhere people get together, there are going to be problems. Haven't you heard the old saying 'Church is a hospital for sinners, not a hotel for saints'? Broken people don't always realize they're broken, even in the church. We've had our share of hurt these past two years—some caused by a few of our fellow church members and things they've said about the divorce. Other friends from church have carried us through our pain and wiped our tears."

Cassie's phone chirped, interrupting their conversation. "It's Nick." She answered and then hung up a minute later. "He has a conflict and needs us to keep Michael earlier than expected. I'd better run shower."

"I'll shower, too." He rose and strode toward the master bedroom. Cassie took off at the same time, her little legs pumping quickly down the hall. Interesting, though. She seemed to be going the same place he was. He stopped midstride… "Are we racing to the shower or sharing it?"

Gasping, Cassie mashed her hand over her mouth. "I was on autopilot."

He couldn't resist teasing her. "Oh, right."

Spinning on her heels, she scurried in the opposite direction. "I'm issuing a gag order for you."

~~~

Five o'clock p.m. on the dot. Perspiration trickled down Cassie's back as she and Dylan climbed the steps to Jill and Nick's home. The day had passed quickly as they'd tended to the little man, and she'd made sure they were on time returning Michael. Punctuality might help to keep things going smoothly between the two parties. The door swung open before they
~~~

rang the bell.

Jill's eyes, traced in dark circles, lit up as she reached for the baby. "Nick's stuck at work, but he'll be here soon. I wanted to keep Michael on schedule. Did you have problems with him sleeping or eating? Were my instructions in the bag clear?"

Instructions in the bag? Cassie hadn't seen any note in the bag.

Dylan's eyes met hers with a quizzical look. "No problems."

A wrinkle formed between Jill's eyebrows. "Nick was supposed to put the note in the bag. He did, right?"

From the street, a woman dressed in black leggings and a strapless yellow top appeared, high heels clacking up the steps. She flung long black hair back from her face. "Where's Jess?"

Jill held Michael close. "Jess doesn't live at this address anymore. He married, and we bought this house from him."

Dylan pulled his hat down over his brows, turned away, and eased toward the van.

The woman stomped her foot. "I know he's married. Did he move down the street into that girl's house?"

Fury flared in Cassie. Who did this woman think she was, coming here like this?

Tame the tongue. James. Remember the words of James.

The woman brushed past Cassie and back down the steps toward Dylan. She leered at him, then yanked his hat from his head. "Dylan Conner, what are you doing here? And why didn't you speak? Or return my calls. You coward."

His mouth formed a flat line as he acknowledged her. "Sophia."

Enough. Cassie hurried to his side. She'd heard about how this woman operated. The look Sophia cast at the two of them sent a bitter taste to the back of Cassie's throat.

Sophia snarled. "You gave me up for that?"

Dylan placed his hand on Cassie's back and set a quick pace toward the street. "Let's go."

Sophia kept up with them. A wicked grin spread across her face as she peered into the minivan. "A car seat and a baby. That's why you quit seeing me. You knocked her up."

Lord, help me. Cassie bristled. Slapping the woman was out of the question. Tackling her came to mind. Screaming, too. But her legal training kicked in. Smacking her with a bit of verbal sleight of hand—a legitimate option.

Cassie planted herself between Sophia and Dylan. "Have you ever heard of godparents? People who commit to being a part of a child's life?"

Wild, dark eyes stared back at her. The depths radiated hate.

Sophia jabbed Cassie's shoulder with her index finger. "You have no idea who you're talking to, and you *will* get hurt."

Dylan started to step in, but Cassie stilled him with one shake of her head.

Looking first at her shoulder, then back at Sophia, Cassie stood taller and shifted further into lawyer mode. "I think it's the other way around. I'm an attorney, and some would classify what you just did as assault and battery. Not only could I have you arrested, I could sue you. From what I've heard, Jess and Dylan could have restraining orders placed against you for harassment, stalking even. And what would that do to your corporate image if it made its way to the tabloids?" She made air quotes with her fingers. "'Fashion Diva Stalking Former Lovers.' So, I'm thinking you should take yourself out of Oxford, Mississippi, and don't look back."

Teeth clenched, Sophia thrust a finger near Cassie's face. "If you think the likes of you can keep a man like Dylan, you're kidding yourself." She spun around and stomped down the sidewalk to a car parked behind the next house.

Only after the woman drove away did Cassie lower her posture. Shaking, she let out a long breath and climbed into the van. "She's creepy. I thought she might stab me with one of her stilettos." Her confidence dissolved as she pictured the wrath she'd seen inside Sophia. That wouldn't be the last they'd hear from the woman. Too many times at the courthouse, Cassie had seen eyes like that—the kind of eyes that committed unspeakable acts.

Dylan let out a nervous laugh. "I think I mentioned she's a sociopath. Most people are intimidated by her, and she plows over them. Not my little redheaded attorney, though."

"Let's pray she leaves and doesn't come back. I hate confrontations like that, but every now and then, it becomes necessary to protect people I care about."

"So, you care about me?" Dylan nudged her arm.

More than she intended. "And Michael, Jill, and Jess."

"She'll look for a way to get even."

A shiver rippled through Cassie's core. "I could see it in her eyes...so cold. I wonder what happened to her. It's sad. She's such a beautiful woman."

Dylan's chin dropped. "I can't believe you feel sorry for her."

"She's human. God loves her, so I'm commanded to love." She allowed herself a grumble. "I'm not commanded to like, though."

Back at her house, Cassie stepped onto the driveway. Dylan circled the van and pulled her into an embrace. "Thanks for sticking up for me. I couldn't think of what to say when she saw the baby seat. I froze."

His arms felt nice around her. Natural. Like home. She'd missed having someone hug her since the divorce.

But she should remove herself. Or...she could wait until he let go. A more polite option.

As she stood in his arms, a pang of guilt tugged at her about what she'd said. "I was trying not to lie. I didn't actually say we were godparents." She groaned. "But it wasn't truth either."

Dylan squeezed her closer, his chin resting against her hair. "Attorney jargon. That's what they teach in law school, right?" He chuckled. "How to lie without lying." His hand stroked her back.

His citrus scent and his arms tight around her—what was she doing? About to plead insanity, no doubt. Cassie pushed him back. "Now you're lawyer bashing? When I just saved your backside?"

His hands found her hair and his fingers sunk between the strands. "And now we're seeing the redhead come out again. Feisty."

Yes. Pleading insanity. No. Pleading guilty. Run.

She pivoted toward the house. "I'm going upstairs to reread the book of James." And maybe a few other books of the Bible.

Chapter 20

Cassie opened her front door with one hand, Michael secure in the other arm. "Hey. What brings you out so early this morning?"

Sarah Beth toed at the thatch welcome mat, both hands behind her back. "Your yard looks nice."

"Thank you." A tiny fist bopped up and down against Cassie's arm. "Would you like to come in?"

"Is Dylan here?" She slipped one finger into the baby's hand.

"He's out back throwing away a smelly diaper. Come inside."

Sarah Beth's mouth took a slight curve upward before she entered the foyer. "Oh, my stars. Who would've thought?"

A thump sounded as the back door closed, signaling Dylan's reentry. "Cassie, I ridded us of the biohazard. We're safe now." His voice moved closer. "Shoo, that was a powerful one." He stopped short when he rounded the corner and saw their visitor. "Oh, hey. I didn't know you were coming by."

The smile disappeared from Sarah Beth's face as she pulled a paper from behind her back. "I hate to be the bearer of bad tidings. This time it's not with me." The front page displayed a photo of Dylan with his arms around Cassie followed by the headline, *Dylan Conner Gets Cozy with Wealthy Southern Divorcee.*

The muscles of Cassie's face flinched, but she managed to close the door. "Quicker than expected."

"Cassie, I'm sorry to drag you into this." Dylan's gaze flew from the gossip rag to her eyes as he moved to her side. "Are you okay?"

"It could be worse. And it will be if they really start digging. We need to prepare." Jaw set, she straightened her posture.

"You, Jill, and Nick will be forced to meet and come to an agreement about how you're going to handle Michael's paternity. Are you going to claim him as your son or try to keep it a secret?"

His arm touched the small of her back. "But what about you? Are you going to be all right now that your personal life's been dragged into this mess? And Benjamin?" Dylan's hand slid to her elbow and squeezed. "Benjamin—we should check him out of school and tell him."

Oh, no. Benjamin. Cassie's mouth fell open, and her gaze flew to Sarah Beth. "I need to talk to him before he sees this."

"I'll ride with you for backup." Dylan swiveled and glanced around the room. "Let me get Michael's bag."

"I'll stay here with the baby, and I'll call Jill to explain." Sarah Beth took Michael while Cassie grabbed her keys and purse. "Don't worry, and take as long as you need."

In the van, Cassie's hands shook, and she blinked hard against the searing heat and the tears behind her eyelids. She needed to compose herself and not drive like a maniac. She glanced at Dylan before putting the gear in reverse. Strange. Dylan's thoughts had gone to Benjamin. A big shift for a single guy. Not that she'd seen a selfish side of Dylan, but still.

Questions barraged her along the short drive. How would Jill and Nick react to the pictures? Would they understand when she explained, or would they end the mediation?

She should have been more careful. She knew Sophia was a loose cannon. The woman had probably followed them and taken a picture from a nearby yard. The thought that she'd caused more trouble pierced her heart. No matter how either party reacted, things were coming to a head regarding Michael.

Twenty minutes later, Cassie's neck burned as she exited the school's front office. Were the ladies at the desk giving her strange looks, or was she imagining things?

Benjamin grinned and set a fast pace to the parking lot. "Got caught, huh?"

Cassie huffed. "You know already?"

"Someone sent a picture to my phone thirty minutes ago."

"Get in the van. We'll pick up your Jeep later." Cassie turned to Dylan who'd slumped down in the front seat, his baseball cap pulled close to his sunglasses. "He already knows."

Dylan rotated toward the back seat. "It wasn't what it looked like."

"I'm cool if you and Mom are dating. My friends thought it was awesome."

Dating? She clawed at her itchy neck. Maybe she should invest in a collection of light summer scarves. Seemed like she was going to be needing them this season. Cassie glanced at Benjamin in the rearview mirror. "We're not dating."

"Living together. Whatever."

Flames licked Cassie's cheeks.

Dylan cleared his throat. "Benjamin." His tone was firm. Almost paternal.

"I'm kidding. Chill. I know Mom is squeaky clean. It gives everyone something to talk about besides Dad. Which is good with me."

But not good for anyone else.

They were home in minutes, and Benjamin stopped outside the van door. "Can I go back to bed, since I'm checked out, anyway?"

"Sure." The knots in her shoulders loosened. "I'm glad you're taking this well. I checked you out of school because I thought you might be upset."

Back in the house, Sarah Beth looked up from her perch on the couch where Michael lay on her lap. "Is he okay?"

Dylan chuckled. "The least of our worries." His expression grew serious. "But this little guy…" He sank onto the couch beside Sarah Beth and caressed Michael's head. "I don't know what's best for him."

"Have you prayed about it?" Sarah Beth's question seemed to catch Dylan off guard.

His eyes moved from Sarah Beth to Cassie. "Will you both pray for me to have wisdom?"

A stab of wonder coursed through Cassie. Was he recalling

the verse from James about wisdom? "I've been praying since I found out about the custody issue."

Sarah Beth gave him a smile. "Me, too. But we can pray now, if you want."

Dylan nodded, and Cassie pulled an armchair close to the couch.

Placing the baby on Dylan's lap, Sarah Beth bowed her head. "Lord, thank You so much for precious Michael who You've given us to love. Dylan doesn't know how to handle this situation, but he wants what's best for his son. Give him wisdom. Show him and all of us what You would have us do, and help us know Your timing. We know You love Michael more than we can ever imagine, and we want to follow Your plan, not ours. In Jesus' name, we pray. Amen."

Dylan pressed his lips together, and Cassie couldn't help but reach out and squeeze his arm. "We're going to have to be really careful when we go out in public and we need to set the alarm when we're home. I'll hire a few friends from the sheriff's department to keep an eye on the house. They can rotate when they're off-duty."

His fingers covered hers. "Again. I'm sorry. I'll pick up the extra expense."

Scooting to the edge of the couch, Sarah Beth nodded toward the door. "I should go."

"Stay and have an early lunch." Cassie stood. There wasn't much else to do about the press for now. "We're having stir-fry."

Dylan nudged Sarah Beth with his knee. "She's a good cook, and I remember how you love to eat."

"You do know my weakness. How can I help?"

"Don't get near the food until it's done." A teasing smirk crossed Dylan's face.

Sarah Beth crinkled her nose at him. "I could set the table or do something else safe."

Cassie motioned toward the kitchen. "That would help, and you can come talk to me while I cook. I want to hear how your new consulting business is sizing up." She zipped over to the alarm control panel near the pantry and punched in the code. She'd call the security as soon as she got the lunch started.

Sarah Beth followed her. "I'm busier than ever. Where are the plates?"

"The cabinet to the left of the sink." Cassie plugged in the wok she'd set out earlier. After adding sesame oil and turning up the heat, she pulled the sliced vegetables and meat out of the refrigerator. Good thing she'd made time to cut them before bed last night. "By the way, I'm not going to take the full-time position at the law library, so maybe I could help with your new venture. I found your work fascinating, and it was great to be able to float in and out. I still had time to be here for Benjamin and my pro bono work."

"Actually, I need advice with the legalities of running my own business and keeping up with the paperwork."

Oil sizzled in the wok as Cassie stirred in a Vidalia onion, which gave off a pungent odor. Good grief. Would her hair smell like an onion the rest of the day? And why did she care? "I'll come by your place one afternoon."

"Great, but I must warn you, I'm really scattered trying to get ready for the trip to Honduras."

"I can handle scattered. Are you nervous about traveling?"

Chewing her lip, Sarah Beth nodded. "Nervous, yes, but no panic attacks. I'm trying not to dwell on it." She smiled. "Jess will be with me, and anywhere with Jess is home."

A bit of sadness surged to tighten Cassie's throat. Had she ever felt that with Evan? "I'm glad you're happy."

"I am, but it's scary. I worry sometimes that it's too good to be true—that it can't last."

"I know the feeling, but you shouldn't think that way."

Dylan rounded the corner. His eyes explored her face as he took a whiff of the sizzling food. "I've been so spoiled here, I'll never be the same."

The light filtering from the sunroom cast a glow through Dylan's auburn hair. The way his mouth cocked up on one side and carved out a dimple on his left cheek as he gazed at her caused Cassie's breath to hitch. A vision of him, shirtless with

Michael on his chest, passed through her mind. She'd never be the same, either.

Chapter 21

Dylan pushed his empty plate away and excused himself. He lifted Michael from the pallet on the floor and carried him to the portable crib in the master bedroom, where he laid him on the small mattress. His son slept with such peace.

Too bad he couldn't sleep like that.

Losing his father's presence in his life had torn something in his heart. A hollowness he'd tried to ignore but had never really gotten over. Today's paparazzi photos forced his hand. Obviously they were Sophia's doing, but now he had to decide how to proceed. At least Cassie had a plan to keep them safe. An unmarked sedan was already parked in the drive.

But questions remained. Would Michael call him Daddy? Or would his son call another man Daddy and think of Dylan as his uncle or something? What was really best for Michael?

One decision seemed right, and then another. He squeezed his eyes shut and shoved his head in his hands. How could he decide?

He knew what Jill would want. She'd made that apparent when she'd left him out of the whole process. Anger bubbled up from his gut. If only she'd been honest from the start. And Nick. How dare that man give Michael his last name?

Dylan straightened and opened his eyes. This was *his* son. Michael would have his real father in his life.

~~~

Another unexpected knock summoned Cassie from the kitchen. Was it the security detail or had someone gotten past them. "Benjamin, are you expecting someone?"

"No," he hollered down the stairs. "I can peek out my window and see who it is."

"Okay." There could be a reporter lurking. "Nick already
~~~

picked up Michael. I hope it's not—"

"It's Dad."

The last person she wanted to see.

Emerging from the sunroom, Dylan carried a script. "You need backup?"

Benjamin tromped down the stairs, but Cassie held up her hand. "Give me a minute alone to talk to him." She eyed Dylan. Would it be rude to ask her guest to hide in the bedroom?

Dylan's angled jaw stiffened. "I'll go back in the other room, but if he gets out of line—"

"He won't." She shot him a pointed stare. The last thing she needed was for Benjamin to find out about his father's behavior the other day.

Placing a hand on Dylan's back, Benjamin guided Dylan away. "I can handle my dad, but I'll wait with you."

The bell rang three more times in a matter of seconds, and Mimi growled and followed as Cassie cracked the door. "Evan, do you and Benjamin have plans he forgot to mention?"

"What in the world are you doing?" Her ex shoved the gossip magazine toward her. "For someone who supposedly only kissed one man, you're sure making up for lost time. Now you're hanging all over some movie star? Have you gone out of your mind? Hasn't Benjamin been through enough embarrassment?"

Blood rushed to her face, and she yanked the door open. "You're worried about embarrassing Benjamin now? Where was all that concern while we were married?"

He scoffed. "At least my picture wasn't plastered on the cover of a national magazine for the whole world to see."

"I'm not married, so there's nothing wrong with me spending time with a man."

"Sweetie, you're so naive." He lowered his voice. "You'll get hurt."

"I just wish someone would've convinced me of that before I married you."

"Come on, now. That actor can't really be interested in you." He reached toward her arm, but she stepped back.

"I told you not to touch me."

Benjamin burst out of the sunroom and bolted to the door. "Hey, Dad." He stepped in front of her, standing a head taller than Evan already. "Let's go take a ride and talk, man to man."

Evan edged to the back of the porch. A moment of tension passed between them before he nodded once and twisted away. Benjamin followed his father to his mid-life-crisis convertible which was parked right beside the security detail. Evan must've known the officer and convinced him to let him by.

After they drove off, Dylan appeared at her side and shut the door. He touched her elbow and nudged her back toward the living room. "Are you okay? Come sit down."

Hot tears filled her eyes as all the anger and hurt she'd locked away broke through the barriers surrounding her heart. She let herself sink into his shoulder as he led her to take a seat in one of the club chairs. "Evan infuriates me. I was so naive when I married him. Singularly focused on academics. Never got into the social scene or dating." She sniffed. "My mom was my best friend, and I was a total nerd, but a happy nerd."

Dylan stood behind her and touched her shoulders. "Lean back and relax. This is a good time for me to finish showing you my massage skills."

Every instinct warned her to make an excuse to go upstairs. It was the practical thing to do. She shouldn't be personally involved with Dylan. But as his hands found her shoulders, she stilled. Couldn't they be friends? She'd never talked to anyone about her divorce.

His hands melted away her tension and her defenses. "My father told my mother in junior high he would marry her someday." Words tumbled out as she stopped trying to hold back the hurt. "He promised to give her a ruby every year until he could give her a wedding ring. She has all these trinkets he gave her over the years. Of course, they weren't real rubies at first, but he was a hard worker, and by the time they were in their late teens, he was giving her real rubies. They married young and have always been so in love." She swallowed at the lump in her throat. "Evan pursued me in law school. He didn't let up, so I thought maybe he was the one. I thought maybe I was Evan's ruby."

Dylan's hand moved to her hair, unloosing the band that held it in place. His fingers massaged her scalp, sending tingles down her back. "You're way out of Evan's league. It's not your fault he was an idiot. Don't be like my mom and close yourself off for the rest of your life."

Close herself off? That was exactly what she'd planned. To never let her heart be broken again.

She swiveled to look up at him. "But haven't you done the same thing? I don't want Benjamin to close himself off because of my mistake like…"

"Like me." He walked around to her side and rested on the arm of the chair. His green eyes fell to her lips. "Maybe we should both leave the door cracked, in case the right one comes along."

Her mouth dried as she tried to speak. "Maybe so."

Dylan's focus dropped to the floor. "I was thinking I should go ahead and buy a place in Oxford. I have people beating down my door to buy my empty condo in Malibu. I can let that go, keep my bigger house there, and have a place here, too." He looked back at Cassie. "What do you think?"

She crossed her arms as she tried to collect herself. "Makes sense."

"Could you connect me with a good Realtor? Maybe I can find something before we go to Honduras."

So soon? Her ridiculous stomach plummeted at the thought of him leaving, but she held her shoulders straight back. She needed to forget Evan, forget the paparazzi…and forget that massage. *Focus.* A Realtor. Dylan wanted to move. "I have a friend in high-end real estate. What kind of place should I tell her to look for?"

Dylan swept his arm around the room. "Something like this, but in a gated community or on some land with a tall privacy fence."

"You'll need to keep away unwanted visitors."

Dylan gave her a crooked smile. "Not you and Benjamin,

though. My casa will be your casa."

"I'll grab my phone and call." She pushed to her feet, headed toward her purse, and sighed. She may as well get it over with. How would life change if Dylan Conner had a permanent residence in Oxford? And why did the thought of it send her heart rate skyrocketing?

~~~

Dylan's heart launched into a run, but he forced his legs to walk a normal stride down the hallway to his room. Cassie's room. The look on her face after Evan left, the pain that creased her forehead and glossed her blue-green eyes, had bitten into his soul. The desire to hold her and protect her overwhelmed him. But he couldn't drag this sweet woman into his world of gossip rags and paparazzi stalkers. She'd been through too much already. Plus, he had to focus on Michael.

Maybe he and Cassie could stay friends. He didn't have many of those. Not real ones. He had to move out and let her life get back to normal. Allow her to heal the scars that jerk Evan had inflicted.

He'd put a call in to his L.A. real estate agent with instructions to sell his condo. All the nostalgia about the place crumbled compared to what was at stake now—being near his son, without hurting Cassie.
~~~

Chapter 22

The country road cut through a sea of green fields and trees while Christian music filled the silence. Not much farther until they reached the house for sale. Cassie tried to drown out the urge to ask Dylan why he'd decided so quickly to move out. Had she said or done something to upset him?

The words of both Sophia and Evan played over in her mind.

If you think you can keep a man like Dylan, you're kidding yourself.

Come on, now. That actor can't really be interested in you.

"Do you know where you're going?" Dylan's voice interrupted her deliberations.

Right now, yes. In life, no. "The Realtor said there's a brown wooden sign at the end of the gravel road six miles after we turn left. We've gone five so far."

"I should know to trust you." His voice soaked into her soul, silencing some of that negative self-talk. "You seem like you're a million miles away, though. What are you thinking?"

Her glance slid his direction to find his eyes locked on her. Jerking her gaze back, she flipped the air conditioner up a notch. "All the strange comings and goings in the last few days. Trying to process whether I handled Evan and Sophia in a Christ-like manner—among other things."

"It's my fault." His words lowered to a half-whisper. "If it weren't for me, you wouldn't be dealing with any of this drama."

She couldn't let him take the blame. "I would have to deal with Evan regardless, and I know for a fact Sarah Beth and Jess have been hassled by Sophia for some time now." The turn came into sight, and she flipped on a blinker. "Here we are. Start drinking in the landscape and see if this is the place for you." With her head, she pointed. "Look, a six-foot iron fence to keep out crazy fans." Or me.

Yellow wildflowers blanketed the meadows on either side as they entered the long, gray stone road. What looked to be hundred-year-old oak trees lined the drive until they reached a circle in front of the house.

Cassie parked next to the steps that led to the porch, stepped out, and blocked the sun with her hand to take in the full view of the two-story Greek revival home. "I like the stone chimney and green shutters. Looks like the trim's been painted recently."

The Realtor pulled up behind their car and hurried to join them. "Hey. I hate to do this, but this was so last-minute, and I have an appointment in town. So maybe we can come out again another day. We need to make it a quick tour today, if you don't mind." She turned to Dylan. "I wanted to go ahead and show you this property, because I think this house is perfect for you, Mr. Conner. Lots of privacy. The owner is a writer who is pretty well-known. He completely gutted and remodeled every room three years ago but wasn't able to get away from the West Coast as often as he'd planned. He only put it on the market yesterday, so you couldn't have timed this any better." Her arms spread in a dramatic wave across the view. "It's like a match made in heaven."

What a sales pitch.

"The inside is pristine." The Realtor unlocked the door. "The grounds need a manicure, but I have some great landscapers I could recommend. This used to be a cattle farm a long while back. There's a creek and a pond about a half mile down the hill. I'll have to lock the house when I leave, but feel free to walk the grounds as long as you like." The Realtor's phone rang. "You go ahead. I'll be along in a minute."

Cassie's sandals clicked on the heart of pine floors. Two large columns rose up to high ceilings in the grand entryway. A curved mahogany staircase led upstairs, but they turned left into the living room. A fireplace with an elaborate mantle was centered on a long wall between two windows. The room connected with what must've been the dining room because a massive chandelier hung from the center of the ceiling.

In the kitchen, she rubbed her hands across the white-washed cabinets and marble countertops. "I love this. The perfect appliances. A great set up to do some serious cooking."

"I'd love for you to use it." Dylan beamed. "I'm spoiled rotten with your French toast in the morning and hot lunches. Don't even get me started on dinner."

His compliment boosted her mood again, lightening the heaviness in her chest. It was nice to be appreciated. And she could sure use the friendship. She returned a smile. "Let's see the rest of the house."

They toured the four upstairs bedrooms and large sitting area, then descended the back staircase to the master bedroom.

"This is nice. I love a fireplace in the bedroom." Cassie opened the door that led to the back porch. She stepped onto the screened-in area and sucked in a deep breath. The sweet scent of gardenias filled her nose, bringing back memories of summers in Mobile. She called to Dylan, who was still inside. "Come look at the view. It's spectacular. You can see the pond from here, but it's not close enough for you to worry about Michael falling in."

Dylan joined her, his shoulder touching hers. "What's that luscious smell?" He sniffed Cassie's hair. "Are you wearing perfume?"

With their shoulders so close and his face next to her hair, tingles zipped down her back. Between the sweetness and his presence, she could stand here forever. "They've planted gardenias along the porch."

A breeze blew in through the screened walls, and she glanced at Dylan.

His eyes were closed. "I don't want to move from this moment."

His face, his voice, the breeze—her arms itched to wrap around him. Her heart was betraying her. She had a plan, after all. Never to let herself love a man that way again. And she had Michael's custody mediation to think about.

But those eyes opened and skipped to hers. How perfectly symmetrical Dylan's face was, how long those dark eyelashes, how magnetic those green irises.

He was so close.

"Cassie, I need to lock up." The voice of the Realtor from inside broke the spell. She poked her head out on the porch. "Mr. Conner, if you like the place, I can spend more time with y'all here tomorrow. I apologize for rushing you, but since Cassie's a personal friend, I wanted to give you first dibs. Like I said, you're welcome to walk the grounds."

Cassie took a reluctant step to exit the porch. "Thank you for meeting us on short notice. We'll contact you soon." She opened the screened door and walked into the back yard.

Dylan shook hands with the agent and fell in beside Cassie. As they inspected the grounds, Cassie examined the plants and explained each one. The place had potential once they nursed the gardens back to health. "I could get my hands dirty out here. See those bushes with honeysuckle winding around them?"

Dylan nodded. He hadn't said much since they'd left the house. Since they'd entered it, for that matter. Maybe he didn't like it.

Cassie pulled his elbow, towing him toward rows upon rows of unkempt bushes. "Those are azaleas and camellias. We missed the blooms, but by next year, this place could rival Bellingrath Gardens."

"Where's that?"

"It's near Mobile."

His gaze traveled across the countryside, then back to her, the sunshine gleaming through his hair. An intense look crossed his face. What was he thinking?

At that moment, sprinkler heads popped up and sputtered. Dylan's brow creased. "Uh oh, I know that sound."

"Me, too."

"Run?"

She nodded. Too late.

The sprinklers came to life, spewing lukewarm water. Cassie

took off at a jog. Dylan joined her, but slipped on wet grass near the house and hit the ground with a slap.

~~~

From his landing spot, Dylan looked up at Cassie. No doubt she was trying not to laugh at him as water continued to spray across his chest.

"Are you okay?"

Why not have a little fun? He turned his face away, hugged his knee, and bent over it, letting out a quiet groan—but not without stealing another glance at her. "Yes. Go ahead. I'll be there in a minute."

Cassie took one step forward, but took two back toward him. A cute line formed across her forehead. "You're not acting, are you? Trying to get me in the mud?"

He waved her off and hugged his leg tighter. "I'm fine. I'll catch up."

"Let me take a look." Cassie stepped to his side. She squatted down in the spraying water and put her hand on his back. "I know first aid."

With one quick move, he reached up and pulled her to the ground on the other side of him and laughed. "I can't be the only one with a huge mud stain on the back of my pants."

Squealing, she swiped a dirty hand across his cheek. "I knew you were acting."

Dylan lowered his chin. "I thought someone learned her lesson with the whipped cream."

"No, don't." Her hands flew back to her sides. "I'm sorry."

He caught both of her arms and held his cheek inches from her lips. Another tiny squeal escaped from her throat. He had to laugh. "I'll show you grace, since I started it this time."

Cassie's eyes held his as she sat in the mud. So close and so beautiful. How easily he could've taken her in his arms. He would have, too, if he'd been the same man he was even a couple of months ago. But not now. He couldn't do that. He wasn't good enough for her, and she was his friend. And his custody mediator.

~~~

Cassie touched Dylan's muddied cheek, rubbing her thumb across to wipe away the dirt. His chin lifted. Cinnamon breath met hers, as he sighed. Her eyes wouldn't obey, drifting down to his full lips. Her mouth, joining the rebellion, moved to brush his.

A soft exhale came from Dylan's throat, and he whispered her name before she closed her eyes and kissed him with an intensity she'd never felt before. His arm slipped around her, and he pulled her into his lap, his other hand sinking deep into her hair. Moments passed. The spraying water and the sounds around her disappeared. Hadn't her heart ached for Dylan since that first day she'd gotten to know him? Seen another side of him? And hadn't she longed to kiss him for days now?

Too soon, Dylan pushed her back to arm's length. "Cassie, no. I can't…I can't blow this. I know Evan hurt you. And what Sophia said…"

Heart still racing, her eyes fluttered open. "What?"

He touched a finger to her lips. "Cassie, you're so good." His hands cupped her face as water ran down her cheeks and hair. "I know hurtful things were said to you the last few days. But you're the best friend I've ever had, maybe the only real one. I don't want to do anything to ruin that."

The tepid water on her skin steamed compared to the icy chill that ran through her. What a mistake. She'd made a fool of herself. "I'm sorry." She pulled away as the sprinklers continued their drenching of the grounds. "We should go."

Evan and Sophia were right. She stood and marched toward the driveway.

"Cassie, wait." Dylan caught up with her. "I said that all wrong. I don't want to lose you because of a rash moment."

She lifted her chin but couldn't meet his eyes. Not now. "Let's pretend it never happened. It was inappropriate on my part." At the van, she popped the cargo hatch. There had to be something to dry off with. "Here's a couple of T-shirts." She pulled them out and held one out to him. "That's all I can find to wipe away the mud."

He caught her arm. "Cassie…"

"Please. Don't." She slipped away from him. "Let's just go." She hastily dried off, then climbed into the sweltering van. Her phone chimed as Dylan sat beside her. She glanced at the screen. "It's my sister, Elinor. Do you mind if I put her on speaker?"

He shook his head.

At least the call would distract her from how badly she'd messed up and the awkward ride home. How could she have been such an idiot?

Chapter 23

Dylan entered Cassie's house from the garage to find Benjamin standing in the kitchen with Mimi at his side, wagging her sculptured tail.

Cassie nudged around him. "I told you to keep the security system armed."

"Sorry." After surveying their wet clothes, Benjamin scrunched his brows. "Where in the world have y'all been?"

Mimi sniffed Dylan and turned up her nose. Apparently, all the ladies of this house were unhappy with him.

Cassie threw her keys on the counter with a clank. "Dylan's buying a house."

"Did you have to swim the moat?"

Dylan managed a smile. "Sprinkler system surprise." And a few other surprises he'd handled badly.

Benjamin laughed. "Wish I could have seen that. I'm glad you're getting a place in Oxford, but I'll miss having you and Michael around. How long until you move in?"

"Here." Cassie handed Dylan a towel and a plastic grocery bag to put his wet clothes in. "I'm going to clean up."

Clearly, she couldn't wait to get away from him. How had he always managed to screw things up so badly?

"Hey." Benjamin tapped Dylan's shoulder, and he turned to face the boy. "I can help you move when you're ready."

"It'll be after we get back from Honduras. Speaking of, I need to go shopping at a sporting goods store for a few things. Want to take me after I change?"

"I know just the place." Benjamin gave him a thumbs up.

Maybe that would give Cassie some privacy and time to cool down.

After Dylan had hurried through his shower, Benjamin took

him across the small town to purchase the clothing he'd need in the tropics. Not that Mississippi was any cooler. An hour later, they returned to find Cassie dressed in a delicate ivory pantsuit and heels.

"Whoa, Mom. You look nice. Are we going somewhere?"

Dylan blinked. The soft white material and her creamy skin set against the red hair flowing down her shoulders… He couldn't form words.

"I'm going to dinner with a friend on the Square. I left my card so you can order pizza or something."

"What friend?" Benjamin tilted his chin.

Cassie grabbed her clutch and tucked it under her arm. "I'm meeting Wyatt Meadows."

When she was halfway out the door, Dylan found his voice. "You're wearing your hair down?"

She left without responding. The door slammed behind her.

"She never wears her hair down. And she never dates." Benjamin squared off with Dylan, eyes narrowed. "What exactly happened today?"

"I blew it." Even when he'd been trying to do the right thing, for once.

~~~

Cassie strolled through the large double doors of Oxford's newest gourmet restaurant. Why had she been impulsive enough to accept this dinner invitation? Maybe Wyatt's call had just come at the wrong time. Or the right time, if she were honest with herself. Because she knew exactly why she'd accepted.

To make herself feel wanted. And maybe to hurt Dylan in the process.

Two imprudent decisions in one day. Poor judgment. Clearly, she needed to find someone to take over Dylan's custody mediation. Who could she ask? She ran through a few good attorneys who owed her favors.

Wyatt's sandy-blond hair came into view, and he greeted her with a small gasp. "You look beautiful."

She made small talk as they waited to be seated. Once they'd
~~~

settled into the cozy table for two and given their order to the waitress clad in dress-blacks, Cassie's gut clenched. She'd no doubt given this nice man the wrong idea.

His brown eyes stared as if waiting for her to speak. After years of meeting with legal clients, not to mention socialites at fundraisers, she could get through this dinner somehow.

"So, Wyatt, I've learned something about your professional life, what about the rest?"

Unfolding his napkin, he smiled. "That's a loaded question. Not sure where I should start. But, here goes. Good family. The oldest of four." He took a gulp of tea. "I know you're divorced, so maybe you can relate to my past better than most." The fingers of his left hand tapped nervously against the table. "I married my high school sweetheart the week I graduated college with an accounting degree. I started a job with a prestigious firm in New Mexico. I thought I was on top of the world until Kelly, my wife, left me six months later. There wasn't another man. The only thing I could figure was that her parents divorced when she was in tenth grade, and she'd stayed with me all those years for security."

Cassie gave a slow nod. She certainly hadn't meant for him to open up this much. What kind of signals was she giving off? "Divorce is tough."

He managed a weak laugh. "You know, the heartbreak and feelings of failure were miserable, but the worst thing was losing my best friend. We'd been together so long, when something good happened, I thought, 'I should call Kelly.' When I was sad, my first instinct was to tell her, but I couldn't. The loss of the friendship left a huge hole in my life. I eventually went on to law school, started teaching, and ended up here a few years ago."

Her mouth fell open. *Friendship.* The worst part for him had been losing his best friend.

"Cassie, what are you thinking? Did I say something wrong?"

"You just made so much sense." She'd never been best friends with Evan, but Dylan had called her his friend. Maybe his *best friend.* Something worth saving. She'd been an idiot twice, no, three times in one day.

As soon as she shoveled the last bite of dinner in her mouth, she made her excuses and headed home, leaving a baffled Wyatt at the door of the restaurant. She'd never eaten that fast in her life.

Now to see if Dylan was awake.

At the house, she punched in the alarm code. Mimi greeted her at the door and led her to the sunroom. Cassie peeked her head around the doorframe to find Dylan sipping a cup of tea and reading. "Busy?"

He glanced up from his script and rubbed his drowsy eyes. "Just memorizing. How was your dinner?"

Easing into the chair beside him, she smoothed imaginary wrinkles from her pants. "I'm sorry for overreacting. You were right about everything. We shouldn't ruin our friendship. Plus, Michael's future is too important."

"No, that wasn't what I meant. I need to explain—"

"Hey, Mom." The slap of flip-flops crossed the kitchen floor. "I thought I heard you come in." Benjamin plopped down in a chair across from them. "Guess what? Coach McCoy invited us to go waterskiing tomorrow. I said yes for all three of us."

Cassie's jaw dropped. "You know I can't ride in a boat."

Dylan's forehead creased as he gave a sarcastic chuckle. "And I'm sure they didn't intend to invite me." His curious gaze traveled to Cassie. "Your father's an admiralty attorney and you grew up in Mobile, but you can't ride in a boat?"

He'd caught that one. "I tried to be the son my father never had. Learned to hunt, camp, and even followed his footsteps by going to law school. I can fish on land, but could never get over being seasick on the water." She grimaced at the thought of waves churning her stomach. "I tried every remedy. Luckily, boating is one thing my sister Emma loves to do with Daddy."

Benjamin's eyes pleaded. "They invited us *all* to go. Wouldn't it be rude not to show?"

"Even if that's true, I can't ski." Dylan shrugged with both hands out.

"I'll teach you. It's easy."

"Tell you what…" Dylan thumbed at Cassie. "I'll go if she goes."

Benjamin was up to something. This couldn't have been Jess's idea, but she'd question her son later. "I guess I could set up a base camp on land at the picnic area. I'll cook lunch while you guys come and go on the boat. That's the best I can offer."

A huge smile crossed Benjamin's face. "Deal."

~~~

Dylan had never been so distracted. He'd intended to have this script memorized before he left for Honduras. He had to be on location in New Zealand within three weeks of coming home from the mission trip. How Benjamin had gotten them invited to ski with the McCoys remained a mystery, but it had to be a plot on the kid's part to make things better between everyone. If only a day on the lake could do that. Now, he'd have to be around that arrogant jock, Jess McCoy. More likely, the tension would push things over the edge. But he would do his part and try to be civil. Besides, he couldn't say no to Benjamin.

Or Cassie. Another distraction. Rather, the biggest distraction. Her hair. Her eyes. That kiss. Her lips had ignited the emotions he'd been fighting so hard to quench—feelings he'd never experienced with anyone and hadn't planned to ever explore.

But now she was happy to be friends. Had her dinner date led her to the decision that friendship was the better option? Did she find that guy Wyatt more attractive? The thought seared into his chest like hot coals.

~~~

Cassie arrived at the lake early to prepare, asking Dylan and Benjamin to unload the minivan per her exact instructions. The security detail had parked in the shade nearby. This day would be strange enough without any hitches in the equipment or crazy stalkers. At least the weather was cooperating.

The large canopy she'd brought and erected in a grassy area

near the picnic table sheltered Michael and Jill. Nearby, Sarah Beth and Katie tossed a small plastic ball.

Once more Cassie checked that the tent stakes held fast in the hard soil, then stepped into the scorching sun and poked the charcoal fire she'd started in the grill. The chicken, sliced potatoes, and onions chilled in the rolling cooler beside her feet. She'd done her part to keep things going smoothly. How the group interacted with each other was beyond her control, but she'd prayed this morning before leaving the house. A lot.

Nick inspected her work. "I didn't figure you for the outdoorsy type."

Benjamin pointed at her. "Mom was a leader for our Scout troop. She could teach most of the badges, except for the ones on boats."

Sarah Beth pulled a water from the cooler. "Benjamin, are you an Eagle Scout?"

"Yes, ma'am."

"So is my brother, Mark. That's quite an accomplishment."

He gave her a humble smile, red creeping into his cheeks. "Mom was a lot of help. My dad was too busy working."

The compliment both pleased and gnawed at Cassie. She'd enjoyed helping with Scouts but had hoped Evan would make more of an effort as Benjamin grew older. The only thing Evan had made time for was the baseball games. And then he was too into the games, hollering like a madman and fussing at umpires. If the ballgames hadn't been the only time he could count on his father's attention, Benjamin may've quit playing the sport.

Jess hopped off the bow of the boat anchored close to shore in front of the canopy. He motioned to Benjamin, Dylan, and Nick. "Let's go take a run."

Cassie's grip stiffened around the tongs in her hand. This would be tricky.

Dylan waved them off. "I'll hold down the fort."

Benjamin pulled one of Dylan's arms. "I told you I'd teach you. It's easy."

Jess and Nick exchanged glances and crooked smiles. Jess's

brow raised. "You can't ski?"

Dylan kicked at a clump of dirt with the toe of his leather loafer. "Never tried."

"Be nice." Sarah Beth and Jill told their husbands in unison.

Benjamin hadn't let go of Dylan's arm and now pulled him closer to the water. "I'll watch out for you."

Mumbling as he went, Dylan gave Cassie a wide-eyed look. "Or be a witness to the crime…"

"Don't worry." Benjamin's chest expanded, and he flexed his bicep. "I'm man enough to watch your back."

Dylan clapped his shoulder. "Lucky for me you take after Big Roy."

From under the tent, Katie ran after the boys. "Who's Big Roy?"

Benjamin smiled at her. "My grandfather. He's a lawyer in Mobile for people with huge boats."

Nick's eyes lit up as he lifted Katie to his chest. "Mobile? They have amazing flowers down there."

The guys snickered at Nick's observation.

"Hey, I have a landscaping degree. I'm supposed to know these things. Let's go ski." He rubbed noses with his daughter. "You going on the boat with the guys or staying with the ladies?"

"Michael can stay, and I'll take his place on the boat."

"Good choice."

The pained expression on Dylan's face, despite the fact he was supposedly a great actor, both worried and tickled Cassie. Maybe Nick and Jess would go easy on him since Katie was riding along.

~~~

The boat zoomed back in sight in time for lunch. They weren't gone long really. No doubt because of the awkwardness of the situation. Cassie took the foil-wrapped dinners out of the coals and adjusted the Dutch oven to the center of the heat. Shirtless, Dylan moseyed over with a towel draped around his neck. His skin glistened in the sun as he crossed the grass to stand in front of her.
~~~

"I see you survived." She was anxious to hear about the escapade, but she forced her eyes back to the food. "Could you ski?"

"They only jerked me off the skis once. Otherwise, it was a quiet trip. Really quiet."

"Sean Jessup McCoy." Sarah Beth scoffed. "I told you to be nice."

Winking at his wife, Jess joined Cassie by the picnic table. "Falling is a rite of passage. And the motor's too noisy to sit around chewing the fat." He took a whiff of the smoke drifting up from the grill. "What's that delicious smell?"

Cassie spread out a blue and white tablecloth. "We called them hobo meals at Scout camp. You put your meat—I brought chicken and hamburger—and seasonings on top of sliced potatoes and onions, then wrap them up in a foil tent. For dessert, I have a peach cobbler finishing up on the coals."

Jess raised an eyebrow and let out a sigh. "Sounds delicious."

Sarah Beth jumped up and elbowed him. "Watch it, buddy. I'm getting jealous of you salivating over Cassie's cooking."

He pulled her close and planted a kiss on her forehead. "I didn't marry you for your cooking."

She tried to push him away. "You're getting lake water all over me."

He pulled her closer. "And that's a problem?"

She giggled and returned the hug. "I guess not."

Cassie turned away while Nick took a seat at the picnic table. "Let's thank God for our food and dig in."

After he led a prayer, Cassie passed out the plates. As they ate, Jill and Sarah Beth made attempts to keep the conversation moving. Benjamin brought up football, baseball, and movies. Cassie was proud of his effort. Even if every one of the adults felt uncomfortable, he had the right idea. Maybe he should be the mediator and not her. She'd certainly lost sight of her job. Another reason to be thankful Dylan would move out after the trip.

When they'd finished, Cassie cleared away the plates, and

with Dylan's help, took the canopy down, while Jess and Nick pulled the boat out and hitched it to the truck. A baby didn't need to be in these temperatures for long. Nor did Jill for that matter. And the longer they stayed, the more likely someone would say something they'd regret. It was probably for the best that the guys had been "quiet" on the boat ride.

They trudged across the parking lot with all the gear. Sarah Beth carried the baby equipment for Jill, who held Katie's hand on the way to the car. Benjamin offered to carry Michael. He cradled him in his arms and waited to put him in the seat until the air in the car had run enough to cool the steamy pent-up heat.

Jill patted his back. "You're really good with him."

Benjamin gave her an appreciative smile.

"This was a very gracious invite." Cassie waved from beside her van. Thank goodness they'd made it through the morning without incident. They all got in, she cranked the engine, and turned the air on full blast. She glanced at Dylan in the front seat beside her. "Jill held up pretty well. I hope she rests after this."

Benjamin leaned his head over the console. "Mrs. Jill looks like a model."

"Put on your seatbelt." Cassie smothered a chuckle at her son's assessment. "Jill's tall and thin like a model."

"Your mom's every bit as beautiful." Dylan's voice seeped with warmth.

Cassie gripped the steering wheel tighter. Was he trying to placate her or drive her nuts? Or a little of both?

Chapter 24

Even in the shade of the porch, the stifling humidity caused beads of sweat to form on Cassie's nose. She knocked a second time on Sarah Beth's door. A howl and a thud sounded inside, and she jerked her hand back.

A minute later, Sarah Beth opened the door, holding her dog's collar. "Welcome to the zoo." A black and white cat swished around Gingie's legs, meowing.

"Did you ever name that hole-digging cat?"

"Sort of. I asked Katie to come up with a cute name like she did for Gingie. The suggestion wasn't quite what I was hoping for, but I'd already promised Katie she could name him."

"And the name is?"

"Hairy."

A laugh bubbled out. "It's kind of cute."

"She said the cat got hair all over everything, so…"

"Makes perfect sense."

They strolled down the hall into the living room with both animals at their heels, vying for attention.

"Have a seat, and I'll get the documents I wanted you to look over." Sarah Beth crossed the room to a small desk stacked with manila folders.

As soon as Cassie sat, Hairy sprung onto her thighs, punching claws in and out of her pants as if kneading dough. "Make yourself at home, Hairy." The cat purred as Cassie scratched under his chin. Gingie circled the chair and whimpered.

"Are you jealous of the kitty? Come here. I'll pet your head, too."

"Oh, watch out, Cassie." Sarah Beth ran toward the dog. "Gingie. No."

Too late.

The huge mutt soared into Cassie's lap beside Hairy, covering her entire view of the outside world and weighing enough to take her breath away.

"Outside. Both of you." Sarah Beth took a firm tone.

Gingie lowered her head and edged off Cassie, paws leaving indentions in her pants, and Hairy bounced along behind. Cassie sneezed as fur floated past. She swiped at the black and white hair on her gray slacks. "He is hairy."

"I'm so sorry. I have a basket of those tape roller thingies." She reached to the end table and handed one to Cassie, along with the folder. "What's it going to be like when I add a baby? It'll be a circus for sure."

"You'll do fine." Cassie scanned the contents of the folder. Contracts. This would take a while. "I'd like to do some research with these at home, maybe tweak the wording. I'll have them back tomorrow." She rolled the tape along her legs, and then tossed the contraption back in the basket. "Can I ask you something, not about business?"

"Sure." Sarah Beth smiled and inclined her head closer.

"How did the boating invitation come about? I was a bit stunned that Jess and Nick would have anything to do with Dylan."

Looking away, Sarah Beth mashed her lips together.

"Tell me the truth."

"I promised to keep it to myself, but being together in an informal setting was a good idea."

Cassie crossed her arms. "Benjamin asked you, didn't he?"

"If Benjamin had asked me, I would've been totally behind it. Jess and Nick went along."

"Once you and Jill told them they had to?"

"Something like that, but Dylan seems different with you. More mature."

She wouldn't take credit for that. "Probably becoming a father matured him."

"I'm sure his new role is part of the change, but the way he looks at you and treats you with respect… He has deep feelings for you." Sarah Beth seemed to watch for her reaction.

Could she disappear now? "He has more substance than I expected from the way everyone talked about him. We've become close friends."

A gleam flashed in Sarah Beth's eyes. "Just friends? I think he's falling for you."

Flashback to the sprinkler catastrophe. "He only cares for me as a friend. He may still have feelings for you."

Sarah Beth scoffed. "He had a crush on me for a while, but that's not what I see when he looks at you. Don't tell me you haven't noticed. And you can't tell me you don't find him attractive."

A flush of heat swept through Cassie. "Of course, he's attractive. The whole world sees that." She picked at another clump of cat hair on her sleeve. She'd imagined for a second… "He respects me as a friend and as someone who is trying to assist him with a custody agreement. That's all."

"If you say so. Benjamin seems to have taken to him."

Sweet Benjamin. Cassie bit back a sigh. "Another reason I should keep Dylan in the friend zone. My son doesn't need more drama in his life." Cassie rose and edged toward the door. "I should get on these contracts right away. Thanks again for including us, even if we did kind of invite ourselves."

"I'm glad y'all went. We'll all be together for a week in Honduras, and it was a great way to break the ice." Sarah Beth walked with her. "We'll attempt more outings when we get back. Maybe it'll help everyone get along better."

Maybe they shouldn't push their luck. Cassie stepped back out into the heat. What emotions had Sarah Beth seen in Dylan? Surely it was only the friendship he claimed to feel.

And that was enough. She'd keep reminding herself until the facts plugged the last ebbing of her heart.

~~~

Dylan repeated lines from his script to the large mirror on one side of the workout area Cassie had built. Mimi stood watching, her head cocked to one side. The scene called for a profession of love between his character and the leading lady.
~~~

Normally he'd pretend he knew how this might feel. It had always been part of the act. Until now.

Of course, he'd seen actors fall for each other, giddy and supposedly crazy in love. Two years later, they hated each other. And sure, he'd thought of Sarah Beth a few times in the past as inspiration, but that seemed like child's play compared to the way his emotions had surged the past few weeks.

He spoke the words again with feeling. Every syllable drenched with thoughts of Cassie. Moving closer to the mirror, he repeated the lines once more.

"All we have is today. And today I love you. And today I'll follow you up that mountain. I'll follow you up south, north. Doesn't matter. The torrents will never wash my love away."

"Knock, knock. Am I interrupting?"

Oh, shoot. How had Cassie snuck up on him? He pursed his lips. "You caught me talking to myself."

"Don't worry. I do that, and I'm not even an actor."

"But aren't you?"

She turned and bent to lift a wicker hamper near the staircase. "I told you I wear the glasses and keep my hair pinned up for my profession."

He scanned her petite form as she bent over. "Does that include rolling in some kind of fur?"

Spinning toward the mirror, Cassie craned her neck to inspect the back of her pants. "Really?"

Dylan nodded. "A nest of black and white hair all over your, uh, slacks."

A giggle erupted from her throat as she put the hamper back on the floor. "Yes, that impresses many people. Sets them at ease."

He threw down his script, chuckling at her adorable response. "You are the smart one."

She choked between laughs. "You want a cup of tea or something?"

"Maybe, but I don't think I want you making it, Hairy."

Cassie doubled over.

"What? I'm not that funny."

She sniffed and wiped her eyes. "That's the name of Sarah Beth's cat who…haired me."

He followed her downstairs, laughing. Man, she was cute. He'd never seen her laugh so hard. And at herself. Not many women he knew managed that one. Dylan filled the teapot with water and ripped open two tea bags.

"You look like you know what you're doing." A huge smile still clung to her lips. "I'm going to change."

Dylan called over his shoulder. "You don't need to change. I love you just the way you are."

The clack of her flats against the wood floors halted.

He could punch himself. Freudian slip if there ever was one. He glanced back at her.

Her eyes held his before dropping. "I—be-be back." She shook her head. "I *mean* I'll be back."

And he'd thrown her for such a loop, she'd stuttered. A first. "I be-be here, too."

~~~

Cassie gave a half-hearted chuckle at Dylan's attempt to make light of her clumsy tongue, then willed her feet forward. The *I love you just the way you* are comment nearly knocked her into cardiac arrest.

He was trying to be cute. That was all. She sighed. And he was cute. Okay, more than cute.

She threw on light blue jeans and a white shirt. No more hairy. A quick double check in the dresser mirror just in case.

The glimpse of Dylan repeating his lines to the mirror darted across her thoughts. Obviously a love scene. The passion and force behind his words lit a fantasy of her own. What if he were saying those words to her? What would that feel like?

A tingle pressed its way across her lips. The kiss they'd shared under the sprinkler, even though it had been a mistake, had unsealed a well of emotion. Maybe she could love again. Only it wouldn't be with Dylan. He'd made that clear. She'd have to lock thoughts of that kiss away. Her fingers traveled to her mouth. At least until he was long gone.
~~~

Back downstairs, Dylan greeted her with a steaming mug and a warm smile. "Here you go."

"Thanks." She took a sip. "When's Michael coming?"

His smile and posture wilted. "He had a fever after the lake outing, so Nick and Jill took him to the doctor. I wanted to go along, but they said no." His scoff told her what he thought about that. But at least he hadn't made a fuss. "Anyway, I offered to keep him afterward, but Jill insisted that when Michael's cranky, he only wants *Nick* to hold him."

The flash of resentment on the word Nick had her heart pounding. *Poor Dylan.*

"You know, when Emma would get sick, all she wanted was my dad. I, on the other hand, only wanted my mother. Kids are funny that way. It doesn't mean they love the other parent any less. It means that person gives them security. Nick's probably more relaxed handling a child, and Michael senses it. I'm sure Jill feels let down by that, much like you do, but you have to let it go."

"Do I? The difference is they didn't give me a chance to try to console Michael." His expression hardened. "I'm ready to change the birth certificate, claim Michael as my son, and settle the custody issue. I'd like to draw up a custody proposal before we leave for Honduras. And I'm going to amend my will. Can you handle that?"

This was another sudden move, and a custody issue couldn't be settled so quickly. Probably *should not* be settled so quickly. "I have to revise some contracts for Sarah Beth, and those will take a few hours, but then I can turn my attention to your requests. Could you produce financials for me, and a scanned copy of your current will?"

He nodded. "A phone call away."

Now to broach the more difficult matter. "What were you thinking as far as custody?"

"Shared."

Shared? She stifled a groan. "What do you mean by shared?"

"I understand leaving him with Jill when I travel for work,

but equal custody when I'm in Oxford."

"You want to bounce Michael back and forth? Would that be best for him? If it were Benjamin, sharing custody would break my heart." The words hadn't come out like she'd planned.

Dylan's jaw tightened. "I'm positive I want to be a major part of my own child's life." Dylan's tone was firm. "And my situation is nothing like yours."

Pressing her fingers over her eyes, Cassie tried to think clearly and objectively. She was supposed to be the peacemaker, so she held her tongue to Dylan's curt response. How would Jill react to the demand? And Nick? Wouldn't be pretty. "I'll be in the sunroom with my laptop trying to come up with a plan that might be acceptable to both you and Jill." A doubtful reality. "You'll be stuck with pizza delivery for dinner."

"I'll make the calls to have the information emailed to you. Then I'll go back to the exercise room and get out of your way."

Was Dylan angry?

Oh, Lord, please help us all have wisdom and self-control to determine what's best for Michael.

Hours later, the door leading from the garage into the kitchen opened and slammed shut. "Mom, I'm home."

Cassie pushed her computer aside and stood to greet Benjamin. "Hey, you're late."

He traveled straight to the counter and yanked open the pizza box. "Yeah, I went to a bonfire. End-of-school party."

As she hugged him, she sniffed his hair. A woodsy scent mixed with sweat. "Smells like smoke." She eyed him. "I've heard those bonfire parties can get rowdy. I'm not crazy about you getting into that scene."

"It's like ten o'clock. I left before it got *too rowdy*." Benjamin squeezed her tighter and shoved pizza into his mouth with his free hand.

Could she trust him? It was just ten. Parenting a teen alone was tough.

Dylan hit the bottom of the steps and popped around the corner. "Thought I heard you come in. How'd you two like to help me practice my lines?"

A grin spread across Benjamin's face as he let Cassie go. "What movie?"

"The sequel to *Current*. It's called *Torrents*." He handed Benjamin a script. "So you'll help?"

Benjamin raised one finger. "I've never been in a play or anything, but I'll try."

Dylan turned to Cassie. "And you?"

She crinkled her nose. "Me? I'm still working."

Dylan gave her a pleading look, his lips pouty. "What about some of the discipline of flexibility you preach about?"

How could she say no to that? "I'll try. For a few minutes."

Up in the exercise room, Benjamin and Cassie read along, hesitant at first. But as practice continued, they hammed it up. A humorous scene had them laughing. In other scenes they pretended to run and scream. Now they reached the spot Dylan had been reading earlier when she'd walked in on him.

As he continued through the passage, Dylan's eyes twinkled. She had the sudden thought that he'd planned this. Surely not, though. Not after his speech about them being friends. She perused the words quickly, saw that the scene called for a kiss between Dylan and Cassie's characters, so she handed the script back. "I need to finish my work now."

Benjamin caught her arm. "Kiss him. I give my blessing."

Her heartbeat accelerated. Why was Benjamin pushing this? And where was that summer scarf she'd been wearing around lately to cover her blushing neck? "I'm sure Dylan's had plenty of practice with that."

Dylan took two long steps over to Cassie, dipped her back, and made her heart stutter. But he kissed her cheek as if it were her mouth. Smashing his lips around in a circle near her jawbone.

"Stop." Giggling, she pushed at his head. "You're getting my cheek wet."

He ignored Cassie's protest until Benjamin clutched his

stomach, laughing. At last, Dylan released her and blinked innocently. "Practice makes perfect."

"My acting career is over." She rolled her eyes and wiped her face. "Back to attorney work, and I'm taking it to my room, so I'll say goodnight." Cassie fanned herself with her hand as she ran down the stairs. Crazy, but he'd actually handled the awkward situation in a fun way. He must not be miffed with her after their custody discussion earlier. No matter that she wished the kiss had been real. That was her problem.

Chapter 25

After a big yawn, Dylan glanced at his watch through blurry eyes. What kind of people started their day up at four-thirty? Oh, right, his cute hostess who stood by the coffee pot ready to go. But today, for the first time since he'd met her in L.A., dark circles plumped the light skin beneath Cassie's eyes. Had she even slept? Maybe he was asking too much of her. Dylan leaned against the doorframe in the kitchen. "I need to ramp up my workouts before filming, or they'll have to hire a body double." He squeezed the skin around his midsection.

"No ramping up for me." Cassie waved him off and took one step toward the back staircase. "And no discipline of flexibility. I must be vigilant with my schedule today. I have to drop papers off at Sarah Beth's this morning and spend a few minutes with her explaining them. You and I need to go over the will and custody agreement together. There's a lot to work through before we have the will witnessed and notarized." She paused. "You realize, the custody agreement will probably have to be negotiated. I doubt they'll accept this plan."

They'd better not push him too hard on the negotiations. But he didn't want to get into that right now. It was way too early. He rubbed his sleepy eyes and followed as she hurried up the steps. "I could drop you off at Sarah Beth's, and then pick up Michael."

She handed him a gym towel from the stack near the mirror. "That could work. Let's get started."

A few hours later, Dylan dropped Cassie at Sarah Beth's and drove on to Jill's. His knuckles tapped on the front window. No sense making a lot of noise.

Katie slung open the door. "Hi, Uncle Dylan. My brother's still got a cold. I'll go tell Mommy you're here."

Dylan waited near the threshold.

But as the little girl turned, Nick entered the foyer, Michael's head resting against his chest. "Today's not going to work. He's still sick."

The urge to grab Michael and run coursed through Dylan's arms. "I can deal with some crying. You haven't given me a chance to console him. You don't know what I can handle."

Jill joined Nick in the entry hall. "He has to take breathing treatments."

A cold rush of alarm engulfed Dylan. "What's that?"

"Not deathly serious." She spoke with calm deliberation. "He has bronchitis, and the treatments help break up the congestion. Not that big of a deal."

"If it's not that big of a deal, show me how."

Nick scowled. "We don't feel comfortable with it. Why are you being so difficult?"

No way. If this guy wasn't holding his son… "You're calling me difficult for wanting to see my own kid and take care of him?"

Nick shook his head and lowered his voice. "If something happens, you don't even have permission to get medical treatment for him."

Raising to his full height, Dylan stared down his nose at the jerk. "The paperwork is in the works today. Michael's paternity will be corrected. Legally."

A small voice hollered from the living room. "What's paternity, Daddy?"

Nick placed Michael in Jill's arms. "Please, go entertain Katie in her room a minute." He stepped outside and stopped only a couple of inches away from Dylan, shut the door, and shook a pointed finger near Dylan's face. "Don't you think of anyone but yourself? You don't realize how this affects other people. You're willing to hurt anyone to get some kind of satisfaction."

A bomb detonated in Dylan's chest. And Nick wasn't holding his son now. He clenched his fists, ready to send one to Nick's mouth.

The door yanked back open, and Jill stood there, holding Michael.

Dylan looked down his nose at the finger pointing at him. He kept his gaze fixed on Nick but addressed Jill. "Your husband says *I'm* selfish." His jaw contracted as he spit out the words at Nick. "What about when *he'd* planned to raise Michael as if he were his own? To keep a child from his own father?" He narrowed his gaze and leaned slightly more toward Nick. "Who's really the selfish one here? Were you thinking of what was best for your daughter when you married Jill knowing she was carrying *my* baby? I think you were thinking of what Nick wanted."

His face reddening, Nick's eyes flashed. "We need our own lawyer. It's obvious that Cassie can't objectively mediate for us. Your picture was in the paper, for heaven's sake."

"That's what you think is best for Michael?" Dylan scoffed. "You know if we take this to court, I'll get primary custody, considering how sick Jill is. And the way you tried to steal him from me. For the record, Cassie has more class and fairness in her little finger than anyone I've met in my entire life."

Jill stepped onto the porch and offered Michael to Dylan. "Here. Take him. I'll grab his bag, medicines, breathing machine, and insurance card."

Michael settled into his arms with nothing but a tiny squeak at being passed from person to person.

She ran back into the house while Dylan glared at Nick. She returned seconds later towing two diaper bags and a sheet of paper. Frowning, she nudged Nick inside. "Let's all cool down. I can explain the breathing machine."

Nick gave Dylan one last scowl then stormed down the hall.

"Here are the instructions." Jill cleared her throat and held up a piece of paper. "He's not crazy about the mask." As Jill explained the details of how to use the nebulizer, her lips quivered. She ran the back of her hand across Michael's forehead. "Call me if you have any questions."

~~~

Back in the van, Cassie took one look at Dylan and sensed
~~~

the tension surging through him as he held his flawless jaw tightly clenched. "What's wrong?" She turned and looked at Michael.

"Where does Nick get off calling me selfish for wanting to spend time with my son? He's supposedly such a good Christian, but he lied. Jill lied. If they want to push it to court, so be it."

She'd never seen Dylan so angry. Experience warned her it was probably best to let him vent and decompress. They rode without speaking the ten blocks to her house. As Michael grunted and fussed, Dylan hummed and whispered to him. Once inside, she headed to the laundry room and pulled out an old CD player and music from a cabinet.

She found Dylan reclining on the couch, Michael laid across his chest. "I used these classical tunes when Benjamin was irritable. Worth a try?"

"Sure." His voice was flat.

After plugging in the device, Cassie made herself scarce. It wasn't like she didn't have plenty to do. The laundry needed folding. All the suitcases needed to be packed for the mission trip.

She printed lists and taped one to each bag. A list for hers and another for Benjamin's. Normally she'd let him pack, but going to a third world country at sixteen… No. There wouldn't be a convenient store if he forgot something important.

An hour later, she'd found almost every item they'd need. Time to go back downstairs. She hadn't heard any crying. A good sign.

The music still played. Dylan must have started another CD. He sat on the floor bouncing Michael on his knees. Both seemed content.

A strand of auburn hair fell across Dylan's forehead as he turned to face her. "Music's nice. Thanks." A slight tilt of his lips and one cocked eyebrow shifted his expression to something more playful. "Was it Michael you were trying to soothe? Or me?"

"You were upset. I hope for everyone's sake things don't

come to a court battle. You have a long road ahead as a parent. No matter how you feel about the other parent or stepparent, you'll always have to deal with them on some level. It's better to keep things amicable."

A heavy sigh passed through his perfect, white teeth. "One of the many things I love about you. Fair and wise."

Did he have to keep using the *L* word? She shoved aside the emotions bombarding her and prayed. *Lord, what does he need to hear?*

She felt an urge to help explain somehow. "You know, Christians aren't perfect. Only Christ is perfect. The rest of us make mistakes. Me, Jill, Nick, Sarah Beth… We're trying to follow the Lord. But, there's no such thing as a 'good Christian,' only a good God."

"Maybe that's why I left the church."

"I don't think we should leave the church. We still need each other. We need to learn how to love and forgive. That's what Christ gives as a commandment, 'Love one another as I have loved you.' How can you love a God you can't see, if you can't love those people around you, those created in His image?"

"But how can I love someone I don't even like?"

"I've asked myself that question every day since my divorce, and the answer I keep receiving is that I can only do it with God's help."

Dylan's cell chimed. "The real estate agent. Can you take Michael?"

"I'd love to." Cassie scooped up the baby and walked to the wall of windows in the sunroom. Benjamin had always loved to have her point to the birds at the feeder hanging on the tree out back.

Moments later, Dylan found her. "We're closing tomorrow. It's an all-cash deal, and the title is clear. Your friend pushed it through in record time."

Sadness nibbled at her insides. Her eyes closed without permission, and she turned her face away. "When will you move in?"

"Not until after our trip, if that's okay with you." He edged closer until they stood shoulder to shoulder. "I want to ask another favor of you."

She still couldn't look at him. "What?"

"Can you help me decorate my new place when we get back?"

Was keeping up this charade a good idea? Playing house. Playing just friends. Playing havoc with her heart. "I don't think I'm qualified as interior designer for a celebrity. You should hire someone."

"But I want something like what you have here. Like home. How you would decorate if you lived there."

She had to see his face. Search his expression. Opening her eyes, she turned and warmth washed over her at the glimmer in his gaze. Another crazy fantasy to join the rest. "Sure. Why not?" Why not have a load of bricks delivered and dumped over her, too? Maybe she could cook dinner for his dates there and cry herself to sleep every night?

She had to stop. They were friends. These were the kind of things friends did for each other.

~~~

Dylan lowered his cap over his forehead then pulled the aviator sunglasses from his shirt pocket and pushed them on. Stepping into the bright sunlit square, he had to admit this town charmed him. Along with the beautiful attorney at his side.

The will, the house closing, and the financials had consumed the past two days. Cassie had been a trooper, her work exacting, but the whole mess had taxed her. He could tell by the way her eyes drooped. Because of him.

Back in the van, Dylan caught her hand before she shifted the vehicle into reverse. "I'm sorry for laying so much on you. I should've thought of the will and all when I first came, not two days before a trip out of the country."

Her hand felt soft beneath his, but cool. "How can you be cold in this heat?" He enclosed both hands around her fingers.

A smile inched across Cassie's lips, but something in her
~~~

eyes troubled him. Pain?

She shrugged. "You know what they say about cold hands."

His arms took on a life of their own and pulled her fingers to his lips. "Warm heart."

Cassie's gaze dropped to the steering wheel. She reclaimed her hand with a gentle tug, snatched a light blue scarf from her purse, and tied it around her neck. "You're doing well to get all this done. Many people neglect to make a will. A terrible mistake if you ask me. We'll get everything finalized, even if it takes staying up late. Walmart's open all night if we're missing anything for the trip, and we can always sleep on the plane."

"I'm not going to Walmart in the middle of the night. I have to draw the line somewhere."

Again, she moved her hand to put the van in reverse. Dylan tucked his fingers under his thighs. It was bad enough he kept saying the wrong things, now he'd lost further control. If he was honest, he'd lost control of his heart weeks ago.

"Do you think you're too good to run errands?" Cassie kept her eyes on the road.

"I reserve the right to remain silent."

Her lips twitched. "You're learning."

When they arrived to pick up Michael, Jill answered the door, her mouth in a thin line and her hair falling from her ponytail into her eyes. "Hey, can you come in a minute? I don't have the bag ready."

Dylan nodded and stepped inside, the large brown envelope tucked under his arm. "I've got business I need to discuss with you, anyway."

Cassie glanced around the disheveled home. "Can I help you with something?"

"Maybe… If you don't mind. Dylan can hold Michael, and you could help me change the baby bed. Michael's medicine has his stomach upset, and it's not pretty."

"I remember those days. Sometimes you get through one minute at a time." Her smile held compassion. "Let's tidy up."

They disappeared into the back of the house, but Dylan stayed put. Better to keep out of the way, especially from what

Jill described.

A few minutes later, Cassie traipsed through the living room carrying laundry and a diaper disposal, a rancid scent following. The back door opened as she passed.

Great. Nick was back, and he made no attempt to cover his disdain as he seized the diaper machine. "Cassie, I'll take that. You don't need to be dealing with dirty diapers."

"I don't mind. Y'all had a hard night."

"It'll pass." He returned moments later with the empty container.

Jill joined them, her clothes changed, hair combed. "It's funny how a little help makes work go so much faster."

"That's why God gave us friends." Cassie offered another warm smile to each of them.

Nick tapped his fingers. "We'll pick him up at the same time, as usual."

Obviously Nick was ready for them to leave, but they had legal matters to discuss first. At least he and Jill did. Dylan motioned to Cassie. "We've prepared my new will. It was rushed, but since I'm traveling out of the country, I wanted to have it done. Just in case." He bet Nick hoped *just in case* happened. "Cassie did a thorough job of assessing my assets and getting everything drawn up." He lay the will on the sofa table, then withdrew a check from the envelope. "This is child support, plus arrears. I hope you'll cash this before I leave. I can meet you at the bank if I need to."

As she read the figures, Jill's eyes grew larger. "That's too much."

Nick strode over to join her. "We don't need your money."

Catching Nick's forearm, Cassie shook her head. "Dylan's not saying that you need his money. Dylan's giving to Michael what he owes by law. It's his moral and legal responsibility. I've gone through his earnings during the first months of Michael's life, and that's what's fair. If you don't need it, Jill can put it in an account for Michael. It can be used for college, emergencies, Michael's wedding, but it's not yours to turn away."

Nick sighed. "Can we put it in a trust for him?"

Creases found their way between Cassie's eyebrows. "Of course, but I can't do any more paperwork before we leave."

Dylan put an arm around her and squeezed. "I've worked this little lady to death. I owe her." He looked at Jill. "We closed on a house just outside of town today."

Nick squinted. "We?"

Cassie inched away. "He bought a house and would like to make a custody proposal. I've included his offer with the other papers. Jill can consider the terms while we're gone, and we'll talk further afterward."

Nick stepped forward and grabbed the packet. He removed and scanned the custody document. "You're kidding. I can see every other weekend and holidays, but shared custody? Do you realize how difficult that will be on our son emotionally? On what planet do you think we'd give you that?"

The muscles of Dylan's jaw twitched. "I would never kid about *my* son. Or lie either like some people in this room."

Cassie moved between the two. "It's shared custody in Oxford. When Dylan's on location, you'll keep Michael. But when Dylan resides in Mississippi—"

"That's not fair to a child." Nick hurled the envelope back to the table. "We'll get our own attorney."

The sound of Jill's whimper silenced the room. "I'm really tired, guys, and I don't feel well. I can't do this now. Please table this discussion, argument—whatever it is, until after Honduras."

Nick hustled the few steps to his wife's side and slipped an arm around her. "Of course. Sorry."

Dylan studied Jill. If Michael's mother was that sick, maybe he shouldn't leave town. "I can cancel my flight and stay to help you."

"If anyone is staying home to help my wife, it's me." The volume of Nick's voice was low, but the anger was palpable.

Jill whacked her hand against the back of the sofa. "My mother is arriving in the morning, and no one is staying here with me but her. No one. I need some peace. You are all going on this trip, and Michael will be fine. Got it?"

He got it. They all did. Not much chance of missing that one.

~~~

Between the look on Jill's face and Nick's comment about shared custody not being fair to Michael, a stab of guilt sunk deep into Cassie's chest as they strode back to the van. Objectivity and impartiality weren't just words to her. And though she would never intentionally violate her conscience or standards, it was time to step aside. Past time to step aside. "Dylan, I'm going to connect you and Jill with another attorney to mediate."

"Cassie, don't let him—"

"No, it's not Nick's fault. It's mine. I'll phone Jill when we get back to the house and let her know." She paused. "After the mission trip, you can start fresh in your new home with a new attorney. It's best for everyone."
~~~

Chapter 26

Standing in the parking lot of the Christian Student Union, an uneasiness gnawed at Dylan's gut. Traveling had never bothered him before today. Not that he feared for his own safety, but leaving his son to visit a third world country seemed irresponsible. Maybe that was the wrong word. After all, he'd been trying to help this tiny section of the globe for a couple of years now. Before, the risk didn't affect anyone but himself. Now, another human being relied on him.

He eyed Cassie lingering by the van. Was she having the same feelings, worrying about herself and Benjamin?

The smell of diesel and exhaust filled Dylan's nose as he gathered her matching bags, her inventories still attached, and carried them to the charter bus. He chuckled as he removed the extensive lists. Cassie was efficient. He tossed his backpack alongside the suitcases and waited for her to finish checking her van for anything they might've forgotten.

Sarah Beth strolled up, a baggy green blouse hanging low over her jeans. "Are you riding the charter bus to Memphis with the rest of us non-famous peons?"

"I reckon so."

"What about bodyguards?"

"Actually because of a few recent incidents in Honduras, I've asked Juan to send an armed escort for the bus. They'll meet us when we land at the airport." He motioned toward the towering group of football players. "Besides, this group looks like a whole clan of bodyguards." He pointed toward her midsection. "What about you? Should you be going on this trip when you're expecting a baby?"

"Not that again." Sarah Beth rolled her eyes. "I've dreamed of visiting the clinic and chapel for so long."

From behind, Jess handed Sarah Beth a small leather binder. "You might need this."

Her hand went to her forehead. "Thank goodness. My passport is in here." She pulled down the zipper and removed the document. A paper flitted to the ground.

Dylan bent to retrieve it. A picture. Of Sarah Beth's ex… "Here. This fell out."

She gasped and her face paled.

"What is it?" Jess wrapped his arms around her. "Are you having second thoughts?"

"This old picture of Adam fell out. It must've been here since my last trip out of the country." She sniffed. "It just caught me off guard. And you know how emotional I've been."

Jess inhaled loudly and brought his lips to her forehead. "This will be a more difficult trip for you than I realized. Not only the travel anxiety, but all the memories and hopes from the past." Jess squeezed her into a hug. "I'll be right here, and I love you."

She pulled back and tilted her face up to look at him. "I love you, too. I hope I didn't hurt your feelings."

"You know I'm stronger than that…and cocky." He rubbed her nose with his.

Dylan slipped back toward the van. Not that long ago, he would've either had the urge to punch Jess or ram his finger down his own throat after watching that exchange. Now, not only did it not bother him, he was happy for Sarah Beth. Kind of.

Jess still came off as an arrogant jock, but to each his own. He eyed Cassie locking the van. She must finally be satisfied they hadn't forgotten anything. No one would be reminding Cassie about her passport, that was for sure. Wouldn't it be nice to have someone like Cassie always by his side?

~~~

Seated between Benjamin and Dylan, Cassie gripped her armrest. Though the flight to Houston had been uneventful, a thunderstorm rocked the jet now as they flew to Honduras. How could her son sleep while the plane bounced and shook
~~~

over thunder caps? Another lightning strike in the distance sent chill bumps along her arms.

Warmth covered her hand as Dylan's fingers wrapped around her palm. "You okay?"

Her tension must've been pretty obvious. "All this turbulence is unnerving. You'd think after flying around with my father, nothing would bother me."

"You'd think." He raised his chin as he whispered. "This is a pretty bad storm. I wonder how Sarah Beth's faring. Can't make leaving Oxford any easier on her."

Cassie followed his gaze to the row beside them where Sarah Beth was seated between Jess and Nick, her face tucked into Jess's shoulder. Poor Sarah Beth. "You're right. I need to take a breath and trust the Lord." Plus, Dylan's hand was a bit soothing.

"You can lean on me and take a nap." His eyes caught hers and held them. His scent wrapped around her. Another thing about him that soothed her.

She searched his face for some hint of what he felt about her. Heat seared her neck, but she couldn't look away. At least he was distracting her from the storm.

"Come on, relax. Get some rest." He slid his arm around her shoulders, and she let herself melt into his chest. Her eyes closed, but not before she caught a glimpse of Nick scowling.

Another storm brewing. But she was exhausted after the busyness of the past few weeks. Her tired brain slowed, and she drifted into the comfort of Dylan's arms.

A tap on her hand startled Cassie, and her eyes fluttered open. How long had she slept?

Dylan's perfect smile greeted her. "We're *fixing* to land."

She straightened and stretched her arms in front of her. "Picking up the Mississippi verbiage?"

"Yep." He nodded toward the window. "But you might want to hang on."

The plane dropped below the clouds and soared barely above tree-covered mountains. The engines whined as they tilted and lowered. They plummeted, leaving Cassie's stomach somewhere in the clouds, hit the runway, then slammed to a screeching halt.

Even Benjamin woke at the jolt.

Dylan squeezed her hand. "I neglected to mention the really short runway surrounded by ginormous mountains."

"Probably a good choice." She couldn't stop an eye roll.

"At least you got some sleep." Dylan smirked. "You had the cutest little bit of a snore."

"I do not snore." Did she?

Holding up his phone, he laughed. "Got video proof."

"That's a dangerous game, mister." Please don't let it be true. "I'll get you back."

Benjamin grabbed at the phone. "Let me see. I'll upload it."

"Not so fast. I have one of you drooling." Dylan pushed the phone back into his pocket and adjusted his cap and sunglasses. He gave her a slight wink.

Her son's eyes rounded.

Cassie laughed as relief unfurled. He was just playing with them. Which was fun, but he was playing with their hearts, as well.

~~~

Dylan scanned the heavy clouds hovering over the mountain roads. Looked like they were in for more storms. Other trips to Honduras, he'd traveled by helicopter to the clinic. On the bus with the rest of the group, the view was different from street level. With rumors of human trafficking, armed guards escorted them before and behind. The poverty and litter lining the thoroughfare and urban alleys weighed on his heart. These people had so little. He had so much. The readings Cassie had shared from the book of James about helping the poor came to mind. He could do more, and he would.

The students on the cramped bus took in the meager surroundings with rounded eyes and quiet whispers.

Moisture filled Cassie's green eyes. "In my worst nightmares, I never imagined this kind of poverty."

"I couldn't until I visited two years ago. It's mind-boggling,
~~~

and couple the poverty with disease—heartbreaking."

She swiped a knuckle across her lashes. "I pray it will be life-changing for Benjamin and the other students."

The terrain shifted from dense city to small villages with houses built from reused sheet metal and random boards. Some sort of quarry dug into one of the mountains, and large trucks hogged the opposite side of the narrow highway. Fatigue set in. Dylan's lids grew heavy. He should've napped before the ride turned into something more akin to bouncing on a trampoline with a giant.

Another hour and the road narrowed until it was barely a dirt trail. He turned to Cassie. "I recognize this. We're almost there." No sooner had the words left his mouth, the bus jerked to a stop.

The minister Juan and his family ran out to greet their group, trailed by a number of half-bald chickens. He'd forgotten those ugly things ran around everywhere. What in the world was wrong with their feathers?

As each person exited, the short, smiling preacher shook their hand with vigor and introduced himself. When it was Dylan's turn, Juan squeezed his shoulder. "Dylan, my friend. Many good works have taken place because of your contributions."

Sarah Beth squealed and pushed past him. "Juan. I made it."

The small man bubbled with laughter. "I am happy you are here." He embraced her and glanced around at the football players. "You brought many very large friends to work, I see." He motioned beside him. "You remember my wife, Lupe, and my children."

"Of course." She hugged Lupe and each of his three children. "Wow, you've all grown so much since I saw you last. Victoria and Lucas, you're not children anymore." She turned back to Juan. "I can't wait to see all you've done."

A smile crinkled Juan's eyes as he swept his hand toward the compound. "You know this is what God has done, not me. I am a tool in His hand." He spoke to the group gathered behind Jess in a loud voice. "Just as each of you will be tools in God's hands these seven days. Let me lead you to your accommodations. You will be tired after your trip. You have two hours to unpack and relax before we meet in the chapel."

Low hanging smoke and the scent of burning trash, probably from a neighboring village, filled the air as Dylan followed the men to their side of the dorm-style housing. In the past, he'd set up private accommodations, but this wasn't too bad. The concrete floors and cinder block walls at least appeared clean.

Benjamin stayed at Dylan's side as they entered the bunkhouse. "You want top or bottom?"

Something about Benjamin's friendship kicked him in the gut. But in a good way. The kid looked up to him. Respected him. Even liked him. And he wanted to be deserving of those emotions. "Either works for me."

Dropping his suitcase beside the metal bed, Benjamin collapsed onto the bottom bunk. "I sleepwalk sometimes, so I'm safer down here."

Dylan threw his pack to the top. "Wouldn't want you taking a nosedive."

Once settled, they reassembled in the rustic, open-air chapel. More chickens and a few ducks picked at the dirt around and under the old metal folding chairs. He spotted Cassie and took a seat beside her. "How do you like the place?"

Her lips twitched. "Nice enough. I'm a little concerned about that bald chicken that keeps following me." She pointed near her feet at one of the hens that seemed to have lost all but a handful of its feathers.

"Slightly creepy." He grinned at her. "It's no doubt jealous of your hair."

Benjamin chuckled, and other group members took seats around them. A few of the students yawned. It had been a long day already.

Tears ran down Sarah Beth's face as she entered the chapel. "Juan, this is wonderful. I love it."

Boy, the pregnant woman cried all the time.

Juan pressed his lips together as if he held back a smile. "I have a surprise for you." He held up a large, rectangular piece of plywood.

Sarah Beth scrunched her nose. "That's a nice piece of wood."

"It is a nice piece of wood, and we will use it for our chapel sign, if you all will paint it. I need approval for the name first."

"Of course, I'll be happy to help. I know you well enough to give a stamp of approval on any decisions."

"About the name… We would like to have a special ceremony before you leave and hang the sign above the entrance. I would like to call this place Adam's Grace Chapel, unless you can think of something more fitting."

"Oh, Juan." She sniffled. "That's such a beautiful tribute. I don't know what to say."

"You are okay with it?"

She wiped her eyes with the corner of her loose shirt. "More than okay."

His attention focused back on the group. "Then, if I can have your attention, please be seated." The crowd settled on the bench seats as Juan stood behind the podium. "I must give assignments and explain the way things work down here in Honduras. I am Juan Moreira, and this is Dr. Rodriguez." He motioned, and Dr. Rodriguez joined him in the front of the assembly. "We will be your leaders for your week of missions. I would like all of you to have an enjoyable time, but I would also like for you to be safe. Dr. Rodriguez will first explain how to stay healthy here."

Though taller and slimmer than Juan, Dr. Rodriguez shared the dark eyes and complexion. The doctor had grayed around his temples in the past couple of years.

"We set up the clinic in this location due to the large number of outbreaks of dengue fever and the lack of another clinic to care for the ill in this remote area." The doctor described the disease and the area's epidemic. He emphasized using protection against mosquitoes, and he explained that they should only eat the food provided in the compound to avoid food poisoning.

When Dr. Rodriguez finished going over the risks, he turned the group over to Juan for assignments and stepped toward the clinic. He stopped and called back. "Oh Sarah Beth, could you stay on site and help me with some business issues and government paperwork?"

Sarah Beth huffed. "Did Jess tell you we're expecting a baby and ask you to keep me safe?"

Dr. Rodriguez's face lit up, and he returned to shake Jess's hand. "No, but congratulations."

One side of Jess's mouth turned up. "Thank you, Doctor. And I'll feel much better with Sarah Beth staying on the campus."

For once, he agreed with Jess. Dylan couldn't help but laugh at Sarah Beth's frustration.

Her brows knit together. "But I wanted to get out and help people."

Dr. Rodriguez gave Jess a quick knowing glance. "You'll be helping, just in a different way. Using the skills God gave you." He chuckled as he turned to walk away. "It'll be much safer, too."

Dylan smiled. Maybe God had a sense of humor.

~~~

Cassie led Benjamin and Dylan over to squeeze into the circle of football players that formed around Jess.

Jess and Nick exchanged confused looks before Nick shrugged and shook his head. "Cassie, aren't you going to stay and help with the VBS?"

"Mom is better at carpentry than most men, so we signed up for the construction crew. I like working with my hands." Benjamin smiled at his mother. "And she's small, but she can handle her tools."

Jess shrugged. "Can't argue with that. She should be in charge of this ragtag group instead of me." He caught Cole's elbow beside him. "Cole, you're supposed to stay on the campus and work with the Vacation Bible School team."

Cole shook his head. "I know, but I'm not taking any smack
~~~

from anyone." He eyed Grant.

"I'll handle that." Jess gave Cole a pat on the back before he left. "Glad we're on the same page." Once the quarterback walked away, Jess addressed the remaining huddle. "I'm leading this group out into the surrounding area to repair houses and water wells. We'll also be providing vector control."

Grant Vaughn pointed at Cole's empty spot. "What about him?"

"Last time I checked I was still in charge. Got it?"

"Yeah, Coach."

Jess motioned to Nick, and then to Cassie. "These two probably know more about construction, so listen to them. I'm just here to keep you knuckleheads in line."

Taking a step back, Cassie waved him off. "I'll just show you how to use the tools if you need help."

Chapter 27

Something about using tools to build a tangible object both exhilarated and relaxed Cassie. The feel of the cool metal in her hands, the sound of the indigenous birds, called motmots, chirping away in the nearby mango trees, plus the scent of wild tropical orchids engulfed her. A simplicity of life. At least for her.

However, most of the guys labored to dig a new trench leading to the well. They probably weren't enjoying their assignment as much. The old piping had degraded over time, filling with sediment. She and Nick worked to repair the pump and cylinder, a much less physical chore.

An hour into the task, something slid across the side of her leg as she knelt by the well. A chill slithered up her back. "Ahhh, Nick. What's on my leg?" Though her heart pounded, she restrained herself from moving even a fraction while studying Nick's reaction. She'd heard about poisonous snakes in the area and didn't want to instigate a bite.

Nick kicked toward her leg. "Shoo, go on." He clapped his hands. "Only an iguana." He clapped harder and louder.

Cassie's head rotated to catch a glimpse of the reptile. A large gulp of oxygen lodged in her throat. "Only an iguana? That thing's like a little alligator." She sprang to her feet and jumped a yard away.

"Cool." Benjamin ran over, clicking photos on his cell phone. "Smile and scoot closer to it."

She moved to the other side of the pump. "Maybe Nick wants to, since he says it's *only an iguana*."

Nick chuckled. "No, thanks. It is a rather large one, but I didn't want to alarm you. They're not poisonous."

Cassie took another reluctant glance. "But they can give a

nasty bite that could get infected." She pinged a look at her son. "Especially out here, so stay back, Benjamin." The reptile scuttled away, but another crept out from under a nearby tree toward the well. "I have the feeling we're on their turf. Let's hurry up and finish."

"Maybe they're just thirsty." Nick surveyed the reptiles. "But I'll go as fast as I can."

By the time they completed the repairs, a whole line of iguanas studied them. Behind them stood football players, a few half-bald chickens, two small dogs, and a goat.

Jess warned the guys not to touch any of the animals.

After wiping her brow, Cassie packed the last wrench into the toolbox. "Finished. Thank goodness. I love the great outdoors, but those things staring at me…" Another chill shook her shoulders. "Disturbing."

Dylan tromped up carrying two large plastic buckets, his shirt drenched with sweat and plastered to him. He was followed by Grant, who looked nearly as exhausted.

"What's going on?"

"My audience." Cassie swiped her arm toward the odd collection. "Where have you been?"

"That is rather bizarre." His brows furrowed. "I was sent by Coach McCoy to carry buckets of sand from the creek, up that hill, and dump it in the pile at the opposite end of the trench." He scoffed. "Me and *one* other guy."

The huge lineman at his side patted Dylan's head. "You did good for a skinny guy who plays pretend for a living. Oh, and worries about whether he's getting a sunburn."

"Thanks, Grant. Or can I call you Goliath? And I have to make a living with this face."

The two shared a laugh. It was clear they'd enjoyed each other's company, despite the manual labor. Cassie's eyes wandered from Dylan's dimpled cheeks to the damp shirt clinging to his chest. This was going to be a long week.

~~~

Between jobs, Cassie and the crew returned for lunch at the compound.
~~~

Sarah Beth trudged outside to greet her. "I did not come like a thousand miles to sit indoors. I want to get out with y'all."

"I know it's hard to sit back and watch. It would be for me, too." Cassie pointed toward a game of kickball led by Bryan. "Surely, you can play with the kids awhile. No harm in that, and they're so adorable."

Sarah Beth's teeth caught her bottom lip. "I'm going to. Jess'll have to get over it." She craned her neck, looking around. "Where are Cole and Audrey? Jess warned me to watch out for Audrey."

"Any particular reason?"

"Just that the girl had been through enough already, and he didn't want anything else to happen to her. He didn't explain what *enough* meant, but it must not be good."

"Let's go look, then." Around the back of the chapel, Cassie spotted Audrey kicking an old soccer ball with the younger children, giggling as they chased around her. "There they are."

Cole sat on a wooden bench at the rear of the chapel, cheering them on. A smile worked its way across his face.

"Maybe there's hope for Cole. Word is the quarterback has an ego as wide as the Gulf Coast. Three times, Jess had to race off and drag him from a near fight at a bar or fraternity party. Usually because Cole had picked up some other guy's girlfriend."

One little fella kicked the ball over to Cole and pointed. "Football." Cole stood and followed the boy. They joined Audrey and the others.

"Maybe this trip will be just the thing he needs." Thumbing toward the cafeteria, Cassie took a step. "I better get my grub while I can. We're heading back out in a minute."

Hours of work later, Cassie's stomach growled as afternoon showers pulled all the workers inside. It was time for dinner, anyway. She stripped off her muddy clothes, threw on fresh jeans and a T-shirt, and then walked around the building toward the dining hall. A tap on her arm stopped her. She turned to find Nick at her elbow. She'd worked with him all afternoon, and they'd kept the conversation focused on the job at hand, avoiding the elephant in the room—or the great outdoors, as it were. Questions hovered in her mind though on how he was handling these odd circumstances.

"Hey."

Nick kicked the toe of his work boot at the muddy ground. "I've wanted to clear the air, but there's always someone nearby. I know you've been put in an awkward position with the custody situation, and you were only trying to help us. Jill told me you're withdrawing and having another attorney take over."

"It's for the best, and I'm sorry." She'd really made a mess of the whole thing.

"No need to apologize." His lips formed a partial smile. "You did good work out there today. I was impressed. I'd hire you as a landscaper, carpenter, engineer…"

"Just maybe not a custody mediator." She allowed an uneasy laugh. "I love the math involved in carpentry and engineering. I always adored math and science."

Another nudge to her shoulder. "Mom, that's plain weird. You must've been such a nerd in school." Benjamin and Dylan walked beside them.

"Yeah, I was a nerd, but I didn't care. I loved school, and my mom was my best friend, so—"

"Stop. None of the other guys need to hear how nerdy my mom was."

Opening the door of the dining hall for all of them, Dylan grinned. "I think you have a very cool mom. Haven't you heard? Nerds rule the world."

Nick's brow furrowed as he glared at Dylan. "I'm going to get a tray. See y'all later."

Laughing and cutting up, Benjamin and Dylan waited in the food line together. It looked as if they'd known each other for years. How had they become so close so fast? For that matter, how had she come to care so much for the man?

She loaded her plate and took a seat. The steaming chicken and rice did the job. Plain, but filling. Later, Juan would lead a devotion. Would Dylan attend? He came with the mission group, but that didn't mean he'd be participating in worship.

After Benjamin all but licked his plate, he stood and patted his stomach. "Let's go outside and get a seat for the devo. It's cooler out there. At least there's a breeze."

Dylan's smile flattened. "I don't know." He lifted his cap and ran his fingers through his hair. "I have some things I need to do."

"Oh. Right." Benjamin's sad expression gouged at Cassie's heart.

She hated that look on his face. With a father like Evan, she'd seen it plenty.

"You know…" Dylan's voice was quiet. "I can go for a little while. Lead the way."

~~~

No way could he turn the kid down with that look on his face. Dylan squirmed on the hard wooden bench. Maybe Benjamin would be satisfied with him staying fifteen minutes or so. From what he remembered about church, that was about all he could take.

Juan stood before the group. "I want to thank you for coming and giving your time, your hands, and your hearts to the Lord here in Honduras. You will have noticed the poverty by now, but I hope you noticed the beauty and the graciousness of the Honduran people. They have a hard life compared to what Americans live, and they must work hard for very little. I will read from the book of James."

He opened his Bible and read with a loud voice. "What good is it, my brothers and sisters, if someone claims to have faith but has no deeds? Can such faith save them? Suppose a brother or a sister is without clothes and daily food. If one of you says to them, 'Go in peace; keep warm and well fed,' but does nothing about their physical needs, what good is it? In the same way, faith by itself, if it is not accompanied by action, is dead. But someone will say, 'You have faith; I have deeds.' Show me your faith without deeds, and I will show you my faith by my deeds. You believe that there is one God. Good! Even the demons believe that—and shudder."
~~~

The words were familiar. "Hey." Dylan elbowed Cassie. "That's the book of the Bible you study all the time."

The imposing rain clouds that had dampened the early evening dissipated now that the sun sank into the horizon. The orange flame reflected in Cassie's eyes as she nodded and smiled. Those eyes moved him. Unbalanced him. Again.

~~~

Was Dylan Conner really recognizing Scripture? Maybe he did have a photographic memory. Cassie blinked as he stared into her eyes. Even in the low light, the man was her undoing.

Juan was quick to address Dylan's comment. "James does have a good message for all of us." He continued on a few more minutes, but she'd lost her train of thought.

"We are honored to have a young man that God blessed with incredible talent to lead us in songs of praise. Bryan Freeman, I turn it over to you." Juan took a seat, and all eyes turned to Bryan.

The guitar joined the chorus of tree frogs and insects that had taken up their night song. Bryan smiled as he played. "Any requests?" An awkward silence followed, and he started singing "Blessed Be Your Name." Sarah Beth jumped in. Others followed. A sound came from Jess. Poor thing. He couldn't carry a tune in a backpack.

But someone in the crowd had a great voice. By the second song, Cassie placed where the stunning harmonies came from. Audrey Vaughn. Who would've guessed the shy girl had a voice like that?

Bryan must've figured it out, too. He motioned to Audrey. "Come sit over here and tell me what songs you know. You're good. I've never heard anyone harmonize like you do." He rotated toward Sarah Beth. "No offense, Ms. Professor."

"None taken. Where did you learn to sing so well, Audrey? Choir?"

The shy brunette's hands twisted in front of her. "We grew up in a little church that sings a cappella. Momma always said I could harmonize with a vacuum cleaner."

"What's a cappella?" Cole asked.
~~~

Bryan answered for her. "That's when the only instrument you use is your voice. No piano or guitars, that kind of thing. And I love it. Harmonize on."

They sang a couple more contemporary tunes, and then Nick requested *Amazing Grace.*

A new voice joined in beside her. Dylan? Very nice. Chills raced up her arms at the sound of those words on his lips.

When the song ended, Bryan nodded toward Dylan. "Where you been, man? Why weren't you singing before?"

"I grew up in the mountains of North Carolina in a little church where we only sang the sacred hymns."

Cassie patted his arm. "That was almost as good as when I heard you singing to Michael on the baby monitor."

Nick's head turned so fast, he might've gotten whiplash.

Cassie's hand covered her mouth.

Shrugging off her slip, Dylan pointed to Bryan. "I'll sing out if he starts another oldie."

Bryan set aside his guitar and begin "How Great Thou Art."

Talk about wonder. The sounds blended up with such beauty in that dark night, more chills pricked Cassie's skin. Miracles. She should believe in them by now.

Chapter 28

Day two of manual labor. Dylan groaned.

His thighs and shoulders screamed in rebellion. No worries about missed workouts or fattening foods on this trip. Why'd he have to plan to spend the whole week here? Oh yeah, to do good for the less fortunate. At least if he kicked the bucket soon, he'd done a couple of unselfish things in his life.

Dark brown eyes and smiling tan faces circled the work group, chattering. The Honduran people were beautiful. However, the house they were *repairing* needed to be ripped down and burned. For now, a few new cinder blocks, a cement floor, and raised beds for the children would have to do. Of course, Coach McCoy would stick him and Goliath Grant together again, this time mixing the cement.

A small boy tugged at Dylan's shirt. "Jewelry?" He held out a ragged piece of cardboard with necklaces hanging on it, along with one ring, and bracelets made from some sort of cord and painted beads.

Dylan set aside his shovel and wiped his brow. The boy couldn't be more than five. "How much?"

"Two dollars. Each." A snaggletooth grin filled the brown face.

"What happens if you sell them all?"

His dark eyes widened. "Chapel."

"Sounds like a bargain. I'll take everything you've got." He paid the boy and took the treasures to his backpack under the nearby scrappy tree. The perfect excuse to drink his bottled water. A mid-morning break was long past due.

After he sucked down the last drop, he returned to the wheelbarrow. If it weren't for the fact that he was an actor, he might've let on his disappointment of being separated from

Cassie. Again.

She and Nick worked side by side, measuring and supervising. They did seem to know what to do, but still.

Lifting the shovel, he plunged it back into the wet cement. No doubt, Jess took some dark pleasure watching him sweat. But he wouldn't give Jess or Nick a reason to run him down about anything.

At lunch, Dylan spotted the little boy he'd seen earlier. The child made a beeline for Cole and jumped on his back. A smile spread across the singing girl Audrey's face as she joined the two boys. They ran up and down the muddy open area with the younger children, kicking the soccer ball. The sight warmed his heart, and he thought about the pieces of jewelry he'd bought. A handful of necklaces, bracelets, and one ring. Maybe he'd give the jewelry out to some of the little girls, but he'd better ask first. It might start a problem.

The door swung open to Dr. Rodriguez's cabin, and Sarah Beth walked out, followed by the good doctor.

Dylan chuckled. "Sarah Beth, you're like a sad puppy with big brown eyes, watching all the children play without you."

"That obvious, huh?" She pointed across the compound. "The little snaggletooth boy on Cole's back is precious. He was out there yesterday."

The doctor's lips formed a grim line. "Emilio. He lives with his grandmother. She makes jewelry that he sells. He's already had dengue fever at least twice, though, and the more often you acquire the disease, the more dangerous it becomes." He clucked his tongue. "Sarah Beth, you go play with them. You've done plenty. Adam would be proud."

"This whole place and ministry is a God thing, and a lot of people pulled together." She thumbed at Dylan. "Even this guy. You want to go with me to play with the kids?"

Dylan shrugged. He was starving, but a few more minutes wouldn't kill him. "Sure." They jogged out to the group running behind Cole.

Audrey slowed. "Hey, Sarah Beth, they let you out."

"How do we get in on this game?"

"Sorry, but in a couple of minutes, we're going to settle them down for story time. But they'd love to sit in someone's lap."

Dylan checked his watch. "How long is this story?"

"You won't miss lunch." Sarah Beth elbowed him. "Come on."

Cole jogged over with Emilio in tow. "Hey, you ready to tell the story? I feel like I've been through three football practices in a row." He flashed a warm smile at Audrey.

"I'm ready." She held her arms out to Emilio. "Can I have a turn so Cole can take a break?"

The child's eyes bounced from Audrey to Cole.

He squeezed the quarterback's neck. "Mi amigo, Cole."

Audrey smiled. "Cole will be at story time. He'll be here all week. You want to ride on my back over to the chapel?"

With a reluctant look, Emilio agreed and traded onto her back.

"Let's gallop." Audrey took off bouncing like a horse, Emilio giggling the whole way.

Sarah Beth sighed as she watched. "Maybe it's the pregnancy hormones, but oh, I'd love to scoop them up and hug them all."

"You'll be a great mom, Sarah Beth." Dylan pointed to the group of kids. "I'm pretty sure they'll let you hug them."

Once they reached the shade of the chapel's tin roof, Audrey gathered the children close. With an old-fashioned flannel graph for visuals, she told stories about the King Jesus who loved children so much that He went to live in a small, poor village instead of His heavenly kingdom. A young girl translated for the children who spoke no English.

Emilio's little face scrunched up. "Poor like me?"

A pang of sympathy tore at Dylan's heart. There was such great need here.

"He probably was, but He was rich because of His great love. He shared His love with all of us so that we could be part of His kingdom."

"Nice like you and Cole. And that man bought my jewelry."

He glanced at Dylan with a huge smile.

The pain became more of a throbbing, but he'd done what he could to help these people the past two years.

A little black-haired girl inched her way over to Sarah Beth's legs. Sarah Beth smiled down at the child. In an instant, her lap was full of adorable children smiling and holding her hands.

"I'm so happy," she whispered.

Eyeing Dylan, a young boy, maybe three, scooted in between them. Dylan nodded, and the boy climbed into his lap. Could his heart explode? His thoughts turned to Michael. Someday he'd bring him along to work beside him here, like Cassie and Benjamin.

After the lesson, Cole scooped up Emilio. "Jesus was a lot nicer than me. But Audrey… She's pretty and nice."

The girl blushed big time.

"I think you meant pretty nice, and I'm nice because I follow Jesus." She motioned to the children. "Y'all go with Juan now. It's time for your lunch and rest time. Adios."

The children ran to Juan and his family, and the four of them walked toward the mess hall line. Dylan scanned the compound. Where were Cassie and Benjamin?

Flanking Audrey, Cole leaned near to her. "I meant pretty and nice. Not pretty nice."

Giant hands grabbed Cole's shoulders from behind. "What'd I tell you about my sister?"

Cole wrestled himself away and spun to face Grant Vaughn. "Man, I'm not touching her. Back off."

Uh oh, trouble. Dylan stepped closer to Grant. Should he intervene?

Jess appeared and inserted himself between the teammates. "What's going on, guys?"

Dylan stayed near Grant. Something had been troubling the big guy, and now he got it. The quarterback and Grant's sister. But what could he do to help defuse the situation? A gentle grip on Grant's bicep would either earn him a punch in the face or ease the tension. He'd chance his face this time.

"Grant. Let's go get some chow." As Grant's enormous

muscle tensed, Dylan tightened his grip. "Not here. Not now."

Giant shoulders slumping, Grant turned. "Fine." He let Dylan lead him to the cafeteria.

Dylan passed him a tray. "Look, beans, rice, and goat cheese in tortillas. What a surprise."

The anger hardening Grant's features lessened.

Now what to say? Being tired and hungry left him without any clever thoughts. It had been a while since Dylan was twenty-one, but he'd had the urge to slug a number of people over the years. Reporters. Directors. Jess. Nick. The reasons varied, but controlling the impulse had served him well. Maybe that's something he could share with Grant. Besides, one punch from the giant could kill someone.

They took a seat at the table, and Dylan cleared his throat. "You know, I've wanted to pommel a few guys over the years, but—"

"I know you're trying to help, but this is different." Grant swallowed his tortillas in a few bites and picked up the beans that fell to his plate.

Did the guy even chew? "You want my other burrito?"

Grant gave Dylan's food a glance and shrugged. "You don't have to."

Angling his plate, Dylan slid his food over. "I have to drop ten before my next movie. It'll be much easier here than back home. Especially staying in a dorm with a dozen guys who eat beans two or three meals a day."

That one brought a smile from Grant. Maybe he could get him talking later.

~~~

Cassie scanned the crowded tables. She hadn't spoken to Dylan since breakfast, and as much as she hated to admit it, she missed him. A lot. But what was she doing searching him out? The goal was to distance herself from him—from the whole tabloid situation. Now that she'd had time and space to think, there was no way she'd put Benjamin through all the drama again. Or herself, for that matter. She'd steer clear of Dylan. Taking her tray, she spotted him and found a seat on
~~~

the opposite side of the room. She glanced at her plate. Beans again?

A stab of remorse ran through her, and she bowed her head. *Dear Lord, thank you for this food. Sorry I complained. Forgive me. I'll go back home next week, and the people we're helping will be lucky if they have this kind of meal. Amen.*

After she'd finished her meal, Nick pressed a hand on her shoulder. "We need to huddle on materials and maps with Juan. Now that we've established how much work we can manage, we'll route out the rest of the week."

She nodded and followed. Nick was a good man. That was truth. If only she could help Nick see that Dylan was a good man, too.

No.

She was stepping back. And maybe Nick saw something about Dylan that she couldn't. At one time, she'd thought Evan was a decent man. She'd been oblivious to the extent of his betrayals.

Chapter 29

Cassie managed to avoid Dylan the rest of the afternoon and evening. Until he climbed over three students to the seat next to her for devo. His proximity needled at her heart. Why couldn't she move past these crazy feelings?

At least the afternoon of work had sped by. Another water pump repaired, and they'd handed out mosquito netting to a village farther down the road. An outbreak of dengue had been reported only fifteen miles from the clinic. Since they'd showered, she needed to remind all the students to spray with repellent before Juan got started.

Once the group assembled, she passed the insect repellent around. Benjamin only gave her the we're not-babies frown for a second. A few of the football players he'd been assigned to work with had befriended and included him. Thank goodness he'd found someone to talk to besides Dylan.

Juan stood, and the crowd quieted. "Good evening. By now many of you are getting to know some of the Honduran people. I hope you are enjoying your service to the Lord. Are there any concerns or prayer requests? For people you've met—or yourself. Getting away from home to a place like this can give you new perspective on life."

"I would like prayers." Ivy Patterson, one of a handful of girls on the trip, spoke up. "I was assigned to help in the clinic, and I've always wanted to become a nurse. I'm not sure if I can now."

"What happened to change your mind?"

"There's an older lady with dengue fever. She's not doing well, in severe pain, and she confided to me that she's worried who will take care of her granddaughter if she doesn't make it. Her daughter is in the U.S. working to send money to them each month." She sniffled. "I don't know how to help her or what to say."

"Praying, holding her hand, and listening to her is all anyone can do. That is why the clinic and Dr. Rodriguez's research for a cure is so important. Also our work for spiritual health."

"I've tried to keep her hydrated and comfortable. I held her hand and prayed for her." Ivy sniffled again and pushed away tears with her fingers.

Moving to Ivy's side, Juan put a hand on her shoulder. "Let's all join hands and pray for Ivy and her patient."

Cassie bowed her head. The prayer and a distant rumble of thunder hushed the group. It seemed the cacophony of frogs and insects muted. Only a quiet chirping of motmots merged with the falling darkness.

After Juan said amen, he raised his gaze to the group. "Anyone else need specific prayers or want to share something?"

"I do." From across the chapel, Benjamin spoke, his voice low.

Pain pinched Cassie's throat shut. Her eyes itched to turn and stare at her son, but she shouldn't. He didn't need his mother gawking at him.

Dylan's hand slid to cover hers. At first, her fingers twitched and stiffened, but as his thumb traced the borders of her wrist, calm found her.

"How can we help, Benjamin?"

"I'd like to ask for prayers for my father, his new wife, Brooke, and my half-brother. A lot of people in Oxford know what happened… My dad was the one caught cheating with his coworker's wife. Then Brooke's husband, an attorney who worked under my father, pulled a gun, but Brooke begged him not to shoot because she was pregnant. The guy freaked out, ran out in the middle of the street, and killed himself."

A screaming silence followed, and though only for a second, Cassie's heartbeat blasted into overdrive and slammed at her ribcage. She had to stay quiet and let Benjamin handle this. Let God handle this.

"Anyway, my mom and I have been dealing with all this scandal. I've been angry with my dad, but something keeps pulling at me to feel sorry for him. My mom tells me I have to honor my father, because that's what God commands. She says we should love others like God has loved us…" His voice broke. "I try to be respectful, but I'm having a hard time with it—and I want to do the right thing."

The pain of the last two years unleashed and suffocated Cassie, as if the surrounding mountains had collapsed and crushed her.

Dylan squeezed her hand harder, as if sharing her grief, but turned toward her son. "Benjamin, you and your mom have been such a wonderful example of grace and kindness for me. I've been through a situation not too different from yours, and it's normal to be angry for a time. My father was a coach at the high school where he and my mother both worked as teachers. He was caught in a compromising position with one of his female soccer players. It was a similar small town scandal, because she was pregnant and under age."

Heads and eyes flew toward Dylan.

Cassie squeezed his hand now. Why would he let this story get out now? For Benjamin? Her gaze cut to her son to gauge his reaction.

"My mother and I moved away. Never had contact with my father again." He swallowed hard and cleared his throat. "But I should be more like you. I've never forgiven my father or even seen my half-brother, but maybe because of your example, I can find the strength."

Benjamin nodded. "Thanks."

Juan took slow steps around the group. "One can only do the impossible with the strength of the Lord. What is impossible for man is possible for God. Forgiveness is perhaps the greatest miracle God performs. The Bible says we are all sinful, but the good news of the gospel is that we are forgiven. Jesus offers us love and grace when we ask. Then we are to go and do likewise. Benjamin, you are doing the right thing trying to love and forgive. I will pray for both you and Dylan."

"Wait." Nick held up a hand. "Add me to that list. My father and brother ran down the wrong paths. Landed in jail. My mother left to get away from the insanity when I was a young teen. I've never completely forgiven any of them. I see now, that experience hardened my heart toward others." He turned to Dylan, his gaze solemn. "We can all learn from Benjamin's example."

Dylan gave Nick a small nod. Once again, Juan prayed.

A host of emotions descended on Cassie like an avalanche. Weren't they all strugglers, dealing with hefty baggage? No one was exempt from the humiliation and shame of sin. Should she cut off Dylan because of the possibility of embarrassment? Scandal?

But was Benjamin strong enough to withstand the onslaught of publicity that hounded Dylan? Even if they were only Dylan's friends when he visited Oxford?

~~~

Dylan sighed as Juan prayed. If not for Cassie's hand, soft but strong holding tight to his own, he might run out of this place, catch a plane, and hightail it home. Never look back.

But where was home? Boone? He left that small town, only going back because of his mother.

L.A.? He hadn't even missed that crazy city before he knew about Michael. In his heart, home had become another place. A place with a tiny baby, a petite redhead, and a tall, lanky teenager.

The group's singing drifted on the gentle breeze coming down from the mountain, Cassie's voice beside him quiet but joining the praise. A place in his soul he'd long forgotten broke open, and words seeped between the cracks.

Grace. Hope. Forgiveness. Blessings. Love.

Dylan's chest trembled as he struggled to hold back the sobs threatening to spill out. How long had he locked away God's Word, and why? The knuckles on his free hand pushed away the moisture forming in his eyes. He swallowed hard. The reason didn't matter. A sense that he should forget the past and embrace the present engulfed him.
~~~

Forgive me, Lord.

Gratitude filled his heart. He had a son who loved him. He glanced at Benjamin. Maybe two sons who loved him. And he had Cassie—no matter what came of their friendship.

Thank you, Lord. Bless you, Lord.

"Earth to Dylan." Bryan smiled and waved his hands up and down. "Hey, Dylan."

Cassie elbowed him. "Bryan asked you to help lead some oldies."

A request way out of his comfort level. He hesitated and ran his hand across his forehead. "I don't know."

Sarah Beth huffed. "When have you ever been shy about performing?"

Leave it to Sarah Beth. "I'm a little out of my element."

Cassie's hand caressed his. "I think you look right at home in this element." Her eyes found his.

Those eyes gave him strength—confidence that he could be a better man. Dylan smiled. And he'd do anything for this woman. "How about 'Blessed Assurance'?"

Bryan nodded, and Dylan sang praises with a full heart.

Chapter 30

A strange gurgle came from the bunk above Cassie. A second later, Sarah Beth dropped to the floor and ran to the bathroom.

The gray light of dawn filtered through the window. The other girls, all university students, slept like turtles on a log. They hadn't budged. Probably wouldn't until their alarms sounded off a few times.

Cassie sat up. Was Sarah Beth having morning sickness? From the gagging sound in the bathroom, something was wrong. Pushing her feet to the cement floor, Cassie threw on her work clothes, then rushed to check on her friend.

Sarah Beth stood by the sink, splashing water on her pale face.

"Are you okay?" Cassie studied her.

Sarah Beth pressed a wet rag to her neck. "If this is what most pregnant women go through, I have a new appreciation for morning sickness. I don't understand. I've been fine, then boom—nausea rolled over me like a tornado in a trailer park." She turned off the faucet. "I think I'm okay now."

Cassie trailed Sarah Beth as she tiptoed back to her bunk to dress for the day. "A walk outside in the fresh air might help."

After Sarah Beth slipped on a T-shirt and khakis, they crept out the door.

The view of the mountains covered in lush green forests stood before them. They found a bench shaded from the early morning sun and flopped onto it. A slight breeze stirred the air.

Sarah Beth wrapped her arms around her stomach. "Only a little shaky."

"Seems strange that morning sickness would happen at this juncture, when you've not experienced any so far. Maybe you should wake Dr. Rodriguez."

She waved away the suggestion.

"I'll wait until after breakfast and see how I feel. Please don't mention it to Jess. He'll freak. He didn't want me to come on this trip after we found out about the baby. My brother didn't want me to, either."

"If you're still nauseated after you eat, don't keep it a secret. Dehydration is dangerous for you and the baby. Once your stomach rests, you should sip some water."

"When Jill was so sick, she nibbled crackers before she got out of bed in the morning. I'll try that tomorrow."

If the nausea proved to be something more serious, maybe Jess and Mark had been right. Sarah Beth shouldn't have come.

~~~

Dylan rolled over in the bed. Every muscle begged for him to be still. What body parts weren't sore from carrying sand now joined the pity party after a day of mixing concrete. The second day following a hard workout was always the worst. At least that's what he was going to tell himself. He pushed up and climbed off the top bunk.

His stomach growled. He would eat a kettle of beans if that's what they stuck in front of him for breakfast. Rice, too. Didn't matter.

After he dressed in the clothes with insect barrier built-in, he sprayed on more mosquito repellent. Cassie had insisted he and Benjamin follow this routine to protect themselves from dengue fever and other vector-borne diseases. The woman was thorough. And cute. In fact, he could hardly wait to see her at breakfast.

He stepped out the door into the misty mountain morning and drew in a deep breath. Being here felt good, despite the hard work. Especially after the devotion last night. His heart had burst open, but the pain and resentment, long locked away, had been replaced with healing and love and peace. A new feeling of lightness covered him with joy.

Underneath the shade of a pine, Cassie and Sarah Beth sat talking. Maybe they wouldn't mind if he joined them. He
~~~

meandered over. "Am I interrupting?"

"Not at all." The smile Cassie greeted him with held something back, and worry knitted her brow.

He glanced at Sarah Beth.

Her normal glow had been replaced by a drab look around her eyes. "Are you sick?"

Her shoulders sagged. "One look. That's all it took." She stared at Cassie. "How long will it take Jess to know?"

Cassie shrugged. "Just tell him."

Rising to her feet, Sarah Beth shook her head. "Let's go to the dining hall. A little food has to help."

"Mind if I join you ladies? I woke up with an appetite that would shame even Sarah Beth." Dylan grinned.

Cassie returned the smile. "By all means, let's get you some food. I have a feeling Sarah Beth will end up sharing hers with you."

Dylan rushed ahead to open the screen door of the dining hall. "Ladies first."

The scent of eggs and fried plantains sent another growl through Dylan's stomach. "Smells great."

Apparently, Sarah Beth's stomach did not approve. Her hand covered her mouth as she ran back toward the sleeping quarters.

Cassie gave him a troubled look. "I'll go check on her and catch up with you later."

"Let me know if I can help." As Cassie jogged away, his admiration for her soared. She was a caregiver, first and foremost. A woman to be respected.

"Excuse me." Jess's voice caught Dylan off guard.

"Sorry." He hadn't meant to block the door. That's what he got for gaping after Cassie. Not cool, especially in front of Jess. Another thought hit him. If he was Jess, wouldn't he want to know Sarah Beth was ill? She may not want him to, but too bad. Women keeping secrets hadn't done him any favors.

"Jess, can I speak to you before you get in line?"

The coach's eyebrows furrowed, but the look held no malice. "What's up?"

"Sarah Beth was here a minute ago. She's not feeling well. Sick to her stomach. Cassie's checking on her."

Jess's eyes widened, his mouth agape. "What should I do?" He stared at Dylan like a lost pup.

This was a first. Jess not knowing what to do?

Dylan couldn't help but feel sorry for the guy. "Get Dr. Rodriguez and have him check her out. You should stay here today, and let Nick lead us out to work. Between Nick and Cassie supervising, we'll get everything done."

"I'll get the doctor now. You tell Nick." As he turned away, he mumbled, "I knew she shouldn't have come."

~~~

Cassie's hand grazed Dylan's as they worked to build a new cinder block wall for a tiny home about a mile from the mission.

The touch warmed her and made the labor...enjoyable. Creating a sort of human conveyor belt to pass along the bricks had been Nick's idea, and it seemed to be working, thank goodness. The less walking through the mud they had to do, the better.

Overnight, torrential showers had left the short route via pickup trucks impassible, forcing them to travel on foot along a moss-covered trail carrying heavy supplies. A few times, students had lost their footing. Luckily, all they'd endured was ribbing from the other guys and muddy pants.

More rain clouds hovered in the north. A sprout of worry grew as the day passed. The sooner they finished and got back to the clinic, the better. Plus, she wanted to see about Sarah Beth. Nick had led a quick prayer for her before they'd begun their work.

An hour later, the last block was laid. Their home repaired, the owners circled them, offering broad smiles and hugs. Cassie's heart couldn't hold more joy. Helping these hard-working families brought her a sense of satisfaction no amount of money could ever buy. She could see it on the faces of the football players and Benjamin, too. This mission was life-changing. Not only for the Hondurans, but for the Americans
~~~

on the trip.

Dylan caught her hand as they walked back. "You can order me around any day."

His smile and his words unearthed the emotions she'd tried so hard to squelch. "God's working here. I can feel it." That's what she needed to keep her focus on, too. But she'd leave her hand where it was for now.

~~~

After dinner, Dylan joined the others for devo. It seemed to be expected now that he helped lead the *old songs*. Never in a million years had he envisioned a world where he was in a third world country, leading worship songs as the old guy. What happened to being the Hottest Man Alive?

Didn't matter. He was a father now. That fact alone aged him inside and out. His thoughts and prayers reached out to Michael over the miles.

Being with Cassie all day had thrilled him. He only hated that it took Sarah Beth getting sick to make it happen. Jess relinquished his duties as construction leader, and Nick and Cassie would take charge of the crew for the rest of the week. Jess wouldn't be leaving Sarah Beth's side again. If Sarah Beth got well quickly, Dylan wouldn't mind the arrangement one bit. He could offer to have a helicopter pick up her and Jess, so they could go home, just in case. Still, he joined the others saying prayers for her recovery. He did want Sarah Beth and her baby to be okay.

The student named Ivy raised a hand. "I wanted to tell everyone that the woman we've been praying for with dengue fever is better. In the morning she'll get to go home. I was hoping we could offer a prayer of thanksgiving. In fact, I'm thankful that I came on this trip."

Dylan nodded. Praying. How long had it been since he'd done that before this trip? Too long.
~~~

Chapter 31

First thing in the morning, Cassie hustled over to Dr. Rodriguez's cabin to check on Sarah Beth. The doctor had set up cots for both Sarah Beth and Jess in his personal quarters. Of course, quarantining her wasn't a bad idea. Maybe no one else would get sick if Sarah Beth had something more than a pregnancy-related illness.

Cassie's knuckles rapped on the green metal door. Surely either Jess or Dr. Rodriguez was awake. Breakfast started in fifteen minutes.

The door creaked as it swung open. Jess signaled for her to come in and nodded his head. "Our patient is feeling better. And literally begging for food."

Sarah Beth tipped her head around the wall that separated the living area from a small breakfast nook. "Hey, Cassie. I'm well. They won't let me go to the dining hall, but Dr. Rodriguez is bringing me a plate." She clutched her stomach. "I'm starving. I hope he brings a lot of those fried plantains. If they have some fried green mangos, that would be even better."

Cassie released a pent-up breath and smiled at Jess. "I think she's back to normal. I'm glad. We've all been praying."

"Just a twenty-four-hour virus." Sarah Beth waved her off. "Maybe no one else will catch the bug."

"All right, then. I'll check in with you later."

A small smile loosened the tension on Jess's face. "Thanks for coming by, and for taking over. Nick says things went fine without me, so I'll hang with my girl again today."

"Don't worry about a thing."

Inside the dining hall, Benjamin and Dylan had saved her a chair. A swell of happiness filled her, even though all this was probably temporary. No matter how much she let herself pretend otherwise. She pushed back the negative thoughts goading her and enjoyed the time while she could.

"Good morning, guys."

Dylan scrambled to pull her chair out. "How's Sarah Beth? I assume that's where you've been, Ms. I'm-Always-On-Time."

"She's ravenous."

"Sounds like our Sarah Beth." Dylan chuckled.

The fried plantains on Cassie's plate did smell good.

Growing up in the South, she'd had her share of fried foods, but these were a treat. Like a potato mixed with a banana. She savored the sweet fruit.

Across the table, Benjamin took out his phone. "Mom, I haven't even thought about my phone until this morning. Can you believe it? You bought that plan so I can give Dad a call, right?"

Not necessarily so Benjamin could call Evan. She'd keep that thought to herself. "We have international roaming if you can get a signal." She didn't mind her ex and her son being close as long as Evan's ways didn't rub off on him.

After Benjamin pushed the power button, the phone chimed over and over. His eyes widened. "I got a lot of texts." He focused on the screen. "Oh, shoot." His hand went to his forehead.

"Is something wrong? I haven't checked my phone, either."

"I forgot I told this girl I'd go to the Sub Deb Ball with her. She asked me like a month ago, but I didn't realize the ball was this week."

Sounded just like some justification Evan would come up with. Heat and anger boiled through her. How could her son be so insensitive? The plantain in Cassie's mouth soured, and she forced herself to swallow. "Benjamin Brooks, I am very disappointed in you. Letting the poor girl down. You apologize this instant, and don't plan on driving for a while when we get home."

"It's not like we're a thing."

"Don't you dare make excuses for yourself."

Dylan's hand slid across her arm. "Cassie, he didn't stand

the girl up on purpose."

The heat fired up a notch in her gut. "Look. I don't want my son growing up to treat women disrespectfully. Or turn into some kind of playboy, like—"

A flash of anger spilled across Dylan's face. "Like me."

Cassie's jaw clamped down.

Why was Dylan taking Benjamin's side? Seemed like something Evan would've done. "If the shoe fits."

"Everyone can't be as perfect as Cassie Brooks. Sorry but some of us are among the fallen."

"I sent her an apology." Benjamin held out the phone. "I'll be grounded from the Jeep. Y'all don't fight."

The pained look on Benjamin's face ripped the scab off her old wounds. Arguments with Evan she'd tried to cover and keep Benjamin from hearing. She pushed her chair back and lifted her tray. "Okay." What else could she say? No other words formed in her mind. And she couldn't look back at Dylan. Not now.

~~~

Dylan opened and shut his mouth.

What had just happened? Cassie stormed away without a backwards glance. Poor Benjamin. The kid kept the scars of divorce hidden—most of the time.

Dylan forced a smile Benjamin's way. "She'll cool down." But would she? If Cassie saw him as the same kind of man she'd been married to before, how could their relationship ever get beyond that?

An hour later, a pickup dropped the construction crew at a small village a couple of miles further than they'd been all week. Dylan climbed out of the bed of the truck. As soon as his feet hit the ground, the wind and exhaust from the ride dissipated, and another brutal smell assaulted him. He joined the circle standing around Nick. The students groaned and covered their noses.

Dylan raised his hand. "Is it safe for us to be here? This place smells like a dirty diaper bonfire. Toxic."

Benjamin laughed. "That's exactly what this smells like.
~~~

Nasty."

Running his hand through his hair, Nick let out a long whistle. "Something's very wrong with the sewer." He pointed to Cassie. "We'll work on the plumbing. Dylan, you unload the mosquito netting and insecticide. You and the guys can work on vector control away from the…" He directed a small smile toward Dylan. "Diaper bonfire."

Dylan's stomach stiffened. Had Nick actually smiled at him? *Weird.* At least no one made him shovel the sewage mess. Probably if Jess were here…

He opened the truck door and lugged the box of netting to the shaded area where the students had settled. A good distance away from the noxious dump, the smell was a tiny bit better, but he'd miss Cassie. She still hadn't spoken to him since breakfast. Or looked at him, for that matter. And her snub stung more than the noxious scent.

In fact, she was all he could think about.

Chapter 32

After this job, they'd both need to burn their clothes. "Here you go." Cassie stretched her arm toward Nick to hand him the wrench in her fist. Mud covered the poor man. Stinky mud.

He tightened the last joint and pushed himself out of the muddy hole. "I say we break and come back for another day of stench tomorrow. There's no way we can finish. We'll need the guys to dig a ditch for runoff."

Whispers of a storm in the distance sent an alarm through Cassie. She scanned the sky. Ominous dark clouds gathered again in the north, above the mountains. "We should hurry. More rain looks to be headed our way. I'll collect the tools while you round up the others."

Nick smirked. "The guide stayed with the trucks all day. His normal chipper attitude dissipated when he took a whiff of this place." He surveyed the heap of mud and shrugged. "Who could blame him?"

"Not me." The tool box weighed heavy in Cassie's exhausted fingers. She let out a groan as she lifted with her right hand and then brought her left arm under the case for additional support.

Nick reached for the tools and took them from her hands. "Let me help." He paused in front of her. "Cassie, this isn't the time or the place, but I need to apologize. You tried to help us with the custody issue because you care about Jill. And with no fees. I believe you've been as honest and as objective as you could." He sighed. "Something I may've thought I was doing, but my vision was clouded. I never really tried to put myself in Dylan's place or yours, and I'm sorry."

Her heart went out to the guy. After all, Nick had married a woman pregnant with another man's child. And loved that child as his own. She couldn't fault him for the fierce way he wanted to protect Jill and Michael. "I understand what you're going through all too well, thanks to my divorce. There's nothing to forgive." She searched his kind face. "But maybe you and Dylan should have a man to man. As Christian men."

Wetness formed in Nick's eyes. "You hit hard with the truth, lady." He turned his gaze toward the sky. "A truth I've fought in my spirit. I can be hardheaded sometimes—if you haven't noticed."

"We all fight that battle."

A rumble of thunder reverberated through the clouds, and Nick's expression screwed into a frown. "I think you're right about the weather. Let's move."

Before they reached the vehicles, the bottom dropped out. Rain pounded against the truck's roof the whole way back to the compound. Cassie glanced at the boys in the back of the pickup. *Poor things.* She'd offered to trade her seat inside the cab, but none would have it. Though she could've used another good hosing after that stench she and Nick had tackled. At least they were almost to the clinic.

She looked back again. Longer this time. Dylan sat hunched over his knees by the wheel well. Rain dripped from his auburn hair, and his shirt clung to his toned chest. Good grief, he was handsome. Why'd she have to fall under his spell?

Twice in her life she'd allowed a man to get beneath her skin. Evan ripped every bit of trust from her heart and shattered that trust into tiny pieces. Now this actor, the father of another woman's child, took a piece of her heart, and she had not one reason to trust the man. None. When he'd pressed her about her reaction to Benjamin, all the bitterness over Evan's betrayal fought its way back to the surface. The shields around her heart surged up. But how long could she keep Dylan locked out? If only this trip were over. She needed to hold on a few more days. Then the new attorney would take the case, and she'd return to her normal life.

Normal. That thought did nothing now but rip open a well of emptiness and disappointment. But at least normal was less painful. And she was used to it.

At last, they reached the muddy drive that led to the compound, and the rain lessened to a sprinkle. Cassie hopped out and jogged toward the dorm. A large group gathered under the chapel roof. As soon as she freshened up, she'd join them. Better to stay occupied and keep her mind off…just off.

~~~

The rain washed away the mud from Dylan's body but did nothing to rinse away the ache in his heart. On the ride back, Cassie had watched him through the back window. He'd pretended not to notice, but what was the woman thinking? The fact that he wanted to know so badly infuriated him. Why did she have such a grip on his heart? If only this trip were over. He loved the place and would come back, but right now, his mind was preoccupied with a little redhead who'd all but called him a womanizer.

When the truck slid to a halt, Dylan and the other guys bolted toward the dorm. They passed a crowd in the chapel huddled together, their faces serious. When he dressed, he'd find out what was happening.

After showering, he pulled a dry T-shirt over his head and stretched his shoulders. The soreness eased as the week passed.

A playboy, huh? A lot of people believed he was. No matter that he didn't hold a candle to most of his celebrity peers. Not that he wanted to. Sure, in the early days, he'd relished the attention, but empty relationships got old. He'd kept to himself the past few years. Considering the few idiotic exceptions he'd made, he should've stuck to being a loner.

Sarah Beth—kept him in the friend zone.

Sophia—psycho.

Jill—one night and an unplanned pregnancy. Although, having a son was a blessing.

Now Cassie. The woman who held his whole heart in her hands and would probably never know.

~~~

Cassie joined the somber crowd under the chapel roof. She made her way down the row beside Benjamin. His eyes held tears. "What's going on?"

"They said one of the children contracted his third case of dengue fever, and it's turned into... I can't remember the name."

"Hemorrhagic fever?"

He nodded.

A feeling of foreboding settled over her. The faces of the children she'd met over the week paraded through her mind. She'd read what could happen if the disease reached this stage.

Juan stood before the group. He put his hands on the shoulders of two students who looked to be taking this hard. One was the quarterback, the other, the girl who sang so beautifully. "Let's pray once more before we break for dinner. Take the hand of the person next to you."

Before Juan spoke, Dylan darted in and scooted onto the chair beside her. She swallowed back the awkwardness and held out her hand. He covered her palm and entwined his fingers with hers, never making eye contact.

Juan began. "Lord, we ask for Your healing on Emilio. We beg that You take away the disease that pains his small body. We don't understand why the innocent become ill. It confuses us and causes us to wonder if You really love us...until we look at the cross. Your innocent Son stretched out His hands and allowed them to be pierced for us. You do know our suffering. You do understand. Give us all peace as we watch and wait. Lord, we ask again for earthly healing for Emilio, in Jesus' name."

Sniffles filled the chapel as the students rose to leave. She slipped her fingers away, humid air replacing the warmth of Benjamin and Dylan's hands. She missed the contact already.

Chapter 33

"Need help?" Dylan held the door as Jess struggled to carry two food trays out of the cafeteria.

Jess hesitated, but then handed him one of the trays. "Thanks for, you know, telling me about Sarah Beth being sick and taking up the slack so I could stay with her. I appreciate it."

Lifting one shoulder, Dylan glanced around. Maybe Sarah Beth put Jess up to thanking him. "I'm glad she's better."

Jess pointed with his chin. "A couple of the students are taking it hard about the little boy getting sick. Thought I'd bring their trays to them."

Two nice things at once for Jess. Maybe the guy wasn't a total jerk.

Across the chapel, the quarterback, Cole, rested his elbows on his knees, his face buried in his hands. Grant's sister sat beside him. Her arm and hand stretched rigidly as she touched Cole's back. A thread of embarrassment pulled at Dylan's chest at the sight of the athlete's obvious sobs.

He stopped with the tray. "We brought food."

Head jerking around, Audrey flinched. "Oh, I thought you were my brother for a second." She took the tray and sighed.

Cole sniffed and wiped his face on his shoulder. "Your brother's not coming over here, is he?"

Jess took a seat beside him. "He's been warned."

"That guy…" Cole scoffed. "I get that Audrey's pretty and all, but he's insane." He turned to Audrey. "No offense."

Audrey's freckled face reddened as she hunched over her tray and flicked at the beans with her fork. "He's not…I'm not…"

"Eat." Jess pushed the tray in front of Cole. "You'll feel

better. And it's a long time 'til the next meal."

"Can you say a prayer for Emilio first?"

Dylan froze. What should he do? He pictured a boy only a few years older than Michael laying on a cot, deathly ill. Little Emilio had a family who loved him no less than he loved Michael. His heart broke for them all. He'd stand and pray for the child along with Jess.

~~~

Cassie joined the somber group on makeshift benches for a devo around a campfire. Her thoughts united with the songs of praise and drifted into a sky pierced with tiny pricks of starlight. God had blessed her with loving parents, good health, and a precious son. Although her marriage had failed, compared to the problems others faced in the world, her life wasn't too bad. She needed to focus on being grateful. No matter what happened between her and Dylan, her life would be an offering of praise to the Lord. That was what mattered. Her son needed to see faith and joy lived out.

She'd never had much singing ability, but she sang with all her might in the chorus of voices singing "How He Loves Us." Across the circle, Dylan's smooth tenor voice echoed. The light from a lantern flickered in his eyes like fireflies on an August night in Mobile. A pinch of guilt gnawed on her heart. The way she'd spoken to him had originated from bitterness about Evan. It wasn't Christ-like. Dylan deserved an apology, and he'd get one, as soon as she caught him alone.

They sang until the student minister spoke to the group. "Juan's sitting with Emilio and his grandmother, so he won't join us tonight. We've prayed and will continue to lift up this young boy before the Lord. But I'd like to take other prayer requests as we adjourn for the night. Anything else?"

After a pause, Bryan lifted one hand. "I would like prayers. It seems frivolous compared to everything else, but before I left on this trip, an agent contacted me. Someone that Professor LeClair, I mean Professor McCoy…"

Sarah Beth chuckled. "I'm not teaching anymore so you can call me Sarah Beth."
~~~

"Okay, Sarah Beth arranged for an agent to hear me sing last year, rather sneakily, I might add, and he thinks I may have a chance in Nashville. The only hitch is I need five or six original songs to make my demo. And soon. I have plenty of tunes written but no words. I need inspirational lyrics. My prayer request is for help with that."

Grant, the big guy who'd befriended Dylan, spoke up. "My sister writes poems and songs. She probably has a few in the journal she's always carrying around."

The shy girl sitting beside Cassie stared at her brother as if he'd picked her up and dangled her over a pot of hot oil. No doubt Audrey could use some encouragement.

Bryan beamed. "I knew I loved you the moment I heard you singing harmony. Now, I'm thinking I could marry you."

The quarterback's head pivoted toward Bryan, who seemed not to notice.

The minister interrupted. "Let's pray, then we'll be dismissed. After that, y'all can stay and work on the music if you like."

Once the group prayer ended, Cassie turned to Audrey. "Would you read us one of your poems?"

"I guess, but don't laugh." She ducked her head and opened the journal.

"Anyone who laughs will have to deal with me," Grant's deep voice bellowed.

"Um. Here's one… I don't know…"

Cassie nudged her. "Go on."

Audrey took a deep inhale, then spoke in a soft voice.

"*Strong hands to cover my own,*
Strong Love, this You have shown
Use me, bend me, into Your mold
Your beauty inside me begins to unfold
Unraveling the cords that keep me from home
A yearning to heal, to feel, to fall at Your throne
A passion, a deepness, a name not yet known."

She stopped and snapped the book closed. "That's enough. I can email the rest. You can use them if you want, Bryan."

Sarah Beth cleared her throat. "Now, wait a minute. I thought I taught you a few things in my class. You don't give away your work." She turned to Bryan. "No offense."

"None taken."

Cassie nodded. "Sarah Beth's right. If you have more that he can use for songs, they're your intellectual property. If he makes money on them, you should too."

Jess laughed as he stood. "The two businesswomen speak. I think they've got your back, so I'm calling it a night." He put a hand on Cole's shoulder. "Let's talk in a few."

Cole nodded and then fixed his gaze on Audrey. "Read one more."

Though she squirmed and fiddled with the journal, she acquiesced.

"*Ageless, timeless, written in the skies*
Your Beauty, Your Majesty, Your love that never dies
Safe and secure, hidden by Your wing
My Love, my Confidant, my Friend, and my King
Fight my battles before me, I ask and I pray
My faith has become weak so late in the day
You never fail me despite my imperfection
You are sure and kind, the essence of compassion
Holy, blameless, wise and untamed
You hold me, protect me with the power of Your name."

Audrey rubbed a hand across her forehead, partially hiding her eyes. "That's all I'm reading. It's too personal and awkward. And I want to see if Dr. Rodriguez will let us say goodnight to Emilio."

The words sunk deep into Cassie's soul. "That spoke to me, Audrey. Thanks. And I can help you and Bryan hammer out a legal agreement."

"You couldn't ask for a better attorney. She's the best." Dylan's voice came from behind her.

If she could catch him, now would be the perfect time to apologize, so they could start tomorrow fresh. She pivoted to meet his eyes. His face held sincerity. Perhaps their friendship was salvageable.

Grant approached Dylan's side. His broad forehead crinkled, and his brows knitted together so tight they met above his large nose. "Can we talk on the way back to the dorm? About my sister? The entertainment business? Maybe you could give us some advice if she decided to go with that Bryan fellow to Nashville."

"Anything for my construction partner." Dylan rested his hand on Grant's back and inclined his head. With slow footsteps, they followed the trail back to the men's dorm.

She'd have to speak to Dylan in the morning.

~~~

The steady tinkling of raindrops against the tin roof made it difficult for Dylan to pull himself from the cocoon of his blanket and throw his feet over the side of the top bunk. He and Grant had stayed up late into the night discussing the ins and outs of the entertainment business. No wonder the guy worried so much for his sister. They'd been through a difficult time together. The music business would be a tough industry for her. She'd need thick skin.

He didn't mind being tired from the late night, but he hated that he'd missed his chance to apologize to Cassie. He'd stepped out of line interrupting her correction of Benjamin. It wasn't his place. And even if someday they were a couple, he should've spoken to her in private instead.

If they were a couple? Why was he even thinking about—?

A booming rumble of thunder reverberated through the room, rattling the windows. Had lightning struck the dorm?

Working outside in a thunderstorm wasn't a risk Nick would take with the students. Or anyone else for that matter. Unless Nick hoped Dylan would meet an untimely demise.
~~~

Chapter 34

Double rainbows painted the sky north of camp. Dylan removed his sunglasses to inspect the array of colors in the natural light. The arc cresting over the green trees and mountains brought to mind Sunday school lessons he'd learned as a kid. God's promise. What were God's promises for him? Or Michael? He dug deep to make a connection, but came up with nothing. Maybe once he apologized to Cassie, he could ask her.

He'd tried to catch her at breakfast, but Grant, his new large sidekick, never gave him a minute alone. The guy was nice and all, but he needed to speak to Cassie. Meanwhile, Cassie and Nick had been in a serious conversation. What were they talking about?

Nick approached with a grim look. Couldn't be a good sign.

Dylan forced his lips into a somewhat flat form of a smile. "What's up?"

"We're not taking the students off campus today because of the mud. The trails and roads are too slippery, but Cassie and I would like to finish up at that last place today. We could take backpacks and walk. She says she and Benjamin are up for the hike. How about you? I could use another pair of hands."

Treacherous trails with the man who probably wished he'd fall off a cliff? Why not? Cassie would be there to hold him as he reached for the bright light. And maybe he could finally apologize. "Ready when you are."

"Meet at the chapel in ten minutes. I'll gather the materials, and we'll go from there."

After a small nod from Dylan, Nick traipsed off toward the trucks.

Meet Nick at the chapel in ten minutes. That just sounded

strange.

Dylan glanced back to the north. The rainbow remained in place, still splendid. *I might be needing some of Your promises today, Lord. Would you mind sticking close by?*

~~~

When Cassie arrived at the chapel, Dylan and Benjamin were talking baseball, while Nick fidgeted and kicked at a large rock. Not an awkward scene at all.

Nick offered her a radio. "Phone service has gotten worse with the weather. We'll take a walkie-talkie to keep in touch with Jess back at the camp."

"Sounds good." Cassie checked her pack once more before she strapped it over her shoulders. Plenty of couplings, a wrench, small pieces of PVC, plus a few other tools just in case. Oh, and duct tape. Never know what problems a good roll of duct tape could solve. She could duct tape Dylan to a tree or something so they could talk.

The hiking backpack Dr. Rodriguez had loaned her was nice. No expense had been spared for this rig. She lifted it up and down. Lightweight, even with the small tent attached. She could take the two-man tent off to lighten the load a little, but the thing didn't weigh more than two pounds. She'd keep the tent. The years as a Scout mom had pounded the *be prepared* motto into her psyche.

Cassie pulled on the pack. "I'm ready."

Dylan came alongside her. "That pack's as big as you are." His hands met hers as she fumbled with the straps. "I can carry it."

"I got it."

"Looks a little loose. I'll adjust these." He tightened the strap.

Her eyes traveled from his hands to his dimpled cheeks, then to his lips. He was so close. The faint scent of citrus and cinnamon greeted her nose. She took in a deep whiff. How she'd missed being close to that pleasant smell. And to him.

The buckle in place, his attention shifted to her face. A penetrating stare sent ripples of warmth through her arms. She
~~~

yearned to hold him. To kiss him. Why couldn't she stop her thoughts from betraying her?

She knocked away the thoughts and turned her back. "Let's commence." A brisk walk might help shake off these feelings. She rushed to take the lead. "I have our course mapped, avoiding the washed out trails Juan warned me about."

Nick nodded. "We know who the real leader of this crew is."

"Oh, Nick, I didn't mean to overstep."

He waved her off. "I was never a Scout like you and Benjamin. Y'all lead the way. I'll follow with Dylan. I've been wanting to talk with him."

She cast a glance over her shoulder. What now?

~~~

Dylan shadowed Nick across a slick log. The trail laced along the edge of a swollen stream. A waterfall to the left hushed their conversations. Between the falls and the water rushing across the rocks and stones, most other sounds became unintelligible. What did Nick want to say to him, anyway? Curiosity was driving him mad.

The foliage thickened as the trail turned away from the creek. Dylan kept an eye out for snakes. He'd heard of a few deadly ones in the area, and with all the rain, they might be out looking for a new home. So far, only a myriad of lizards and iguana had spooked them. And buzzards. Was that a bad sign? He'd never seen so many of the nasty birds.

Nick dropped back to Dylan's side. "I know this is an odd time and place, but I've been doing a lot of soul-searching and praying while we've been down here." He met Dylan's eyes. "I need to apologize to you. I'm sorry for treating you badly. Somehow in my mind, you were this Hollywood Romeo. I was wrong, and I'm sorry."

A thickness squeezed Dylan's throat. Nick was sorry? Was this some kind of trick to keep him from pressing for more custody rights? "Why?"

One corner of Nick's lips rose, and he let out a sigh. "Because you're a guy doing the best he can in the world. A
~~~

guy like me. God forgives my many mistakes, and I hope you can forgive me, too."

Mud splattered from Dylan's shoes to his pants legs. The sound of tree frogs humming swirled around the forest. He took a deep breath of humid air. Could he forgive Nick? What had the man actually done to him anyway? Other than try to keep him away. And did he need to ask forgiveness, too?

Cassie turned and called back. "It's not far. We'll take a left ahead and come out at the clearing." She laughed. "I can smell the place already."

That place. Dylan met Nick's stare and shrugged. "Forget about it. I haven't been the person I should've been for many years. I'm aiming to make things right, too. But we still have stuff to work out. That hasn't changed."

A smile crossed Nick's face and reached his eyes. "But how we deal with stuff can change. Thanks, man."

Forgiveness. A rush of warmth touched Dylan's heart. Maybe he'd found one of God's promises.

Chapter 35

While Nick finished repairing the sewer, Cassie rushed to change the PVC couplings on the water well. Benjamin carried supplies and tools for all of them. The work was taking longer than expected, and they'd already missed lunch. At least she and Dylan weren't in the smelly mud. The wind stirred the air, reminding her to check the sky.

A thunderhead hovered above the mountains in the shape of a giant anvil. She hoped the storm would blow around them. Either way, she'd feel more comfortable with Benjamin at the camp. "Nick, how long until you're finished?"

Nick leaned up to peer at her from his perch on a small rock wall. "Done. You must be reading my mind."

"I'm close, but would you mind taking Benjamin back? Now? That storm cloud's worrying me, and I'd be less distracted if my son was safe and sound."

"What about you and Dylan?"

If she thought they'd let her, she'd send Dylan back, too. But no way they'd leave her alone, though they weren't far from camp. "We'll be right behind you. Only a few more minutes."

Nick shot a look toward Dylan, who nodded. "We'll be fine."

"Okay." Nick gathered his leftover supplies. "Leave it if the weather gets bad and find shelter. Don't wait too long."

Relief swept over Cassie as Nick and Benjamin disappeared down the trail. The sun chose that moment to burst through the clouds. Maybe she'd overreacted, but on the way back, she could talk to Dylan alone.

~~~

Now that the sun had beat on Dylan's neck for over an
~~~

hour, he missed the clouds. How much longer could the repair take?

Cassie made a satisfied huff. Finally, water gushed from the pump. Now all they had to do was clean up.

A serious look covered Cassie's face as she packed her backpack with precision. No stuffing things in that bag. He chuckled. She was a bit of a perfectionist, but he adored her all the more for it.

Her head popped up. "Are you laughing at me?"

He bit back a smile. "A little."

"What?"

"I've never seen someone so good at packing. That's all."

What was that crinkle between her eyebrows?

"And I was just about to apologize to you." She huffed, then a grin twinkled in her blue-green eyes. "I'm sorry. I never should've reacted the way—"

"I'm the one who should've waited until we were alone to express an opinion. Wait. I mean, I shouldn't have gotten into your business, at all."

"We're friends, so it was your place. Private would've been better, but still that was no excuse for me to be ugly. Forgiven?" Her small hand reached to shake his.

"Forgiven." He clasped her hand, not wanting to let go.

Her eyes held his a moment longer. "We better get back on the trail before they come looking for us. I'll radio Jess that we're on our way."

~~~

Only a few yards down the trail, a colossal crack split the air. And it wasn't thunder. Cassie's feet dug in. Her skin tightened, and chills covered her scalp. A mudslide.

Higher ground. They needed to move. *Fast.*

She grabbed Dylan's hand. "Follow me. Now!"

Her mind traveled the different routes she'd mapped. A bellowing rumble shook the earth. "Run!"

They tore up a path toward a small rocky hill. About midway on her course, Cassie tripped over a jagged tree root and sailed forward. Dylan's hand pulled her back, his other arm
~~~

cradled her against him.

"We have to keep moving." Once she regained her footing, she picked up speed again.

Cracking and splintering were followed by ground-shaking thuds that crashed through the forest below like a giant dinosaur thrashing through the trees. Scrambling faster, she dropped Dylan's hand to claw up a rocky crag.

She halted at the crest of the hill and bent over. Her breath came in ragged waves.

Dylan caught her chin and studied her face. "Are you okay? Are we okay? That was a mudslide, right?"

Dirt had splattered and plastered to their arms and pants from the run, but they'd reached high ground in time. This stony place had no mud left to wash off. "We're okay."

Then a wave of terror crushed against her chest, almost smothering her. "Benjamin."

Chapter 36

Oh, Lord, let Benjamin and Nick be back at the camp. Helplessness enveloped Dylan. *The radio.* "Cassie, call Jess on the walkie-talkie. They probably made it back before…"

Cassie's hands scrambled to her belt, and she yanked the radio to her mouth. "Jess. There was a mudslide. Are Nick and Benjamin back at the camp? Jess? Jess?"

Dylan caught her hand. "Take your finger off and give him time to answer." He inched closer and brushed a loose hair from her face. "Breathe."

Her head dropped back as she sucked in air and waited for Jess to respond. "Come on. Please." She ran a hand across her forehead. "Lord, please. Keep them safe. Please. In Jesus' name, protect them. Please, Lord."

A voice crackled through the radio. "Mom? Are you okay? We heard the crash." He panted. "Mom? Mom?"

Cassie held the speaker to her cheek as if she were holding her son's hand. "Thank You, Lord." A smile lifted her lips. "He needs to let go of the button so I can answer."

Dylan chuckled. "Like mother, like son." Nothing in the world could stop him from holding her in his arms at this moment. He reached out and pulled her close.

Her arms encircled him, and her face relaxed on his shoulder. "Oh, Dylan. That could've been the end. We could've died." She squeezed him tighter. "A miracle. That's what it was. God's timing." The radio quieted. She lifted it to her lips once again. "Benji, honey. We're safe."

"Thank God. Mom, if I lost you… Or Dylan…" The crack in Benjamin's voice plucked at Dylan's heart. The young man had included him—cared for him.

Cassie's chest rose and fell next to his. "We're fine. We'll need to figure out another way back. Have Juan contact the authorities to find out the extent of the slide. Maybe he could check with the locals to see if any of the trails are passable." She glanced around. "Meanwhile, we'll stay put. We're in a safe place, and I can set up camp here until we get word."

~~~

Pure adrenaline must've allowed her to run as fast as she had with the added weight. The small isolated hill would be uncomfortable, but safe. Cassie scouted out an overhanging rock for shelter and unstrapped her backpack. She removed smaller rocks from the flat area where she would pitch the tent.

Dylan joined her effort, launching a stone down the hill from a pitcher's stance.

Cassie laughed. "Curveball? Really?"

His green eyes twinkled. "May as well have fun."

"May as well." She removed the hiking tent from her backpack. "I'll pitch the two-man here, just in case we're stuck after dark."

Holding her gaze, he flashed a smile. "Lucky I'm with the Cub Scout Mom of the Year."

"You are pretty lucky." A bit of mud dirtied his cheek. The urge to touch his face tugged at Cassie. But if she touched him, she might start imagining a kiss. Again.

Dylan removed his cell from his pocket and held it up. "No service. You?"

"Coverage has been spotty all week outside the camp." She paused to pull her phone from the pack and glanced at the display. "Nope." After returning the phone to her pack, she went back to pitching the tent.

"Can I help?" Dylan hovered beside her elbow, distracting her.

"I've got it." It'd be much easier if he weren't so close. She rushed to shake the tent open away from her body. After positioning it, she worked on the pegs and guide lines.

The sun gradually dropped lower in the western sky. Although she'd endured camping, sometimes even enjoyed camping, staying out in the Honduran jungle all night wasn't
~~~

an idea she relished. And two-man tents were small. Really small.

Not even going there right now.

It'd be a good idea to make small talk and distract herself. "How do you feel about the mission trip? I mean, up until this point?"

Dylan's eyes roved over the green, mountainous landscape. "I love coming here. This place reminds me of what's real. The first time I traveled to this part of the world, it was for all the wrong reasons. I wanted to upgrade my image and…"

"Impress Sarah Beth?"

His eyes landed on hers, captivating her. He took two large steps to stand face to face with her. "Hollywood can be a tough place sometimes. She stood out with her disarming ways."

She searched his face. Why was he moving so close?

"She's real. That's hard to find sometimes." His hands took hers, his thumbs caressing her fingers. "You're like that, once you get past the attorney disguise."

Her breath caught in her throat as the skin on her fingers seared beneath his touch. She should move. Slipping her hands from his, she sat on the stony ground. "May as well get comfortable." As if that were possible now.

He let out a deep exhale and plopped down next to her. "May as well."

His shoulder touched hers.

Someone better figure out a clear path soon, before she said or did something stupid. Again.

She'd struggled to keep the conversation light and ignore how much she delighted in the feel of his shoulder against hers.

After a while, she ran out of conversation ideas. And he wasn't helping. Maybe she should be quiet now.

The sun dropped lower, extending sweeping tendrils of pink and orange in wavy wisps of clouds.

"Majestic, don't you think?" He nodded toward the western sky. "A sunset to remember."

"Why do you say that?"

"Miracles. We're safe. Benjamin's safe. Nick apologized

today." He gave her a gentle nudge with his shoulder. "I'm with you."

What did that mean? "Being out here in this wilderness after dark isn't something I'm looking forward to." She glanced from side to side. "Hard to navigate in the dark, plus there's bound to be reptiles out after that rain."

"Way to ruin a romantic sunset." He chuckled. "Just when Nick quasi-accepted me, now he'll think I orchestrated this mudslide to get you alone."

"I'll radio the camp again. Maybe they found a way back for us, so you won't get into trouble." *Or me.* She pressed the call button. "This is Cassie. Any word?"

There was a pause before Juan answered. "We've been working to find a way to come to you, but it would be unwise to do so after dark. Dr. Rodriguez says you have his tent, and Benjamin claims you won't have a problem setting up camp. We are all praying for your safety."

"Benjamin's right. I know camping. Don't worry. We'll get back in the morning. We appreciate the prayers, though."

Camping didn't worry her at all. She glanced at Dylan. The smudge of mud still speckled his cheek. Being with Dylan and not saying or doing something to embarrass herself—that was another worry altogether.

Chapter 37

A restlessness stirred Dylan. Hadn't his spirit and heart been dry and empty until a couple of months ago? The moon washed the dark sky with light much like Cassie, Benjamin, and Michael had brightened the dark void in his life.

No. More like they illuminated his life like the sun on a summer day in Mississippi.

Now he yearned for a life he'd been denied, partly by his father, partly by his own choices. Meeting and caring for Sarah Beth, though painful at times, may've been the catalyst to moving to a higher place.

He'd heard the Lord worked in mysterious ways. But would He work despite Dylan Conner's sinful ways?

Even though he'd run from small-town life to escape the gossip and narrow-mindedness, rumors and judgment had followed him in Hollywood. Now more than ever, he was hounded by those very things he'd tried to escape.

Ironic. All roads seemed to be leading him to the Lord. A baby. An adorable redhead. And a small town. Oxford, Mississippi.

Cassie worked beside him. With a little flashlight in her mouth, she pulled mosquito netting and a few other supplies from her pack and stored them at the entrance of the minuscule tent.

Maybe he could help, but this wasn't really his area of expertise. "Should we build a fire or something? I could take the flashlight and pick up a few sticks."

Despite the low light, her eyes gleamed when they met his. "It's kind of hot for a fire, and we don't have anything to cook, so I think we're good."

A small but distinct prick on Dylan's skin sent his hand

swatting at his arm. "Bugs are out in full force."

Cassie scrambled to unzip the tent and pull the insect repellent back out. "Please tell me you remembered to spray yourself this morning."

"It's been a long time since breakfast. I know I did the first few days, but to be honest, I can't remember today."

"Here. Coat yourself." She sighed. "How could you forget? You might get dengue fever. You're taking the antimalarial meds right?"

The smell of the spray tingled in his nose, and his eyes watered. Maybe that's why he forgot. The stuff was potent. "I'll be fine."

She huffed. "But you don't know that, and you've got people depending on you now. People who care. You need to be responsible."

Her words stung. *Responsible*. "Haven't you noticed? I'm not careful. That's why we met, after all." His voice came out sharper than he intended.

No response. No movement.

Why did he have to be such a jerk? "I'm sorry. You're right. I should be more responsible."

"I shouldn't have scolded you." She reached for the can of spray and covered her arms and legs with a fresh coat of the stout repellent. "Maybe that's why Evan cheated on me. I'm too rigid and pushy."

A spear of guilt rammed into his gut. He scooted next to her and touched her chin with his fingers. "Oh, Cassie, no. Don't ever think you caused your marriage to fail." His thumb traced her jawline. "You deserved better than Evan."

Her lips drew him. The slim line of her ivory neck captivated him. The way her eyes widened awed him. His pulse quickened. Wouldn't he love to kiss her? To hold her in his arms and take her pain away?

But she deserved better than a Dylan Conner, too.

A thud, followed by the sound of scurrying came from behind the tent.

Cassie jerked her head toward the noise. "Maybe a fire

wasn't a bad idea." Her neck craned toward the source, and she popped on the flashlight. The beam sent a confused and frightened iguana scurrying toward her. "Good gravy." She squealed and popped up.

Dylan jumped to his feet and stomped at the reptile. "Shoo. Get." He flailed his arms in front of it. The lizard ran in a circle and zigzagged between them. Dylan hopped on one foot away from its path. "Go. Shoo."

At last, it scuttled past and hid under a nearby rock. Dylan let out a loud exhale. "Can we get in the tent now?"

~~~

Cassie caught her breath, then doubled over. Her stomach and chest trembled as laughter exploded from her throat. Tears formed in her eyes.

Dylan closed the distance between them. "Are you okay?" His hand caught her chin. Again. "Wait. Are you laughing? At me?"

The laughter intensified. Through broken giggles, she tried to push out words. "Sorry. So hilarious."

"I heard a squeal coming from your direction, too."

Before she could answer, louder, scruffy slithering turned both their heads.

Dylan's eyes widened. "I think our visitor has friends."

"Those things are unnerving. Time to squeeze into the two-man and zip up tight." Once they'd both slid in, with no room to do much moving, Cassie double-checked the zipper and snaps, then turned off the flashlight to save the battery. Her hands searched for her backpack. "I may have food."

"I'd like steak and potatoes. Maybe some of your sweet tea."

"We should start with a salad first, don't you think?" She chuckled and felt through the items in the bag. Her fingers touched something rectangular with a little give. *Gold.* "Actually, let's split this protein bar."

"*Yes.* I'm starving."

The wrapper crinkled as she yanked and pulled at the ends. For all her twisting and tugging, the package wouldn't tear.

Dylan's hands nudged hers. "Are you crushing it first?"
~~~

His touch sent warmth up her arms. "I can't get it open."

"May I?"

"Be my guest."

A second later, he offered her half. "Here. Funny, you can make all manner of repairs, chart a course, and put up a tent, but you can't open a candy bar?"

Her stomach growled as she took a bite. She chewed for what seemed like five minutes before she swallowed back the dry bar. "Resembles a candy bar, but sadly tastes like tree bark. Need to find the bottle of water." There better be one or two left in her pack. Her elbow rammed Dylan. "Sorry."

"Ouch. Tight space problems."

"I'll use the flashlight." The light popped on, and the bottle materialized. As did Dylan. His smile took her breath. "Here. You can open it."

Propped on one elbow, he twisted the cap and took a swig. "Ah. You saved my life for the second time today. That was the driest thing I ever put in my mouth." He offered her the bottle.

"Probably why it was still in the pack." She lay the flashlight on the floor of the tent and took a gulp.

"You'd have to be stranded in a third world country to eat it." He raised the flashlight close to his face, his eyes open wide. "Boo. Wanna tell spooky stories?"

So funny and cute. Help me, Lord. "Turn that off. We need to save the battery." Maybe she should stay outside. But the wildlife. *Goodness.* He just wanted a friend, anyway. So she should be safe. But being here with Dylan felt anything but safe. Not that her body was in danger. Just her heart.

The flashlight dimmed with a click, but Dylan's face stayed in her thoughts.

He cleared his throat. "I've been wanting to talk to you about the day we looked at the house."

"You don't have to. Friendship is better. I appreciate that we still feel comfortable after my major faux pas."

"But I wanted to kiss you. Badly." His voice moved closer, became more intense. "You had to know I was kissing you back. I've wanted to kiss you since the day I first saw you with your hair down. Shallow, I realize. But as I got to know you, my feelings grew deeper. And I wasn't sure why you were kissing me that day. The visit from your ex...the Sophia run-in. You'd been hurt."

"You thought I was kissing you to get back at them?"

"Not on purpose, but maybe subconsciously. I couldn't bear that." He paused. "I've fallen in love with you, Cassie. But I don't want to lose you. Your friendship means the world to me. I've never met anyone like you. I know you don't trust love after all you've been through, and I haven't trusted love, either."

Cassie's body stilled, but her heart exploded with emotion.

Dylan sighed. "I've blown it, right? But I wanted to be honest, for once." His voice was soft. "Please. Tell me what you're thinking."

Tears filled her eyes. *Here's the man everyone thinks has it all. That he's strong and carefree, but he's so vulnerable. Fragile.* Her heart burst for him.

His voice cracked. "Can you give me any hint of what's going on in there?"

Rolling to her side, she leaned on one elbow above him and turned on the flashlight again to shine between them. "I'm thinking I want to kiss you, but I'm scared that once I start, I won't be able to stop. And it's not to get back at anyone." She leaned close to his lips. "I love you, too, Dylan Conner."

Her lips grazed his. Her hand dropped the flashlight and caressed his face. She trailed his cheekbone with soft kisses, then his chin and back to his lips. This time, she kissed him the way she'd wanted to for weeks, tears streaming. How she loved this man.

Minutes later, Dylan caught her arms and pushed away, breathless. "You're right. I don't think you'll be able to stop kissing me. I love you, but one of us has to be the adult."

She rolled onto her back and laughed. "Who would've guessed it would be you?"

Chapter 38

First light and the soft droning call of a motmot woke Dylan. Cassie lay nestled in the crook of his shoulder, her arm across his chest and one leg over his knee. The sight and feel of her at his side took his breath away. What could be more perfect? Except maybe something softer than a rock to sleep on.

With her so close, it seemed a wonder he'd slept at all. Was last night real? Had she really said she loved him? His heart squeezed. Could he be the kind of man she deserved?

Her eyes blinked open. Other than God and Michael, there was nothing he wouldn't give up for this woman. Nothing.

"Morning." She smiled and turned her head to the side. "Now I wish I'd packed a toothbrush."

He covered his mouth. "My breath's that bad?"

"I meant I wish I had mine, silly." She gave him a quick peck on the cheek before crawling to the entrance to pull the zipper. "We need to get up and figure out how to get back to civilization, such as it is." Once she'd cleared the tent, she stood. "Good news. Sunny skies."

He stretched as much as possible in the cramped space, and then made his way out to join her. The bright rays assaulted his eyes. "Nice and hot. Got more water?"

"I know where a few newly repaired water wells are." In a flash, she collapsed and folded the tent.

"Can I help?"

"Thanks, but this was designed to be quick and easy." She clipped it shut, stood, and switched on the radio.

Dylan caught her in his arms. "This was all just an elaborate plan to kiss me. Right?" He grinned. "Which is fine as long as I can do *this* whenever I want." He sunk his fingers into her red hair and nuzzled her soft cheek with his lips. How could he be so blessed?

Juan's voice burst over the radio. "Cassie, are you and Dylan well?"

Breaking from Dylan's embrace, Cassie returned his grin. "Whenever you want." She moved the radio to her mouth. "We're great. Ready to hike."

"Thank the Lord. I have a guide with me who will instruct you where to meet him to the north of the mudslide. The route will take longer, but you should be back in a couple of hours."

"Put him on."

After Cassie spoke with the guide, they set out down a rugged trail. Hand in hand.

~~~

The feel of Dylan's fingers entwined with her own sent warmth through Cassie's arm to her heart. He'd said he loved her. She glanced up at his perfect face, and her breath caught. Never in a million years would she have imagined a future with a man like Dylan.

Until last night. How sweet and mature he'd been. Not to mention gorgeous.

They neared the meeting site, and she glanced at their hands. "Maybe we shouldn't let everyone know yet?"

He slowed and brought her hand to his lips. "I need to speak to Benjamin first." His eyes popped open wide as he dropped her hand. "And maybe Big Roy."

A chuckle passed through her lips. "Don't worry. They both like you."

Once they'd reached the destination, they took a seat on a flat boulder and waited. Dylan swatted at a mosquito on his arm.

"Good grief." She hated that he kept getting bit. "Even the mosquitoes adore you." She unzipped her pack and pulled out the insect repellent. "Stand up and let me cover you."

His eyes cut to hers. "Interesting proposal."

Rolling her eyes, she sprayed his legs and arms, front and back. "Arrogant actors."

A voice called from a nearby thicket of trees, "You are from
~~~

the clinic, no?" A man not much taller than Cassie emerged wearing a light blue T-shirt and baggy black pants. A toothless smile filled his wrinkled face from under a dirty baseball cap.

"Are we glad to see you." Dylan returned the smile. "We're ready to get back to camp for breakfast."

"I'm Carlos." He pulled a mango, a folded tortilla, and a water bottle from a pack on his shoulder. "You are hungry. You have this."

"Thanks." Dylan reached for the food.

Cassie elbowed him. "We don't want to take his meal." *And we don't know how well it's been cleaned.*

"Oh, here." Dylan reached in his pocket and handed the guide a wad of twenty dollar bills. "For helping us back to camp and for the food."

Carlos's eyes widened as he took the cash. "I will get you back safe and bring you more fruit and tortillas. All you want."

"We should go." Cassie shuffled her feet. "Which way?"

Dangling the mango in front of her, Dylan raised his brows. "You want half?"

Though her stomach rumbled, she'd wait. "No, thanks."

Their route back to camp was more difficult terrain than they'd traveled before, but after a couple of hours, Cassie caught site of the roof of the chapel. At last.

Before they crossed into the courtyard, Dylan caught her arm. "I love you, Cassandra Jane."

Could she feel more complete? "I love you, Dylan Conner."

~~~

A crowd emptied from the chapel as Dylan followed Cassie along the last few steps of the trail.

Cassie turned to face him. "I wonder what's going on."

A new sign hung above the chapel entrance. *Adam's Grace Chapel.* Sarah Beth stood arm in arm with Juan near the entrance.

"They must've held the dedication ceremony," Dylan said. "I hate that we missed it. Sadly, the week's coming to an end."

"We'll have to pack up tomorrow to be ready for that hair-raising bus ride the next morning."
~~~

Dylan laughed and nudged her. "Can you pack for me? Now that you love me?"

"I'll need compensation in return."

"I think I can arrange something."

Her blue-green eyes lit up, but not at him. Then she waved her arms. "Benjamin."

Her son ran to embrace her. "You're back. We were worried about you. I mean, they were. I knew you could take care of yourself." He released Cassie and gave Dylan a quick hug. "She's good at camping, right?"

A pleasant warmth spread through Dylan. "I wouldn't have wanted to get stuck in the jungle with anyone else." He grinned and gave Benjamin a little punch. "I want to sit down and talk with you, but first…" His hand went to his stomach. "I need more food. Half a power bar for dinner and a mango-tortilla breakfast just doesn't cut it. I'm heading to the kitchen to see what I can scrounge up." He glanced at Cassie. "You coming?"

"I'm going to speak to Sarah Beth and take a shower." Her hand covered her mouth. "And brush my teeth. I'll catch up with you later." She winked.

"You sure will."

~~~

Warm hugs greeted Cassie as Juan, Sarah Beth, and Jess surrounded her.

Sarah Beth squeezed her arm. "I was freaking out, but Benjamin kept telling me you could handle it. He was so brave."

"I hate that I missed the dedication. The sign is beautiful, and it's such a wonderful tribute."

Sarah Beth motioned to Juan. "I have this man to thank, plus I videoed the whole ceremony if you want to watch. I might send it to Adam's parents, even though they blame me for his death."

Juan nodded. "I think you should send it to them. I will pray about it tonight, though. You pray about it, too."

Jess neared. "How was being stuck in the middle of nowhere with Mr. Hollywood?"
~~~

"About like having Mr. Hollywood live in my house." A surge of love and respect washed over Cassie. "He was a perfect gentleman."

Jess opened his mouth to speak, but a woman's wail tore through the air. Juan hustled toward the distraught older woman staggering from the clinic.

Sarah Beth caught hold of her husband's bicep. "Oh no. Emilio's grandmother. That can't be good."

Worry shadowed Jess's features, his strong jaw flinching. "I better find Cole. The kid meant a lot to him. He's gonna take this hard."

Cassie rested a hand on Jess's elbow. "I'll be praying for the family and for Cole. I'm going to clean up, but I'll get back as quick as I can to help out." A child's death would be difficult for everyone.

Chapter 39

Cassie showered and dressed as fast as possible, but she took a good long time brushing her teeth. Although her stomach protested, she skipped the dining hall and jogged straight back to the chapel. *Lord, give me words of comfort and peace.*

Dr. Rodriguez stood before the group. Dark circles shadowed his eyes, and tears etched crooked pathways down his cheeks. "Emilio did not make it. Though he was brave, this latest case of dengue became hemorrhagic fever. His small body…" The doctor covered his face with his hands.

Cole and Audrey fell into each other's arms and cried. Other students openly wept, even those who hadn't interacted with Emilio. They'd all come to love the Honduran people.

Sarah Beth rushed to the doctor and embraced him. "You did everything you could."

The student minister, Chris, held up his hands. "Let's pray." He bowed his head. "Father, we're brokenhearted about the loss of this little child, Emilio. We know he was ushered into Your loving arms, but we still grieve. We can't understand *why* on this side of Heaven, so we ask for Your peace to fall on us.

"We need You, Lord. Please strengthen us for the hours to come, Lord. In Jesus' precious name we ask these things."

Chris cleared his throat. "Guys, this is a hard one. We ask why. We'll grieve, and our hearts will hurt, but God will stand with us as we cry. If you let Him, the Lord will wrap His arms around you.

"When Jesus' friends, Mary and Martha, lost their brother, even though He knew Lazarus would rise, both here on earth and again in heaven, the Bible tells us that Jesus wept.

"He wept for the hurt and pain His friends were going through. And He weeps with us now as we mourn." With a broad sweep of his arm, Chris added, "I'd like the leaders to spread out. Students, we'll be available to talk or pray."

Cassie, Sarah Beth, Jess, Chris, and Nick split up in different parts of the chapel. Students hugged and prayed in groups. Cole and Audrey made their way over to Jess and talked with him for some time. Juan's wife, Lupe, took the local children out to the playground.

After an hour of praying with and comforting students, Cassie glanced around the chapel. Five rows away, Benjamin stood with Grant. Dylan hadn't returned from the dorm, or at least, she hadn't noticed him. Where was he? Maybe he'd fallen asleep. After all, they'd had quite an adventure.

No.

Something's wrong.

Was she being ridiculous? Maybe one of them should check the men's quarters just in case.

She caught Benjamin. He agreed and set a fast pace to the dorm with Cassie on his heels. As he opened the door to the sleeping quarters, she stood back.

Benjamin stepped in the quiet room. "Dylan?"

The sound of a bunk bed creaking brought Benjamin further inside. "Dylan? Is that you?"

Cassie's ears pricked.

"Not feeling too good," a hoarse voice answered.

A chill scampered down Cassie's back. "Are any other men here? Because I'm coming in." No way could she stand outside any longer.

Benjamin beat her to the bunk. "What's wrong?"

"Don't know." Dylan's voice was a hoarse whisper. "Maybe bus hit me."

The sound of his chattering teeth fired another shudder through Cassie.

She stood on the bunk railing and pressed her lips to Dylan's forehead. "You're burning up. I'm going to get help."

She sprinted from the room.

Where was Dr. Rodriguez? Zigzagging the campus, she still couldn't see him. Maybe he'd returned to his personal quarters.

She pivoted and crashed into Nick.

He caught her arms. "Whoa. You're galloping all over this place. What's wrong?"

"Dylan's got a fever, and I can't find Dr. Rodriguez."

"I'll help you find him." Nick let out a deep breath. "Don't think the worst."

The words made sense to Cassie's brain, but her heart wouldn't absorb them. Her chest trembled. What if it was *the worst*?

~~~

With red, tired eyes, Dr. Rodriguez studied Cassie. "Are you sure?"

"He has a fever. His teeth were chattering. You need to come with us." She swallowed down the lump in her throat.

"Of course." Dr. Rodriguez shook his head as if clearing out the fatigue from the previous days and stood. He brushed tears from his cheeks. "I'm sorry. I never get over losing a patient. Especially a child." He grabbed a leather bag and led them to the men's quarters.

After Dr. Rodriguez had taken Dylan's temperature, Cassie strained to see the thermometer, praying she was wrong. "It's high, right?"

The doctor gave her a sober look, upping her anxiety another notch. "Gather his things. We need to move him to my quarters."

In an instant, Nick climbed the side of the bunk and slid an arm under Dylan's shoulder. "Let me help you over to Doc's place. From what I hear, you can get some cool air over there."

Rolling to his side with a quiet moan, Dylan allowed Nick to help him up. "My devious plan to get AC."

Cassie motioned to Benjamin. "Will you bring his stuff?"

"Yes, ma'am." Eyes wide, he scrambled to gather Dylan's bag.

After they trudged to the doctor's quarters, Benjamin and Nick offered to help if needed, then left.

Two horrendous hours later, Cassie sat on the concrete floor of the air-conditioned bathroom and held a cool rag to
~~~

the back of Dylan's neck. The color drained from his face as he retched into the low toilet. Not even sips of water stayed in his stomach.

Oh Lord, please heal Dylan.

Helplessness played havoc with her nerves, but she forced a calm expression to her face. Like when Benjamin had split his chin open as a toddler. The memory of her little boy's screams returned to her mind. Fatigue and anxiety threatened to overwhelm her. Muscles ached. The mudslide, the precious child's passing, counseling the students, plus the treacherous trek through the mountains earlier in the day. She closed her eyes. *And Lord, some strength sent my way would be appreciated.*

Dylan rotated and leaned against the wall of the tiny room. "Not many girls get to see their new boyfriend in this position."

She forced a smile. "You're a keeper."

His weak eyes met hers. "You don't have to do this."

"I want to do this."

"I'll owe you."

"Okay, next time we're in Honduras, I'll be the sick one."

"I owe you for more than just this. You've been the catalyst that helped me change my life. Always remember that."

Looking at his sunken features constricted her throat, but words squeezed through the tightness. "You've helped me love again. Trust again." She ran more cool water on the rag and wrung it out in the sink. "You make me smile. I'd say we're even."

After a tap on the door, Dr. Rodriguez stepped in. "He still can't keep anything down?"

"Nothing."

"I'll start IV fluids. We have to keep him hydrated." He left and returned a few minutes later with a nurse and IV pole. "She's good at getting these hooked up. You'd rather her stick you than me."

Cassie moved out of the way until the nurse finished.

Another hour passed before Dylan felt he could return to a cot. Wrapping two arms around Dylan's chest, Dr. Rodriguez steadied his patient's rise from the floor. The IV pole scraped across the cement floor as Cassie followed behind.

Once Dylan settled on the mattress, the doctor examined him again. His mouth twisted as he pressed on Dylan's tender belly. "Cassie, I'll sit with him tonight."

"I'm not leaving. You rest. You were up the past two nights with that sweet little boy. I'll wake you if anything changes."

The doctor nodded and turned down the short hall toward his bedroom.

From a canvas lawn chair, Cassie kept watch. The hours crept by, her unease heightening and heart wrenching as Dylan moaned in a fitful sleep. *Please Lord, don't let this be dengue hemorrhagic fever. I love him so much.*

The small of her back ached. She shifted in her seat, banging her elbow on the slim metal that held the chair together. The slight noise pierced the quiet.

Dylan mumbled and rolled to his other side.

Thank goodness she hadn't woken him. At least they'd stayed out of the bathroom since he'd gone to bed, but maybe because Dylan had nothing left inside. The doctor was world-renowned, but was Dylan getting adequate care?

She studied Dylan's pale cheeks. How she wished for his famous smile pressed between those dimples she loved. The others would be packing to leave today. What should she do?

Maybe she should phone her father. He could fly down and pick them up. But the thought of moving Dylan at this point seemed more dangerous than keeping him here. Another day could change things.

The sheets slid on the cot as Dylan rolled toward her and moaned. Grabbing a fresh cloth, she rushed to the sink to dampen it. She pressed the rag to his forehead. When would this fever break?

"Cassie..."

She kissed his forehead. "I'm here. Get some rest."

His eyes closed again.

Sometime before dawn, Dr. Rodriguez joined her. "How is he?"

"Still has a fever, but hasn't thrown up any more." Her own eyelids were heavy, but unease needled her muscles and skin.

"Let me examine him and check for any signs of a rash. You get some sleep."

"I don't think I can. I'm too anxious, but I'll freshen up while you look him over."

Cassie's feet followed the path to the women's quarters, her brain stalling with exhaustion. She grabbed a fresh T-shirt and pants from her suitcase and made her way to the showers.

Silent tears fell as she prayed for Dylan. The stress of the divorce, the humiliation and betrayal, none of that compared to the thought of losing this man who'd claimed her heart. The warm water washed away the dirt and grime of the past day and night, but it did nothing to scrub away the hopelessness and fear that clung to her.

Chapter 40

Once she dried and dressed, Cassie found Sarah Beth sitting on her bunk, waiting.

Her friend pointed to the door. "Let's get you something to eat."

Cassie wanted to argue, but her stomach growled and gave her away. She followed Sarah Beth out of the cabin toward the kitchen. Most of the campus still slept. Though she knew she should eat, Cassie eyed the door to the doctor's quarters. Her stomach churned, and she longed to be back at Dylan's side. Or rather, she longed for him awake and well, making his usual adorable quips.

Sarah Beth nudged her. "I asked, how's Dylan?"

A picture of his drawn-up features and gray complexion filled her mind. "Can't keep anything down, and still has a high fever. He was able to sleep some."

"How about you?"

"No sleep, but I'm fine."

They entered the side of the kitchen. Sarah Beth opened the refrigerator and poured juice in two paper cups. "But how are you, in here?" She pointed to Cassie's heart.

Raw emotion and exhaustion overtook her. Her vision blurred, and a tear escaped, opening up a deluge that streamed down her cheeks. Her chest shook as she sobbed. "Scared. I love him. I'm praying it's not dengue fever or malaria, or some other virus, especially after…" She couldn't finish that thought. She couldn't go there.

Sarah Beth's arm circled her shoulders. "It's probably something else. And Dylan's a strong, healthy adult, even if it is something like dengue. I mean, it could be food poisoning. Not that fun, but travelers get it here all the time, especially if they eat something outside the camp. In this kitchen, they take special precautions for our western digestive systems." She released her, opened the refrigerator again, and retrieved a plastic container. "Speaking of food. Eat." Sarah Beth handed her a tortilla, rolled and filled with chicken and beans. "Not a traditional breakfast, but it's filling, and you need to keep your strength up."

The aroma brought a growl from Cassie's stomach. She nibbled down the fare, and then knocked it back with the juice.

The tortilla brought back thoughts of their guide the morning before. He'd given Dylan breakfast. Cassie stared at Sarah Beth. "So people get really bad food poisoning here… How quick can it hit? And can it cause fever?"

"It can. Plus that virus hit me out of nowhere the other day, and I was being really careful."

Cassie set aside her plate. "I need to go back now."

"Go. I'll clean up."

She burst out of the mess hall and sprinted back into the doctor's quarters, her heart fluttering. "Dr. Rodriguez, Dylan ate food."

His graying eyebrows knitted together above brown eyes. "Cassie, I think you need to go get some sleep."

At the sound of her entrance, Dylan cracked one eyelid. He winced as the doctor continued pressing on his belly.

"No. I mean our guide gave him food and water yesterday morning when we were stuck in the jungle after the mudslide. Who knows if the mango had been washed or if the water came from a proper filtration system? Maybe Dylan only has food poisoning."

She bent over Dylan and brushed a strand of hair from his forehead, then scanned his shirtless chest. "He doesn't have a dengue rash, right?"

"No rash. His symptoms could be food poisoning." He let out a sigh. "I've been so colored by Emilio's death. You might be right."

The corners of her lips rose. "Great. Food poisoning."

Rolling to his side, Dylan groaned. "Let me get this straight.

You guys are happy I *might* have food poisoning?"

Dr. Rodriguez covered Dylan's upper body with the blanket. "Not happy. But a course of antibiotics could help if it is a food or waterborne illness."

~~~

At a soft tap on the door, Dylan opened his eyes. Not that he'd slept very soundly, but at least he'd slept. Cassie tiptoed away to answer. The woman hadn't left his side in twenty-four hours. The sheets beneath him were dry and cool, and his skull no longer seemed to be pressing his brain through a funnel. Maybe he was going to live. His stomach gurgled. Maybe.

Thank you, Lord, for Cassie. At least, if I die, she'll be with me.

Or would she? The bus to the airport would leave soon. What time was it? He lifted his arm. Where were his watch and phone? His hands rubbed along the edges of the cot.

The hinges whined as the door opened and shut. Footsteps followed. A lot of footsteps. *Such noise.* He cringed at the pain it caused his head.

Above him, Benjamin appeared, flanked by Nick and Sarah Beth. Jess wasn't far behind.

Sarah Beth let the back of her hand run across his forehead and looked toward Cassie. "How is he?"

Resuming her guard in the lawn chair beside him, Cassie slipped her fingers over his. "The fever broke. He seems a little better."

Benjamin bent and hovered near Dylan's face. "He looks a lot better than when we brought him over."

Nick nodded. "He does, but he's not gonna be ready to ride that bus today."

Mashing his eyes shut, Dylan pushed out words. "I'm right here. I can hear you. And no. Not getting on any bus today. Maybe ever." He reopened his eyes. Such hard work.

Casting a pleading look toward his mother, Benjamin pointed toward Dylan. "Mom, you're not leaving him here, are you? He needs you, and I'll be fine staying by myself. I can drive to baseball practice and eat out for dinner."

"You don't have to, Cassie." Dylan forced out more words
~~~

and tried not to think of her leaving.

Her hand tightened around his. "I do want to wait until Dylan is well enough to travel, Benjamin, but I'm not comfortable with you staying by yourself yet."

"Not much room, but you can stay with us," Nick offered.

Sarah Beth pivoted and tugged on Jess's sleeve. "He could stay in our pool house, couldn't he?" She gestured toward Benjamin. "That way you're kind of on your own, but we're right there."

"We'll do anything we can to help." Jess nodded. "Look, Dylan, I've been a jerk, and I'm sorry. I'll be praying you get well, so you can come back to Oxford soon."

The apology sent a squeeze of contrition through Dylan. After all, hadn't he wished many times that Jess would somehow disappear from the planet? "Been a jerk a few times myself."

A small smile lifted Jess's lips. "Let's leave it in the past."

"What about my dog?" Benjamin looked to Sarah Beth.

"You can bring her. I think Gingie's okay with other dogs, but I can't be sure. If we keep them apart, they should be fine."

Dylan groaned. "Monster dog at Sarah Beth's. Beware."

"I think Dylan's going to live." Nick smirked. "Mimi and Gingie together should be interesting. I'll have to come by and see that, after I get back to my family."

Nick's family.

A knifelike pain speared Dylan's chest. *Michael.* How he'd love to be going home to him.

Cassie cleared her throat and shot a hard look at Nick.

"Oh, man, Dylan. Sorry." Nick knelt by the cot. "I wasn't trying to be rude. I mean it. I'll be praying you get well. Your son needs you. And I know we'll be able to figure something out with Michael. We all want what's best for him. I see that now."

The pain lessened. Deep down, Nick was a good guy. His son would be fine. His Heavenly Father would be there for Michael, too.

Dylan licked his dry lips. "And if something does ever

happen to me, I'm glad my boy has a good man like you to be a father to him."

Chapter 41

Damp early morning air hung around the bus as students dropped their bags near the rear door of the vehicle. One by one they formed a loose circle, many still rubbing heavy eyelids. Locals came by and exchanged warm hugs with the volunteers. When finally the group had all been accounted for, Cassie stood by Benjamin as Juan prepared to address the gathering.

Juan held out his open, tattered Bible. "I have clung to and shared this passage with Sarah Beth during the years we have dreamed and planned and prayed for this clinic and this chapel. It comes from Isaiah 61.

"'The Spirit of the Sovereign Lord is upon me because the Lord has anointed me to proclaim good news to the poor. He has sent me to bind up the brokenhearted, to proclaim freedom for the captives and release from darkness for the prisoners, to proclaim the year of the Lord's favor and the day of vengeance of our God, to comfort all who mourn, and provide for those who grieve in Zion to bestow on them a crown of beauty instead of ashes, the oil of joy instead of mourning, and a garment of praise instead of a spirit of despair. They will be called oaks of righteousness, a planting of the Lord for the display of his splendor.'"

Looking up, Juan made eye contact around the group. "I pray that you will remember the Lord's words. When our hearts break, the Lord binds them up and proclaims His love for us. We cannot lose faith during the difficult times. As athletes, you understand that you must not give up when things are tough. We press on, we push harder, but unlike an earthly game or battle, we have the confidence that our side wins.

"You will never truly know the difference you made here, but my prayer is that what you did in Honduras will make a difference *in you* when you return to your homes and communities. That you will carry us with you in your hearts, carry us in your prayers."

Jess strode over and shook Juan's hand. "I think I speak for most of us when I say that Honduras has changed me more than I could ever change Honduras." He looked toward members of the local community and smiled. "I plan to take you all with me in my heart and in my prayers. Sunday mornings, I want to think of the Hondurans singing and worshiping here while I worship in my own home church. We are bound together eternally in the family of Christ."

After Benjamin hugged Cassie's neck, he climbed onto the bus. She stood in place until they rambled out of sight and then turned back toward Dr. Rodriguez's cabin. Her heart hurt. She wanted to stay with Dylan, but it was still difficult to allow Benjamin to travel such a great distance without her, even with people she trusted.

Please, God, keep them safe.

Once she crossed the threshold, Dylan's head lifted, his green eyes already brighter than an hour ago. "Thanks for staying. You didn't have to."

She closed the distance between them, bent down, and brushed her lips across his cheek. "I know. I want to be here for you, and Benjamin will be fine."

Dimples etched his cheeks as he smiled. "Uh-huh." His eyebrows lifted. "Trying to kiss me as soon as they left."

"Get some rest." Her neck scorched. "But when you're well, watch out."

~~~

Dylan edged one foot from under the sheets. For the first time in three days, the cool concrete floor didn't send a shiver through him. Cassie's red hair spread across the pillow on the cot they'd finally brought her and set up only a couple of feet from his. Tempting, but he wouldn't touch those locks for now. His legs held firm as he made his way to the shower.

The warm water streamed over his head. Man, that felt good. After a good lather and rinse, he dried and dressed.
~~~

Where was his shaving kit? He'd seen it through blurry eyes earlier in the week.

Rotating his head, he spotted the leather bag. Days of stubble grew from his chin. After a good shave, he let out a sigh. Better.

He opened the shaving kit wider, searching with his hand. *It has to be in here somewhere.* His fingertips touched the cord. Got it.

After pocketing his find, he gathered the dirty clothes and towel and exited. Cassie sat reading her Bible. She spoke without looking up. "Good morning, sunshine. Someone must be feeling better."

"Thank the Lord, I can hold my head up by myself and can think about food without… you know all too well."

"Yes." Her gaze met his. "Thank the Lord."

A box of garbage bags rested near the bathroom. Dylan unrolled one and threw his dirty clothes in the sack. "I don't know if anyone would want these, but I'm not taking them. Maybe we should burn them."

A grin covered her face. "Good idea."

How he cherished the view of her. His insides warmed with the thought of this woman loving him. "What do ya say we get our stuff together and bust out of here? I like this place, but I'm ready to go home."

Cassie's smile faded. Her brows knitted together over her cute sloped nose. "You have been gone from home a while now. You must miss California." Pain flashed through her eyes.

Dylan knelt beside her, words dancing on his tongue. Words he never thought he'd say. His hands brushed her beautiful red hair away from her face. He nudged her chin with his thumb. "I'm not sure what you're thinking, but I'm not talking about Malibu." He reached into his pocket and retrieved the small ring of braided cord he'd purchased from the little boy earlier in the week. "This is the only ring available, and I'm not sure if it's your style." He took her petite hand in his. "But Cassie, I love you. If you think you'd marry a guy like me, my home is going up South with you."

Tears shimmered in Cassie's eyes. Lip quivering, she nodded, and Dylan slipped the ring on her finger.

"Perfect fit." Her arms wrapped his neck as she showered his face with light kisses. "I love this ring." Her forehead rested on his. "And I love you, Dylan Conner. Let's charter a plane—*not* my dad's—and go home. Up South."

Don't miss the next book in the series.

Tackling the Fields

Cole Sanders is a changed man. The university quarterback questions his direction in life after serving on a mission trip in Honduras. Things that used to fill Cole's ego seem empty after witnessing the developing country's extreme poverty and the death of a precious child. The one glimmer of hope through his confusion is the fresh perspective he now has about his tutor, Audrey. She possesses something beautiful inside and out—something that might help him become the person he wants to be.

University senior Audrey Vaughn tutored Cole Sanders for an entire year and never imagined the popular quarterback would see her as anything more than a friend. After partnering with him on the mission trip, they are drawn together. And he appears to have changed for the better. To let Cole into her life, Audrey will have to overcome not only her brother's distrust, but also the paralyzing fear still lingering from a past she's tried to leave behind.

Cole can't walk away from Audrey now that they're back in Oxford. He'll have to figure out how to keep her giant of a brother, a lineman on his football team, from killing him when the coach has his back turned. But can Audrey trust her heart to a player so similar to the one who stole so much from her in the past.

Dear Reader,

Thank you for your time and resources you spent on this little book. My one desire is that you know God loves you more than you can ask or imagine. We've all suffered hurt feelings and broken hearts. God is the ultimate healer for your heart and soul.

I was able to go on a mission trip to Guatemala while editing this novel. What a beautiful country with beautiful people! There's nothing like ministering to others to lift the spirits. The Guatemalan people ministered to us, as well.

Blessings in Him who is able!

Did you enjoy this book? I hope so!

Would you take a quick minute to leave a review? It doesn't have to be long. Just a sentence or two telling what you liked about the book.

Would you like to be the first to know about new books by Janet W. Ferguson?

Sign up at www.janetfergusonauthor.com.

About the Author

Faith, Humor, Romance
Southern Style

Janet W. Ferguson grew up in Mississippi and received a degree in Banking and Finance from the University of Mississippi. She has served her church as a children's minister and a youth volunteer. An avid reader, she worked as a librarian at a large public high school. She and her husband have two children, one really smart dog, and a few cats that allow them to share the space.

https://www.facebook.com/Janet.Ferguson.author
http://www.janetfergusonauthor.com/under-the-southern-sun
https://www.pinterest.com/janetwferguson/
https://twitter.com/JanetwFerguson

Copyright © 2016 Janet Ferguson
Southern Sun Press LLC
All rights reserved. No part of this publication may be reproduced, distributed or transmitted in any form or by any means, including photocopying, recording, or other electronic or mechanical methods, without the prior written permission of the publisher, except in the case of brief quotations embodied in critical reviews and certain other noncommercial uses permitted by copyright law.

Publisher's Note: This book is a work of fiction. Names, characters, any resemblance to persons, living or dead, or events is purely coincidental. The characters and incidents are the product of the author's imagination and used fictitiously. Locales and public names are sometimes used for atmospheric purposes.

Oxford, Mississippi, is a real town, but other than the name, the events in the location are fictional. None of the events are based on actual people. The charming city made the perfect backdrop for a novel and a wonderful place for my character to call home.

33185444R00158

Made in the USA
Middletown, DE
03 July 2016